KU-446-342

SARAH WISHART

FOUR
good
LIARS

HarperCollins *Children's Books*

First published in the United Kingdom by
HarperCollins *Children's Books* in 2023
HarperCollins *Children's Books* is a division of HarperCollins*Publishers* Ltd
1 London Bridge Street
London SE1 9GF

www.harpercollins.co.uk

HarperCollins*Publishers*
Macken House, 39/40 Mayor Street Upper
Dublin 1, D01 C9W8, Ireland

1

Text copyright © Sarah Harris 2023
Cover illustrations copyright © Adams Carvalho 2023
Cover design copyright © HarperCollins*Publishers* Ltd 2023
All rights reserved

ISBN 978–0–00–864195–5

Sarah Harris asserts the moral right to be identified as the author of the work.
A CIP catalogue record for this title is available from the British Library.

Typeset in Times New Roman by Palimpsest Book Production Limited,
Falkirk, Stirlingshire

Printed and bound in the UK using 100% renewable electricity
at CPI Group (UK) Ltd

Conditions of Sale
This book is sold subject to the condition that it shall not, by way of trade
or otherwise, be lent, re-sold, hired out or otherwise circulated without
the publisher's prior consent in any form, binding or cover other than
that in which it is published and without a similar condition including
this condition being imposed on the subsequent purchaser.

No part of this publication may be reproduced,
stored in a retrieval system or transmitted in any form or by any means,
electronic, mechanical, photocopying, recording or otherwise, without
the prior permission of HarperCollins*Publishers* Ltd.

This book is produced from independently certified FSC™ paper
to ensure responsible forest management.

For more information visit: www.harpercollins.co.uk/green

For Darren, James and Luke, with love

'*Where's the money?*'

Donald Trump presses the gun to my forehead, ripping off the gag with a gloved hand. Holding my breath, I gaze up into the prosthetic mask. Vivid turquoise eyes stare back – contact lenses, right? It's part of the disguise, along with the voice distorter. In my peripheral vision, I catch another glimpse of blood pooling around my dead classmate. I shudder. The bindings bite deeper into my wrists. The weapon trains on the trembling person kneeling next to me in the cave. I try not to show any emotion; that's a sure way to get my head blown off next.

'Tell me where you've hidden it,' the tinny voice says.

A horrible choking noise rings out. The gun swerves in the direction of the muffled sobs. The question is repeated. Another gag removed. And another.

We're all in this together.

That's what the four of us agreed after the crash last week, but we all lied. Now only three of us are left. Who will break first?

'No one?' the metallic voice demands. 'Okay, have it your way. Let's play a game.'

My heart hammers against my ribcage as the gun swings towards me.

'Truth or dare.'

'W-w-what?'

'Don't make me repeat myself.'

'Fine . . . Dare . . . No, truth. I want to tell the truth. I've always wanted to – from day one. It was the others . . .' The words die on my lips. *Yet another lie.*

'Let's start with an easy one. Which school do you go to?'

A sigh of relief escapes from my lips. 'Kingsborough High School.'

'Wrong answer. Dead kids don't go to school.'

The masked figure pulls the trigger.

1

LAYLA

I'm not a thief! I've never stolen anything in my life.

My hands tremble with anger as I spray my hair with a ton of dry shampoo in the bathroom mirror; I didn't have time to wash it. I slept through my alarm after *finally* falling asleep around 4 a.m. I'd lain in bed replaying that awful scene in my head when Mrs Cavendish had accused me of stealing a ring from a guest's room. Someone supposedly saw me going into the hotel suite on Saturday. What a lie! I told Mrs C they were either mistaken or deliberately framing me.

But she wouldn't listen. She fired me on the spot.

Be grateful I haven't rung the police.

Before I'd headed to the sea tractor in tears, Rachel, one of the full-time housekeepers gave me a hug and insisted she believed me. She told me jewellery, money and a silver

3

leopard ornament have disappeared from rooms in the Sea Haven over the last few months. Mrs C was looking for a scapegoat – she'd smoothed things over with the old lady by sacking *someone* over her missing ring, but she didn't want the police turning up again. She'd claimed a dead drunken guest had been bad enough for business this season.

Still, why me?

Mrs C hasn't said anything outright racist, but she never attempted to pronounce my surname, Abdullatif, correctly and thought it was hilarious to call me Q. L. short for Queen Latifah on the rota. Of course, all the staff born and brought up in north Devon miraculously escaped her witch hunt. Mrs C hadn't even punished the estate manager for forgetting to restore the DANGER sign on the clifftop behind the hotel where that guest fell to his death.

'Hurry! It's half past,' Mum hollers up the stairs.

'I'm coming!'

I can't tell her what's happened – her worry list is full. I'll pretend I quit my Saturday job after getting sick of cleaning toilets. That part of my story is true. I've texted Frankie, the Lobster Bar's manager, and she's agreed to a trial waitress shift on Saturday night. I can shadow Liam – the brainiest student in my maths class and the entire school. Probably the whole of Devon.

4

'Layla!' This time it's my stepdad Leon. 'The bus won't wait for you!'

Tell me about it.

Silas the Sadist closes the bus doors and pulls away to make me run whenever he spots me in his wing mirror. I regularly do the walk of shame to my usual seat, three rows from the front while the other kids slow-clap, the ones who are awake anyway.

'I'm almost there!'

I head to my bedroom, past Salih's door. I peer inside – the floor is a Lego death trap as usual, deliberately designed to cause maximum pain to bare feet while posters of famous footballers plaster every wall. His head rests on the pillow – bald, where once there were dark brown curls. I pause, listening for his breath, but he's completely silent. I pick my way around tiny bricks and lean over the bed, frantically scanning his mouth and chest for movement.

Suddenly he sits bolt upright.

'Get out before I throw something at you!'

I jump guiltily. 'Sorry, *habibi*! Do you want anything?'

'A less annoying sister? And I'm not *your darling*!'

I retreat, limping as a tile maliciously clamps to my heel. 'Okay, I'm outta here.'

'And close the door behind you, MM!'

I hate that nickname – it's short for Mini Mum – but I leave the door open a crack before hurrying downstairs.

'Don't forget to arrive early tonight to bag a good seat,' I tell Mum as I sling my rucksack next to the washing machine. I leave the tickets on the table as she and Leon peer at a message on her phone. I stick bread into the toaster and put water, ground coffee and sugar into the kanaka. I'll never survive maths first period without caffeine.

I place the long-handled pot on the hot plate and check my mobile as I wait for the mixture to heat up and froth. My friend Alvita has messaged:

Don't miss the bus. Save a seat for Kai!

She's attached a GIF of two teddy bears kissing. I reply with a blushing emoji. I should never have admitted I fancy him. She'll keep bugging me to flirt on the way to school. Luckily Alvita gets on after him, at the biggest pick-up point, and he'll be sat down already. I need to get a move on. There's only one morning bus for kids who can't get lifts. I've zero chance of Mum or Leon dropping me off, and I can't start driving lessons until I turn seventeen in January.

I pull the pot off the heat as the foam rises and put it back, the way Baba – Dad – taught me. I glance at Mum and Leon but they're glued to her phone.

'Did you hear me? The concert starts at five but the doors open from four thirty.' I peer into the toaster – it works okay for everyone else, but I must have crossed it in a previous life. It always cremates my bread with its malevolent death rays.

'What's that?' Mum looks at me blankly. She has dark shadows under her eyes – another disturbed night as she checks on Salih every few hours. She brushes back a tendril of chestnut-coloured hair that falls loose from her unwashed ponytail.

'Is something on the calendar?' Leon chips in.

'Hello? My choir concert – we're performing songs from *The Greatest Showman*.'

'Has that come round already?' Mum asks, frowning.

They've forgotten! Ever since Salih was diagnosed with neuroblastoma seven months ago, he's come first, which is only right. We've all had to give up things, make sacrifices. But scraping into second place . . . well, it hurts sometimes.

Mum tuts as she scours the dates on the fridge door. 'I *did* write it down. I got caught up in Salih's trial – it slipped my mind to find a babysitter – sorry.'

'It's okay.' I fight to keep the disappointment out of my

voice. This experimental US medical trial is all Mum and Leon can think about since they applied last month.

'I'm on the back row. You wouldn't see much of me anyway.'

'I thought you were one of the soloists?' Leon asks.

I shrug. 'I didn't get the song I wanted.'

That's a lie, but they don't need to know the truth. Mr Grange relegated me to chorus after I missed too many rehearsals. He'd switched the sessions from lunchtime to 4 p.m. and I hadn't wanted to bother Mum and Leon about late pick-ups. I'm also supposed to attend after-school homework club to catch up with my music and drama assignments. Lack of sleep is wrecking my concentration. I jiggle the toaster before turning it off at the wall and stabbing a knife inside. My bread is being incinerated. Smoke drifts out as I free the smouldering black slabs. I drop them into the bin and turn to the kanaka. The coffee's boiling over. Seriously I give up.

'No, Layla, it's not okay!'

I spin round as Mum covers her face with her hands, her shoulders slumped. Leon puts his arms round her. I'm a horrible selfish person. I wish I'd never mentioned the concert. It's probably best they don't come. I don't want them to bump into Mrs C – her daughter, Fliss Cavendish, is one of the soloists. Wait, did Fliss get me sacked so she could spread fake news around the sixth form? I wouldn't put it past her.

'It doesn't matter, honestly!'

Mum shakes her head, wiping her eyes with her sleeve.

'What is it? What's going on?'

'The doctor in the US has emailed about the trial,' Leon says quietly.

A tiny dagger stabs my heart. 'He won't take Salih?'

'No, your brother's been accepted.' Leon's eyes mist up. 'We could fly out and begin treatment straight away.'

'I d-d-don't understand. That's great . . . right?' I scan their faces. They look anything but happy. 'This will make Salih better. You said the treatment was experimental, but it could get rid of his cancer for good.'

'You're right,' Mum says. 'It's his only—'

'Sandy!' Leon interjects.

'I mean . . . this is Salih's *best* chance of getting well.'

I inhale sharply as her meaning sinks in. This is Salih's *only* chance of recovering from his cancer – a rare but aggressive one. I catch hold of the worktop as the room spins. At his last hospital appointment the doctor said he was *responding well to treatment*. Mum and Leon had hugged and performed a goofy dance around his bed. But as I look at their stricken faces now, I realise I've been dumb. The

9

tumour is still there. It could grow, spread, like Baba's lung cancer. He died a year after his diagnosis, shortly after Salih's third birthday.

'What's the problem?'

I bite my bottom lip as Mum stares at a stack of bank statements and unpaid bills on the table.

'How much do we need?' I pause, doing a quick calculation in my head. 'I can help out – I've saved about four hundred pounds.' If I land this waitressing gig, I could beg Frankie for weekday shifts as well as weekends.

'Layla, it's two hundred and fifty thousand dollars,' Leon says quietly.

My knees weaken. Icy fingers crawl up my spine. He may as well have said £2 million. Mum looks after Salih 24/7 and Leon's back injury has ruled out building work. He's only found a part-time delivery driver position since we moved to Sandstown, a village outside Kingsborough, nine months ago.

'What are we going to do?' My voice falters.

'That's not your problem. We'll think of something.' Leon frowns. 'I'll plead with the bank for a loan. Perhaps my parents could remortgage and—'

'I'm setting up a JustGiving page today,' Mum cuts in. 'And I'll ask your grandma for help.'

I raise an eyebrow. Teta stopped talking to Mum when she married Leon three years ago and she rings me to get updates on Salih. Before retiring, she used to own a ful medames shop in Cairo, which was successful and served scores of hungry customers a day, but she's never been mega wealthy.

'I'm sure lots of people will want to chip in when they hear how –' Mum's voice wobbles horribly – 'how important this is.' She means *vital, lifesaving.*

They both attempt fake smiles, but they won't earn Oscars for their acting skills. The pain in my chest grows sharper, pincers grinding deeper and deeper into my flesh.

I open my mouth to speak, but Leon thrusts my rucksack and coat into my hands, steering me into the hall. 'Silas will go without you!'

He manoeuvres me out of the front door and shuts it behind me before I can protest. I don't know how I'm making it down the hill; my legs feel like leaden weights. I'm half walking, half lurching to the bus stop, my stomach churning queasily.

If we don't find a way to come up with $250,000 my super-irritating, funny, football-loving little brother could die.

I can't let that happen.

I'll do absolutely anything to save him.

2

FLISS

I'll do anything to stop those photos appearing online.

My hand trembles as I reread the text:

I have yr pix. £5,000 IN CASH or they go viral.

When the first message landed late last night, I only just made it to the bathroom in time. I'd vomited repeatedly into the toilet until there was nothing left to bring up. Another wave of nausea hits me now. I take a swig of latte, but it makes me feel worse. I push my travel mug into the holder and sink deeper into the cream-leather seat, swallowing hard, as we leave the hotel grounds and cross the causeway. Usually I enjoy the morning commute to school. I'll post a cute picture on Insta from the back seat of our driver Aaron's Range Rover to make everyone jelly before checking Daddy's

Facebook to see what he and Amanda got up to over the weekend. I always 'like' his photos, even though a tiny part of me shrivels and dies inside. But it's worth pretending to be happy for them. It reminds him to check *my* socials before he goes to bed. He'll make a 'funny' comment and I'll reply with an eye-rolling emoji. Or he'll FaceTime if I lay it on thick enough about how much I miss him.

That's not a lie.

It's hard to schedule regular calls when he works such long hours in California, weekends too. Some days the time difference feels more like a century than eight hours. But there's nothing usual about this morning. No way can I take a selfie after my sleepless night – my concealer barely covers the dark circles under my eyes. And I definitely can't tell Daddy about my blackmailer. He'd go ballistic and want to know *everything*. Mother says it's our secret; he must never find out what really happened this summer.

I study the message. I don't recognise the mobile number. Who's trying to ruin my life? If they hacked my phone over the weekend, it narrows down the culprit. The mobile was only out of my sight on Saturday afternoon. I'd paid for the gang to share a private lesson at the surf school. Has one of them guessed my password? Maybe Tristram or Spencer found my mobile in the changing hut. They could have scanned through my pics for a laugh and stumbled across the incriminating ones. But they wouldn't demand cash. All my friends – or, rather, frenemies – have generous monthly allowances.

Kim, who runs the surf school, rakes in thousands from holidaymakers and can't be short of cash. But that kid from my art and psychology classes was teaching a beginners' surfing group. What's his name? Something short and snappy and beginning with 'K'. *Kit?* No idea. It *could* be him. He looks like he sleeps rough on the beach. Whoever sent this message thinks I'm a rich bitch and needs money quickly. They believe £5,000 isn't a big deal for someone like me – probably thanks to *Devon Life*. Earlier this year, the magazine carried a feature about our renovations to the Sea Haven – it was built in 1895 and had belonged to a local family for decades. The piece casually mentioned 'the multimillionaire Cavendishes – the picture-perfect family who currently run north Devon's top luxury hotel'.

As if.

By the time the glossy article was published, Daddy had left us and moved to Malibu to be with Amanda, a stick-thin influencer who's half his age. Sure, we're wealthy, on paper, but Mother has gone all Ebenezer Scrooge since the refurb and scours my bank statements. She'll notice if I dip into my savings account, and no way can I beg Daddy for cash. He negotiates massive property deals in the States and pores over contracts, challenging every figure that looks out of place. He'll see straight through my lies. He and Mother are no longer on speaking terms, but he'll force his PA to ring and find out what's going on. That will spark another furious row over money. I have to sort out this mess myself.

I scroll through my album for the millionth time. All four photos are missing. In hindsight, it was a mistake to keep them. But I'd wanted evidence in case the police ever returned and I'd needed a defence. The pictures would help back my version of events. But now they could seal my fate after I've lied to cover my tracks. Whoever hacked my phone must have deleted the pics and kept copies. Or are they just trying to freak me out? If so, they're succeeding. I take a deep breath and open the second – and worst – message, which landed shortly after the first:

If u don't pay, EVERYONE will find out what u did.

Cold shivers run up and down my spine. My blackmailer isn't bluffing. *They know.* But how? They can't possibly . . .

I close my eyes, but that makes everything far worse. Terrible images flash into my head, one after another, like a sequence from a horror movie. Shame floods me, followed by white-hot anger and dizzying panic. I'm spinning out of control.

Bang!

I scream, my heart racing. My eyes fly open as sand thuds into the windscreen.

Aaron glances in his mirror. 'Sorry! My bad.'

He sweeps a thatch of ginger hair from his forehead and brakes, before fiddling with the radio button. His hand is covered in freckles, along with his nose and cheeks. The slightest ray of sunshine and he fries – like bacon, he claims.

'No music.' My voice is strangely high-pitched. 'Turn it off!'

'Okaaaay.' He raises an eyebrow, but his hand returns to the steering wheel.

I feel a small twinge of guilt for snapping. Aaron always looks out for me – he's driven me around ever since we moved to Sandstown when I was ten. Mother probably doesn't pay him enough to put up with my crap.

'Sorry.'

'A bad case of Monday-morning blues?'

'The worst!' I stare out of the window at the deserted beach. The wind is picking up. Huge waves are crashing swathes of seaweed on to the sand. Mother and I used to hunt for lost washed-up treasure during weather like this in those early days, when Dad ran the hotel, and she was less hands on.

'I know a way to cheer you up.' The skin round his bright blue eyes crinkle at the edges. 'You used to love me and Mrs C doing this when you were little.'

'No, I didn't.'

I'm not in the mood. Plus, I've outgrown childish games.

'Get ready!'

Before I can protest, he turns on the radio. Loud house music blares out. He rams his foot on the accelerator and we fly across the beach, deliberately spattering sand on to the windows.

'Noooooooooo!'

I grip the seat, laughing, as Aaron whoops loudly and beats his hands on the wheel. All my worries and fears slip away. I'm eleven again, squealing with delight, as we head to a birthday party, racing against the incoming tide that could cut us off. Mother would smile and say, 'Can you go faster, Aaron? Fliss wants to travel at the speed of light. She's our little record-breaker.'

The touchscreen console lights up as his phone rings.

'Whoops, it's your mum.' His shoulders tense and his foot eases off the pedal.

17

I roll my eyes. She must have a sixth sense that we're having fun. Aaron manoeuvres the Range Rover off the beach and pulls on to the narrow road that leads to the car park. I glance at my mobile – no reception as usual. Mother must be trying his phone to apologise to me for working solidly all weekend.

Aaron's voice is bright and professional when he answers. 'Hello, Mrs C. I'll pass the phone to Fliss.' He fumbles with the mobile holder.

I lean forward, yanking at my seat belt.

'No need, it's you I'm after, Aaron,' she says, sighing. 'I want you here. I have an urgent appointment.'

My cheeks smart as I slump into my seat.

'Understood, but we've only just crossed the causeway. I'll be another ninety minutes or so.'

'Drop Fliss at the nearest school bus stop and head back, please.'

'You have to be kidding!' I interject.

'See you soon.'

An awkward silence stretches between us as she hangs up. Aaron puts his mobile back in the holder and restarts the engine.

'You're driving me to school as planned. Agreed?'

'I don't have a choice, sorry. Mrs C is the boss.'

My mouth falls open. 'B-b-but she can't mean it.'

It's bad enough my parents never sent me to private school – the nearest decent one is more than thirty miles away – but there's no way I'm slumming it on public transport.

'What will everyone say when I roll up to school on the Poverty Express?'

'Come again?' Aaron flinches in the mirror. He hates me making digs about the 'less fortunate' kids at school.

'I meant the bus,' I mutter.

'You might enjoy a different journey. You could see someone you know.'

I shudder. 'I hope to God not. That would be beyond embarrassing.'

He sighs deeply. 'There's nothing I can do. The bus stop isn't far away. I doubt you'll have long to wait.'

I punch the seat with frustration until I remember that the kid from the surf school will probably catch the bus. This is the ideal time to confront him about the hacked pics away from my gossipy friends.

I'm not the only person about to have the journey from hell.

3

LIAM

'I don't think *we'll* split before uni.' Tristram taps the steering wheel of his mum's old Volvo. 'I'm just saying lots of couples went their separate ways at the end of sixth form last term.' He sighs. 'I'll be so wrapped up with my training and after-school rehearsals – you could be sick of me by the time we have to apply!'

'That will never happen,' I say quickly.

'Thanks, babe.'

I wait to hear the same reassurance, but silence stretches between us for what feels like eternity. Oh God. I want to be swallowed by a black hole and spat out in another universe. *Is* Tristram fed up of me? I'd only said it would be stupendous if we both applied to Cambridge – he's previously described the university as a conveyor belt to the England rugby team, and the stage via Footlights. But bringing it up again was a miscalculation. He did all the chasing a few months ago and messaged me dozens of times a day, but he didn't text back this weekend or last. The probability of us being together this time next year is 63 per cent and decreasing rapidly.

Is it because of the way I look?

However hard I work out, I'll never have the perfect body like him, his rugby teammates and all those surfers at school.

He reaches over and squeezes my hand. 'Stop catastrophising.'

'I'm not, honestly!'

He eases his foot off the pedal as we crawl behind the tractor.

'Let's just enjoy *us* and not stress out making plans. Live for the moment. Right?'

I clear my throat. 'Affirmative!'

Another lie. I feel stressed *without* plans. I draw up lists every day. I have my heart set on studying maths at Jesus College followed by a PhD at Stanford. Is it misguided to hope that Tristram could share my medium-to-long-term goals?

'Do you need another cushion? I can pull over and get one out of the boot. It's not a problem. The traffic's practically stationary!'

'I'm good, thanks.'

I wince as my neurons fire and retrieve a memory buried deep in my brain. Dad had asked the same question on that torturously slow drive back from the hospital when I was twelve. I'd had surgery on my back to correct the curvature and was dosed up on painkillers, but every bump in the road was agony despite the pillows. Worse still, Mum and Dad were arguing. Dad had announced he'd accepted a building job in Dubai and would be gone for months. I'd guessed by Mum's reaction that he wasn't coming back. I'd thrown up and screamed, 'Don't go! Don't leave us!'

Panic claws at my throat. I fight back the temptation to repeat the same pleas to Tristram by thinking of all the prime numbers between forty and sixty.

Forty-one, forty-three, forty-seven, fifty-three, fifty-nine . . .

'Aargh! You'll miss the bus if we're stuck behind this much longer.' He applies the handbrake as the tractor labours up the sloping, twisty lane.

A ray of hope creeps into my heart as he checks his watch. His parents presented him with a vintage Breitling timepiece for his eighteenth birthday last week, but he's wearing the £200 Samsung Galaxy I gave him. He catches my glance and ruffles my hair affectionately.

'Best present ever!'

My heart flutters the way it always does when he gazes at me with those gorgeous bluish-green eyes. His dark brown hair is tousled, his cheekbones high and chiselled. He is the most devastatingly attractive boy I've ever seen. As he leans over and kisses me on the lips, I inhale citrus, woody aftershave, and butterflies dance in my stomach. All my insecurities slip away. Tristram was held back a year due to glandular fever but has returned to captain the rugby team *and* take the lead in this term's production of *Phantom of the Opera*; he'll probably be head boy in the upper sixth. But despite the long trailing scar down my back, he chose *me*.

We spring apart as the motorist behind us toots his horn. The traffic is moving.

'Okay, okay!' Tristram stalls the engine and struggles to get it into gear. 'Dammit. Why can't I have a decent drive, like a Jeep? That's what I'll pick if my parents ever offer a set of wheels.'

That's unlikely in the short or medium term. He's in his dad's bad books after the Merc theft. Tristram had borrowed his car during an overseas business trip. He couldn't admit he'd left the keys inside while he'd grabbed a Coke in a pub after rugby training – his dad would have gone ballistic. Instead, we'd agreed to tell the police it was stolen from outside my house, two days before we got together.

He hits the accelerator as the tractor takes a left turn. 'Okay, we should have enough time,' he says.

I check my watch, a scratched Sekonda. We have three minutes and forty-five seconds before my bus arrives. He's dropping me at the nearest stop before heading to the coach pick-up – his team is travelling to a match at a local school.

'Thanks for doing this.'

'We needed quality time together after I missed your calls over the weekend. Talking of which, have you thought any more about Verbier? The lodge deposit is five hundred pounds each.'

My heart sinks. I can't ask Mum for money. Her hospital trust is being restructured and members of her nursing team could be made redundant or relocated elsewhere. I only have a few hundred pounds saved from my Saturday job at the Lobster Bar. There's no way I can afford the deposit, let alone the £3,000 cost of jointly hiring out the ski lodge with his friends over New Year.

I did something despicable to buy his watch. I can't do it again. I'll tell him no.

'Please say "yes". New Year's Eve will suck without you. I'll die of loneliness.'

My resolve crumbles and I hear a small voice say, 'I'll get the deposit to you.'

'Brilliant! We need it by the end of next week.'

'It won't be a problem. Promise.'

Inwardly I groan. How can I come up with £500 by next week? Plus another £2,500 before Christmas? It's a mathematical impossibility.

What have I done?

4

KAI

How did I let this happen? What the hell am I going to do?

I run down the hill to the bus stop, cursing myself. Lack of food has left a gnawing pain in my belly and scrambled my brain, which is foggier than usual. Energy bars for supper and breakfast barely touched the sides, but I couldn't risk stealing food from the cupboards. The rich Londoners who own my crash pad have laminated lists for everything, including the number of bags of pasta and bog rolls, which the cleaner checks each weekend. Anyway, I'm not a thief. Not yet. Kim has paid this month's wages in advance, and I can't ask for another sub; surfing lessons are drying up. Soon I'll only have Mrs Gibson's weekly gardening to tide me over – maybe I can charge extra for odd jobs around her house. She's always been warm and supportive, offering drinks and big slices of her home-made cakes after my shifts.

I've been dead careful – not trampling in sand or showing any sign someone is secretly sleeping here. I put the spare key under the flower pot, but this morning I overslept. In my rush to leave, I left the key on the kitchen table and slammed the back door shut. I'll have to smash a window to get in. The cleaner will report a break-in and the last thing I need is the police turning up.

I'll have to move on, which is a pain in the butt. I can't afford rent – the cash Mum left me ran out, and our old landlord has changed the locks. This house has a great view of the beach, and I can check out the surf without listening to the radio. Best of all, it's in the middle of a ghost village, surrounded by other empty holiday homes. I don't have to worry about turning on the lights now it's off season. Mrs Gibson – the last remaining local on this road – lives six houses down. Her grounds are vast, and I need a garden tractor to mow them. No one knew I was here until I screwed up and ruined Plan A. I catch a glimpse of the school bus in the distance and sprint across the road. I'll have to figure out where to go next – Plan B. Maybe I could—

Tyres squeal.

Shiiiiiiiit! My hands slam on to the bonnet of a blue car. Luckily I haven't bounced off it. Or been dragged under the wheels.

'Sorry, sorry!' I mouth at the smeared windscreen, my heart hammering against my chest with the adrenaline. *Jeez, that was close.*

The driver – dark-haired, skinny and probably in his thirties – winds down his window and screams his head off. I'm tempted to give him the finger back, but his eyes are dead and soulless. I imagine this is the way serial killers gaze at you, right before they gut you from throat to belly with a knife.

I tap my head, pretending I'm an idiot – honestly that's not a stretch for my acting skills. I make it to the other side of the road and jump on the bus, trying to look casual rather than like someone who's almost shit their pants. If I'd been knocked down, doctors would have asked awkward questions about my home address and next of kin. The police too. I need to blend in, the way I do at school – telling my D&T teacher I'd volunteer to meet and greet next week. It helps distract from the fact that Mum *unfortunately* can't make parents' evening. *She sends her apologies.*

I stagger past Silas.

'What did that guy say to you?' he demands.

I double back. 'Come again?'

This is a first. Silas took over the morning bus service after Bob, *rest in peace,* was killed in a hit-and-run two months ago. Since then, the only word I've heard him mutter is 'Morning'. Today Silas has the same pale listless grey eyes and hair the colour of stale ginger biscuits, but his skin is greyish and his brow has a slick of sweat. He looks ill. I edge back; I don't get sick pay.

'I'm talking about *him*.' Silas jerks his head at the window.

The car, an Audi, has pulled over, engine running. The guy has a mobile clamped to his ear – he's not a local. Maybe he's lost and accidentally ended up in Shitstown. Frankly I'm surprised – and touched – by Silas's concern. Obviously he's not a patch on lovely old Bob, but I should give him a chance.

'I'm okay, honestly,' I say brightly. 'No damage done.' I tap my skull. 'Hard on the outside, but soft on the inside. That's what everyone says.' I wink.

'Tell me what the driver said.'

Apparently we're done with pleasantries.

'An A to Z of all the swear words in the dictionary.'

'Did he ask you anything about me?'

'Erm, why would he do that?'

He shakes his head, drumming his fingers on the wheel.

I peer out of the window. 'Wait, do you know him?' I'm not sure what's more surprising – the fact our monosyllabic driver has a friend, or that his mate happens to be a total psycho.

'Sit down!'

He rams his foot on the accelerator and the bus pulls away before I have a chance to grab the handrail. My forehead bounces off a rail.

'Jeez!' Gingerly I touch the skin. A lump swells beneath my fingers.

Silas glances at me but doesn't apologise. What is it with everyone this morning? One-handed, I chuck my rucksack into the usual place – the baggage rack closest to his seat. It lands on top of a large blue holdall.

'That's fragile!' he shouts. 'Sling your stuff elsewhere!'

Whatever. As I scoop up the rucksack, my fingers brush his bag. It's bulky and hard. 'Do you have bricks inside? *Fragile* bricks?'

Silas scowls at me in his mirror. My forehead's pounding. I don't think today can get any worse until I look straight ahead, out of the back window. The Audi's following us. Is that a coincidence? Or is the driver waiting for me to climb off . . .? I duck down but realise that's a dumb move because he watched me get on.

I steal a look to my left and get that familiar fluttery feeling in the pit of my stomach when I spot Layla three rows from the front. Her eyes look teary as she sweeps her long dark brown hair off her face and leans against the glass. I will her to notice me, but I'm the invisible man. I'd tried asking her in registration last week why she's stopped uploading her music, a fusion of Arabic and western influences, on to her YouTube channel. But she must have thought I was a weird stalker. She'd changed the subject and called me Kyle.

Do I look like a Kyle? Please, God, no!

Most of the seats are empty today; only three other students are on board. Maybe it's a bad case of Mondayitis. Liam – or HMG (Hot Maths Geek) as my best friend, Lou, calls him – is sitting in the row opposite Layla. He pushes gold-rimmed glasses up his nose as he checks his phone, a maths textbook balancing on his knee. He's an actual genius and has probably memorised it by heart. Or written it himself.

'Where's everyone else?' I mumble.

'Inset day for lower school,' he replies.

I catch a glimpse of the Insta photo on his phone – it's his douche bag boyfriend Tristram mid-tackle, or rather mid-pulverising his latest victim to a bloody pulp. Liam 'likes' the pic. Personally I'd prefer to delete Tristram and not only on social media.

I look up and immediately wish I hadn't. A girl with long auburn hair and green eyes glares at me from the back row.

What is Fliss Cavendish doing here? She gets chauffeur-driven to school. And why does she look like she wants to murder *me*? We're in the same art and psychology classes, but she never usually registers my existence.

'It was you, wasn't it?' She flies out of her seat. Correction, *my* seat. Mascara is smudged beneath her eyes. She swings from side to side as the bus picks up speed.

'Sit down!' Silas bellows.

She ignores him and ploughs on.

'Erm. What are you talking about?'

'I left my mobile in my bag at the surf school on Saturday. *You* were one of the instructors.' She glowers at me accusingly.

'Yeah. And?'

'You must have found it and worked out the password.'

I pause for a beat. 'Why would I want to hack your mobile?'

'Because you were looking for something incriminating?'

Interesting.

'Wait, you have dodgy stuff on your phone?'

She ignores the bait. 'You're the only person I recognise who was hanging around. Kim said I could leave my bag in the hut. She wouldn't go through my stuff, but I bet *you* would!'

'Nice!' I exclaim, clinging on to the rail. 'What about your so-called friends? One of them could have nipped back from the beach while you were in the sea.'

'Ha, you did notice when I was surfing!'

'*That's* what you were doing? Thanks for clarifying. I wasn't one hundred per cent certain.'

'Wow!' Layla stands up, facing Fliss. 'What a surprise! A Cavendish pointing the finger without bothering to learn the facts.'

My heart beats faster as she heads over, swaying from seat to seat. I'm picturing the sparks flying between us after I thank her for coming to my defence. I'll lean towards her and—

Tyres screech. A loud bang rings out, followed by a searing jolt. The bus stops and Layla flies forward. Fliss's forehead crunches into my eye socket. My grip on the rail loosens. I slam on to the deck, air squeezing out of my lungs as she lands on top. Groaning, I shift position and notice glasses and a phone by my hand. Both are cracked. Beside them lies Liam, clutching his textbook like it's a life jacket.

'Is everyone . . . okay?' My voice cracks.

'Think so.' Fliss rubs her temple as she scrambles off me.

Liam gropes for his glasses. I push them closer, trying to catch my breath.

Layla crawls towards us on her knees, taking short, sharp breaths. 'Are you hurt?' she asks softly.

'Kai not Kyle,' I gasp.

'What?'

'My name.'

'Huh?'

She doesn't remember our last encounter, and I feel stupider than before if that's humanly possible.

'Doesn't matter.'

'I think you might be in shock.'

She helps me on to a seat, flashing me a warm smile. She has hazel-coloured eyes with green flecks and long, long lashes. I touch my temple tentatively. A bruise the size of a duck egg is no doubt rocketing me up the attractiveness stakes.

Liam joins Fliss at the window. He breathes out deeply. 'Did we hit something?'

She peers out. 'I think a car went into the back of *us*.'

I kneel on the seat. *Jeez*. Psycho Driver's car is totalled.

'Why did you hit the brakes, Silas?' I holler.

He's staring in his wing mirror. Maybe he's in shock because he hasn't done responsible adult-in-charge things like make sure we're not bleeding to death or get out to swap insurance details.

'Aren't you going to check the other driver is okay?' Fliss chips in. 'The bumper's hanging off his car.'

'I think he's injured,' Liam adds.

Silas doesn't turn round or speak.

The guy falls out of the Audi, holding a bloodied tissue

to his head. His eyes are dark with fury as he staggers towards us. Oh God. We're miles from anywhere – stuck in no-man's land between two villages. Not many cars use these lanes at this time of the morning – there are more direct routes to Kingsborough.

I pull myself out of the seat and make a beeline for Silas. 'Call the police! That guy's certifiable.'

As if to prove my point, the driver slams a hand against the bus, smearing blood on the window like a returned-from-the-dead-murderer in a horror movie.

Fliss screams and white-hot panic courses through my veins.

'Silas?' I need him to take charge because I'm crap in emergency situations.

Too late.

The man's bloodied face appears, contorted with fury, at the door. He beats his fists on the glass as Silas starts the engine. The bus pulls away.

'You can't escape!' he yells, stumbling after us. 'I know where you live. You're dead meat!'

Shiiiit!

'Silas! What the hell?'

He finally speaks as he changes gear. 'I can't risk letting him on my bus.'

I gape at him. 'But you'll call the police, right? Or an ambulance?'

'Of course! What do you take me for?'

A frigging lunatic obviously.

'But—'

'Sit down and I'll report it!'

I stagger towards the others as the bus picks up speed. Out of the back window, I watch the guy limp to his car. He pulls off the damaged bumper and climbs inside.

Within seconds Psycho Driver is burning rubber, chasing after us.

5

LIAM

'Hold on!' Kai shouts, slumping into the nearest seat.

The bus swings round a tight corner. Brambles and branches thump into the windows in violent protest. Clinging on to the handrail, I shove the glasses up my nose. The right lens is cracked, and the other arm is twisted, but it's better than nothing; I'm practically blind without them.

'Slow down, Silas!' Layla cries.

'For God's sake!' Fliss hollers, gripping the handrail tightly.

I must stay focused despite my throbbing lip. I've memorised the registration plate of the Audi and jotted it down in my maths book, along with a description of the motorist and the time of the crash. Kai explained why Silas didn't stop, but the police will need precise details later and I wouldn't trust this lot to accurately describe a food fight in the school canteen.

I check my phone for signs of life but it's officially dead. I toss it aside as we veer on to the opposite side of the road. Oh God! I'm stuck in a remake of Stephen King's *Duel*. I touch my swollen lip and a small red smear appears on my fingertips. My chest tightens. I hate the sight of blood. The air is squeezed out of my lungs. Black dots multiply in front of my broken lens. I need to hear Tristram's voice. He'd help calm me down, the way Mum does whenever I feel a panic attack coming on. I close my eyes and breathe slowly.

I love maths, classic horror movies with shock twists and Tristram. Not necessarily in that order.

Concentrate on the numbers. Count prime numbers forwards and backwards.

Two, three, five, seven, eleven, thirteen, seventeen.

Seventeen, thirteen, eleven, seven, five, three, two.

'Does anyone have mobile reception?' I ask when my breathing is normalish. 'We should call school to say there's been an accident. Silas will have to pull over soon and we'll be late after giving statements to the police.'

'Seriously?' Layla snorts. '*That's* what you're worried about? Missing maths?'

I can't admit this is my way of coping in stressful situations – I distance myself and organise. I draw up plans, spreadsheets and logic diagrams in my head and analyse the relevant data in order of priority to stop myself from totally freaking out.

'We could call Kingsborough police station. Tell them what's happened in case Silas misses out any pertinent information.'

Layla shakes her head.

'One bar,' Fliss says. 'Not enough to make a call.'

Kai checks. 'Nope. Not yet.' He covers his head with his hands as we take another bend too fast. 'Jeez!'

I check my watch. Silas will stop in approximately three minutes and thirty seconds at the biggest morning pick-up. It'll be a short jog to the nearest house and a landline. If we don't get off, it'll be twelve to thirteen minutes before we clear the coastal roads and regain decent mobile reception.

'Get ready to jump off at the next stop!' I tell the others.

We career past a lay-by where a cyclist is fixing his tyre. At least that's what I'm guessing the man is doing. He dissolves into a blur of silver. The engine roars deafeningly as we begin a steep incline.

'You mean this stop?' Fliss points out of the rear window as the road levels.

'Alvita!' Layla pounds on the glass to one of the girls at our school who's waiting to get on.

I hear a snatch of cries. Puzzled students point and

gesticulate as we speed past. Now they're reduced to matchstick figures in the distance.

'They'll get detentions for being late,' I say.

'Well, at least they'll be alive!' Layla exclaims. 'We're about to enter Sick-bag Pass!'

'W-w-what?'

'The coastal road – it's windy. I don't think my stomach can take it.'

'I'll talk to Silas. Get him to slow down.' I'm hoping I sound brave. The others are making my anxiety go through the roof. If I stay around them much longer, I'll throw up, *Exorcist* style.

'Good idea. I'll come with you.' Fliss brandishes her phone.

We plough forward, grabbing for the rails. I make the mistake of looking ahead. My vision is partially obscured by the cracked lens, but my stomach heaves at the grey expanse of ocean beyond the windscreen.

'You'll be done for dangerous driving.' Fliss pushes past, filming Silas on her phone. 'Mother knows everyone. She'll—'

A loud roar fills the air as the Audi overtakes, swerving in front of us.

'Hold on, kids!' Silas yells.

I grab Fliss's arm as the bus smashes into the back of the

car with an explosion of grinding metal and splintering glass. The Audi spins round and round.

Fliss screams.

'Silas!' Layla yells.

Blood pounds in my ears. Did Silas mistake the accelerator for the brake?

We slam into the side of the car. *That* wasn't an accident. I hear dull thumps behind me – rucksacks dropping from the baggage rack into the aisle. I fall, spread-eagled, on to a seat as the Audi loses control and careers off the road.

'W-w-what are you . . .?'

The words catch in my horribly dry throat as we veer after the vehicle, bouncing downhill through long grass.

'Stop!' My voice is barely a whisper. It's not nearly loud enough.

'Let us the hell off!' Kai bellows from the back.

Silas must have heard that, but doesn't slow down.

'You'll get us all killed!' Layla cries.

'Please, Silas!' Fliss says, sobbing. 'The cliff is . . . there!'

She touches my arm, her eyes wide with fear. 'He'll stop in time, right?'

I gulp. My throat feels as coarse as sandpaper. Silas will come to his senses and brake! This will be like an action movie – the motorist will perform a last-minute handbrake turn, missing death by inches. But we're skimming over the grass towards him. The probability of us dying is 80 per cent and increasing exponentially.

Holy moly! The driver has wrestled back control of his steering wheel. Only one blinking brake light remains intact. He's slowing down within less than ten metres of the cliff edge.

'Brake, Silas!' Fliss shouts.

The bus picks up more speed.

Bang! Our bumper slams into the rear of the car.

'No!' Fliss's fingernails dig into my arm, but I don't feel a thing.

I hear a gasping sound and realise it's coming from my mouth. Metal rips and glass explodes. The car shoots over the edge. It soars into the blue sky in a perfect arc before disappearing. Screams stab my eardrums. An agonising bang rings out followed by the faint boom of an explosion.

I blink repeatedly but can't get rid of the swarming dots before my eyes. The roaring in my ears grows louder.

Silas deliberately rammed the car over the cliff.

He tugs on the steering wheel. We career violently to the left and swerve away. The bus bumps over uneven ground alongside the drop.

'Stop the bus, you fricking psycho!' Fliss screams.

'I can't!' Silas pants. 'Something's caught beneath the brake. Help me!'

My legs are trembling intensely, jelly like, as Fliss drags me forward. I look down. Lodged beneath the brake pedal is a can of Coke. Silas pulls hard on the handbrake.

'Can you reach it?' Fliss asks.

I can't speak. I can't move. Numbly I hang on to the handrail. Making lists and analysing spreadsheets can't help me.

We're going to die.

The words replay on a loop inside my head.

'I'll try.' Fliss falls to her knees and reaches into the footwell. 'I've almost got it!' She stretches further.

'I can't control the bus!' Silas gasps.

I see a flash of red as the can rolls away from Fliss's fingers.

'Strap yourselves in!' Kai yells. 'We're going over!'

My throat makes a strangled sound. My body is paralysed with fear.

Fliss leaps up, shoves me into a seat and swipes at our seat belts, clicking them in as we swing wildly to the right. My glasses fall off as the world shifts. High-pitched screams pierce my ears and I'm hanging upside down. Glass cascades in a waterfall around me. I catch a flash of blue. A bulky holdall slams into Fliss seconds before crushing me. More yells. Hers? Mine? I cradle my head in my hands as we flip over again, but something small and sharp shoots past, slicing my cheek.

Now I'm upright and a strong breeze slaps my face. A nauseating mixture of salt and petrol drifts into my nostrils. Thick gloopy liquid drips down my face and creates a red pattern on the blue bag by my feet. My brain scrambles to catch up.

The bus rolled over. I'm alive. What about the others?

An arm presses against mine. 'Fliss?' My throat contracts.

She's slouched forward, eyes shut. Blood drips from her nose. I almost vomit. Tentatively I press a finger to her wrist the way Mum showed me and feel a pulse.

Indistinguishable moans, followed by cries, ring out behind us. '*Omigod*' and '*We're all going to die!*' That's Layla.

Another voice becomes stronger and more insistent.

'Stop the bus!' Kai yells.

It takes a few more seconds to register that we're still propelling forward.

I look up, trying to focus. Silas's head lolls, the airbag activated. More red spatters. I blink and stare through the gaping hole in the smashed windscreen. It's blurry, but I can make out the cliff edge a few metres away. I hear a whoosh, followed by a deadening crunch and the sound of waves crashing on to rocks.

This is it. The end.

Fliss's eyes flicker open. Breath catches in her throat as she looks ahead. She grabs my hand even though she doesn't give me a second glance at school. She thinks I'm punching far above my weight with Tristram; I *know* that's true. As we embrace, I imagine his arms wrapped round me. I remember the terrible thing I've done for him. It'll come out before I can make everything right. That's how Mum will remember me.

As a liar. A criminal.

She'll be ashamed and wonder what mistakes she made as a mother. But it's not her fault. I knew what I was doing was wrong. I chose to do it anyway.

Metal creaks. The floor lurches and we tilt forward.

Fliss hugs me tighter.

'*I should never have done it,*' she says over and over.

Me too.

I close my eyes as the bus slowly tips nosefirst off the cliff.

6

FLISS

I open my eyes. My mouth widens into an 'O' shape.

Inwardly I'm screaming at the terrifying view. We're hanging over the cliff edge. White surf crashes on to the jagged rocks below. That's where we'll end up, smashed to pieces.

I wish . . .

It's too late for that. I wish I hadn't done a lot of things.

Panic balloons in my chest, squeezing out the air as my gaze rests on the motionless slumped figure at the wheel. The detonated airbag is streaked with sticky dark redness. Vomit rises in my throat. I struggle to keep it down.

'Silas?' I raise my voice. 'Anyone?'

The silence is more horrifying than any screams. Am I the only one left alive?

I'm clinging on to Liam the Limpet – the gang's nickname

for Tristram's latest conquest, not mine. Blood drips down his shirt from a gash on his cheek. His lip is bleeding, but his chest moves gently up and down. Thank God! He's breathing.

'Liam?'

I squeeze his arm, but he doesn't reply. I pinch harder. 'Please!'

This cannot be happening. It's all Mother's fault. I should be in the back of Aaron's Range Rover. I exhale slowly, trying to breathe through the pain. I shift in my seat, making a grenade go off in my ribs.

A girl's voice rings out. 'Help me!'

I've never been so grateful to hear Layla. Kai quietly consoles her. Now he's shouting over to check we're okay.

'Only just.' My voice sounds distant.

I disentangle myself from Liam, trying to avoid looking at the sea.

'Liam? Can you hear me?'

His eyes open. They're glazed. I've read that some people die immediately after a plane crashes even though they've survived the initial impact; they're too numb to run for the emergency exit before the fuel tanks explode.

My hands shake violently as I unclip our seat belts. 'W-w-we have to get to the back.' My tongue feels too big for my mouth.

Liam stares ahead blankly. He's gone into shock and I'm stating the bloody obvious like a doomed female extra in a horror movie.

Oh God. We're *definitely* going to die.

Maybe I deserve to – it's karma for what I did this summer. If I survive, I'll finally confess to the police.

Clutching my ribs, I turn to Liam. 'We'll go together. Nod if you understand.'

He jerks his head. Slowly I get up and turn. Kai is five rows away, attempting to knot a sweatshirt round his knee. His face is contorted with pain. Layla is lying on her side, three quarters of the way back. Her blouse is spattered with blood. I grab Liam's hand and pull him out of his seat, gasping as spasms shoot up and down my ribcage.

A hideous tinny creak rings out as Liam stumbles. The floor shifts.

'Stop!' Kai yells. 'Don't come any closer.'

The bus tilts and rights itself like the world's deadliest seesaw.

'That's okay for you to say from over there!' I hit back. 'What about us?'

Liam's hand feels like marble in mine.

'We have to keep the bus level like we're balancing on a giant surfboard,' Kai insists.

I grimace. I know where I'd like to shove *his* surfboard.

'I'm closest to the emergency exit.' Layla nods over her shoulder. 'I should be able to get it open. I'm gonna try.'

Wincing, she pulls herself along the floor, commando-style. The bus gives a small moan as she heaves herself on to the back seat.

'She's leaving us here.' I grip Liam's arm tighter.

'Of course she's not!' Kai snaps.

'How can you be sure?'

'Because she's not you!' he retorts.

'Stop it! All of you!'

We jump as Liam finally finds his voice.

He clears his throat. 'It's simple. We work together or we die.'

Layla flinches. 'You're right.'

'We have to trust each other,' he continues falteringly. 'Can you all do that?'

Kai shrugs noncommittally.

'Sure,' I mutter.

Layla nods. None of us look convinced, but this is about survival.

Liam's chest rises and falls rapidly. 'Layla, don't try to open the window until we're all over there with you.' His voice wavers before gaining strength. 'Kai, you move first.

Get over to Layla and take those rucksacks with you. We need as much weight as possible at the back.' He pauses, breathing out through pursed lips. 'But do it slowly. No sudden movements – from anyone.'

Kai bends down and yanks the rucksacks. He moves carefully down the aisle, dragging his injured leg behind him. The bus creaks gently. Bile tastes bitter in my mouth. If Kai doesn't get a move on, we're . . .

I turn away, retching, but nothing comes up. By the time I look again, he's dumped the rucksacks by the back row.

'Now it's our turn.'

Liam catches my hand. 'Just me.'

'What? You can't abandon me!'

He holds tighter as I lunge forward. 'No one will be left behind.'

My head swims and my chest constricts at that familiar feeling of danger – trying to escape but knowing deep down it's too late. I'm trapped.

'Look at me, Fliss,' he says.

I peel my eyes away from the emergency window.

'Count prime numbers in reverse from twenty.'

'What?'

'I mean, just count backwards.'

I swallow hard.

'Honestly it helps.' He lowers his voice. 'I do it whenever I'm anxious.'

I give it a go.

Twenty, nineteen . . .

'This isn't personal,' he continues. 'It's basic maths. You're lighter than me. We need more weight over there, which means shifting that.' He jerks his head at the blue holdall. 'Can you move it if you're in pain?'

My fingers curl protectively round my ribcage. I hate to admit it, but he's right. There's no way I can push anything.

'You're the next person to go,' he stresses.

I stop counting.

'The *last* one,' I clarify. 'The one you all left behind.'

'That won't happen, I promise. Okay?'

Reluctantly I nod. Every fibre of my body is telling me to get to that side – by staggering, crawling, knocking the others out of the way . . . *trampling over them if I have to* . . . I'll do anything to survive. I force myself to stand still as Liam gets on his knees and manoeuvres into position. He tentatively pushes the holdall.

'What's inside? Bricks?'

'That's what I said,' Kai remarks.

He tries again. This time the bag moves a few centimetres.

'Can you go any faster?' I ask.

Liam sighs, rubbing his back. 'I can't get in the right position. It's heavy.'

'Let me help,' Kai says.

'No, I'll try dragging it.' He stands up cautiously.

The bus makes a tiny squeak as Kai walks slowly towards us.

'Stay there!' Liam shouts.

'It'll be quicker if we both do it.'

He reaches Liam and grabs hold of the strap. The bag shifts as they both pull.

'You're doing well,' Layla says encouragingly.

I bite down on my lip until I recognise the coppery taste of blood.

'Did you feel that?' Kai asks, as they pass the halfway point.

'W-w-what?' I stutter.

'I swear the bus is levelling.'

'It is!' Layla throws her arms round the boys as they reach her.

I step closer. 'I'm coming.'

'No, wait!' Layla cries. 'We can't leave Silas.'

'He's dead!'

'Are you sure?' she asks.

'Look at him! He hasn't moved.'

We stare at the bloodied figure slumped over the wheel.

'Layla's right,' Liam says. 'He could be unconscious.'

'Tough,' I mutter. 'He caused this.'

'We should check,' Kai insists. 'He'll go over with the bus when we climb out.'

I jab a finger at the windscreen. 'I could fall through that gap!'

'The bus is more stable,' Liam points out. 'You can do this. I know you can.'

I shake my head. 'How can you? None of you know me.'

'Whose fault is that?' Layla demands. 'You don't want to mix with passengers from the *Poverty Express*. That's how you and your snotty friends describe this bus service, isn't it? I overheard Lisa call it that at choir practice.'

Liam scrutinises my face. I force myself to hold his gaze. He doesn't realise his boyfriend came up with the name at a party and it stuck.

'I've never called it that. I swear!'

That's a lie, but I need their help to get out of here.

Kai sighs heavily. 'Arguing isn't helping. Why don't you try to edge closer to him? If we feel the bus move, stop. It's not like he'd help us.'

'Fine!' I shuffle towards Silas, careful not to look directly at the smashed window. I bite my lip at the sound of a large wave exploding on to the rocks below.

'Silas? Can you hear me?' I take another step closer.

'Check for a pulse,' Liam calls out as I reach him.

I don't want to look at, let alone touch, a dead body. It reminds me of . . . I force the image from my mind and shake Silas's shoulder. Nothing. I prod the side of his neck. It's cold and clammy. *Gross*. I can't feel anything. Am I touching the right place? *God knows*. I'm not a medic.

The bus groans and shifts.

'Jeez!' Kai exclaims.

'Like I said, the homicidal maniac is dead!'

My legs give way and I drop to my knees. I take a deep breath before I crawl towards them. Tears patter on to the floor. I didn't feel them forming. My arms are heavy. My legs too. My ribs are burning like *Dante's Inferno*.

Keep moving.

I repeat the words under my breath. No encouragement rings out as I edge closer. No one hugs me when I reach them. I pull myself on to a seat next to Liam, panting through the red-hot pain. I turn away as more tears form.

'At least we tried,' Liam says. 'Which is more than Silas deserves.'

'Sure. Let's get outta here. Do your thing, Layla.' Kai nods at the emergency window.

She reaches up and yanks the lever.

I hold my breath, barely daring to hope. *Don't be jammed.*
Layla tugs again and pushes the handle.

'Yes!' Kai punches the air, as the window swings open widely.

Liam inhales and breathes out deeply through pursed lips.

'Who goes first?' Layla asks.

'Not who – it's what.' Liam rubs his glistening eyes. 'We need to wedge the holdall through the window. We can't risk it slamming shut and trapping us inside.'

Kai gazes at the gap. His mouth falls open. 'We have to get it up there?'

'No way can I lift my arms above my head,' I say quickly.

'I'll try,' Kai says. 'But my knee's knackered.'

'Layla?' Liam asks.

'We should manage it between the three of us.'

'Okay,' Liam says. 'Grab a side. I'll count us in. One, two, three!'

The holdall lands on the seat. After another countdown, they move the bag closer towards the gap and on to the window ledge.

'There!' Kai stands back, wincing. 'That should do it, right?'

'One more push,' Liam insists.

They both kneel on the seat and hoist it, like they're lifting dead weights. Liam has surprisingly muscly arms for a nerd. The bag hangs half out of the window. His plan might actually work.

'You girls should go first.' Kai looks at us.

'Do our nineteenth-century carriages await us?' Layla says jokingly.

'What? I'm not being sexist. You look slim . . .' His face flushes scarlet. 'I mean, you and Fliss are the lightest.'

'I'm ribbing you, but thanks.' Her cheeks match his.

Liam coughs. 'Do you want to go first, Fliss?'

Yes, obviously!

I force myself to shake my head. After all, Layla could break my fall.

She scrambles nimbly on to the seat and stares out of the window, judging the distance to the ground before sliding gracefully through the gap.

'You next, Fliss,' Liam says.

'Are you sure?' I deliberately make my voice sound small and weak.

Liam nods. Kai helps me up to the opening. I blink as salty air stings my lips. I try to follow Layla's example – she made escaping look easy – but there's nothing simple about clambering out of a window when every movement is agony. My vision swims as another gust of wind strikes my face. I try to breathe through the waves of pain as Liam suggested, but my chest is tightening. I close my eyes.

'I can't do this!'

'Yes, you can!' Layla shouts. 'Look – it's hardly any drop.'

Slowly I open my eyes and stare down. Layla's standing on brittle yellowish grass studded with jagged shards of glass.

She kicks them out of the way. 'Sling your leg over. I'll help you down. It won't be as bad as you think.'

I don't take my eyes off her as I try to manoeuvre into position.

'That's right. Take it slow. Now the other leg.'

Suddenly there's a loud bang. Metal groans and grinds. I scream as the bus creaks and tilts. I cling on to the holdall, half in, half out.

'What's going on?' I shout.

'It's Silas!' Liam exclaims. 'He's unstrapped himself.'

'But he's dead!'

My words hang balloon-like in the air as a man screams, 'You thieving bastards!'

'What?' Kai cries.

Silas's voice rings out again. 'My holdall!'

'We're not nicking it,' Kai explains. 'We're using it to escape!'

'I'll kill you all!'

I force myself to look back into the bus. Silas is on all fours, crawling towards us with a crazed expression on his bloodied face. The boys' lips are moving, but I can't hear what they're saying. The buzzing sound in my ears is deafening. How is this possible? Silas felt dead. He *was* dead.

Kai screams in my face. 'Let go!'

I try to move my leg, but my shoe is caught on the holdall strap.

'Jump!' Liam hollers.

He gives me a hard shove. I fall through the window and land on my back. Pain rockets in every nerve ending. Blackness descends behind my eyelids. I must pass out momentarily, because when my eyes flicker open, Kai is standing nearby. The bus is groaning and shaking precariously, caught on a rock.

'What about Liam?' Layla yells.

'This was his idea,' Kai counters breathlessly. 'Give me a lift.'

Layla makes a cup with her hands, and Kai hoists himself up the side of the bus. Dangling from the window, he tenses his muscles and pulls the frame down.

'Get out, Liam!' he shouts. 'I can't hold on for ever.'

The bus judders, tipping backwards.

'Hurry up,' Layla hollers. 'It's going over!'

Liam levers himself through the gap, clinging on to the holdall. He's slithering out when a hand grabs his ankle.

'Give me the money!' Silas yells.

Liam blanches white, attempting to struggle free. 'What money? Let go!'

The hand tugs harder.

'Stop it! We can both make it.'

Silas's gashed face appears, twisted with fury. He swipes for Liam's arm. The bus rocks precariously.

'Get off him!' Kai yells.

He stretches up and rips Liam out of Silas's grasp as a loud, terrible rumbling noise fills the air. Liam falls headfirst out of the window, on top of Kai, as the vehicle slides backwards. Silas screeches, swiping for the holdall, but it falls out with a dull thud on to the grass, next to the spread-eagled boys. Silas's eyes lock with mine as he clutches at air, wide-eyed and terrified, before the bus tilts and disappears.

There's a silence, a vast empty space where the bus was a second ago. Sea and sky replacing twisted metal and paint.

The four of us are frozen, unable to move or speak, for what feels like an eternity.

'Oh God!' Layla's stricken voice breaks the silence.

I place my hands over my eyes and press hard, trying to

get rid of the image of Silas's petrified face. It doesn't work. I gaze at the vast azure sky, one of the last glorious days before autumn. My friends will head to the sands below the Sea Haven after school. They may have a barbecue and a few sneaky beers and joints on the beach. But life will never be the same for any of *us* after today.

We've witnessed a murder and a gruesome death. We almost died.

Kai staggers to the cliff edge, peering over. He shudders. 'What the hell . . .?' He falls back a step. 'I don't get it . . . Why would Silas . . .?'

'He accused us of stealing.' Liam tries to stand but his knees buckle. He sinks to the ground. 'He kept yelling at me to give back his money.'

'What money?' Layla asks.

'No idea,' he says shakily.

'Does anyone have their phone to call 999?' I cut in.

'Nope,' Kai replies.

Layla clears her throat. 'Me neither.'

'We have to flag down a car,' Liam says quietly.

I can't move. I close my eyes. I'm icy cold. I've survived, but my problems aren't over. My blackmailer is coming for me. I'd pledged to hand myself in to the police if I survived. That's the right thing to do, isn't it? Ignore Mother's orders and tell *my* version of events. If I do, the blackmailer won't hold any power over me. I can end this.

'Maybe Silas kept a phone in his holdall?' Kai says.

I hear the metallic ripping of a zip.

Layla gasps. 'Tell me that isn't . . .'

'Holy crap!' Kai says, laughing.

Liam whispers, 'Impossible!'

Something flutters lightly on to my forehead and hand.

And again.

It feels like fragile butterflies are landing around me, a final, fleeting reminder of summer before they are all doomed to die.

I open my eyes.

Fifty-pound notes swirl above my head.

7

LAYLA

I forget the pain rippling through my body as I pull out bricks of fifty-pound notes from the holdall. Some have escaped from their elastic bands and dance wildly above our heads. Kai makes a grab for a couple, but they flutter over the edge.

'I've never seen so much money in my life.' I hold up a note. Vivid redness is smeared on the torn corner. I stuff it back into the bag, wiping my hands on the grass. I shudder as I study my fingers; blood has dried deep beneath the nails.

Kai staggers towards us, clutching a few escaped fifties to his chest. He drops to his knees, grinning. 'Ha, ha. We're rich!'

I can't help but smile as he runs his hands through his dirty blond hair, his grey-blue eyes sparkling. I'd deliberately called him Kyle when we last spoke. My cheeks were burning, and I hadn't wanted him to guess how much I like him. I try to ignore the butterflies that tickle the pit of my stomach.

Liam sighs, picking up more escaped fifties. 'It's not ours, *unfortunately*.'

Fliss crawls over, shaking her head with disbelief. We watch the cash, transfixed, like we're afraid it could disappear into thin air if we blink.

'How much is that exactly?'

Fliss checks over her shoulder, as if someone might be eavesdropping, but I haven't heard any cars drive past. We're completely alone except for the caws of gulls circling over a spot beyond the cliff. Is that where the bodies are floating? Bile rises in my throat. I don't know how Kai had the stomach to look over the edge.

I swallow hard. 'Slightly more than your monthly allowance?'

'Funny.' She grips her ribs tighter, her face grey and taut with pain. 'Liam?'

He traces his fingers over the wads of money.

'Approximately one million pounds.'

'Seriously?' Kai lets out a low whistle.

'Well, that's a guesstimate.'

'One million pounds,' I repeat slowly. 'Imagine what you could buy!'

Tiny sharp blades pierce my chest as I think of Salih – this would fund his treatment in the States. Plus four other sick kids. It would be life-changing.

'I'd help Mum with the rent and bills,' Liam says. 'It would stop her from worrying about her job. She might not have to work if she doesn't want to! We could find somewhere nicer to live around here. Next, I'd buy an investment flat ready for when I head to Cambridge with . . .' He coughs. 'I'd pay my tuition fees upfront and fund my mathematics PhD at Stanford.'

'Wow!' I exclaim. 'You've got it all planned out.'

'Doesn't everyone fantasise about winning the lottery?' he asks.

I shake my head. Apart from saving for driving lessons and a flight to Cairo to visit Teta, cash has never dominated my thoughts, until this morning.

'I'd buy presents – designer clothes and watches – for the people I love,' Liam adds. 'Maybe a Jeep to show them how much I care.'

'Wow. That's specific!' Layla remarks.

Colour rises in his face. 'I'd also pay for my New Year ski holiday and buy all the equipment.'

Fliss frowns. 'Tristram has invited *you*?'

Liam doesn't notice the edge in her voice. He nods happily

and turns to Kai. 'I guess you'd be sorted with surfboards and camper vans for life!'

'Sure, that's the only thing I'd think to buy.' Kai's eyes moisten as he clears his throat. 'What about you, Fliss?'

She stares up the hillside, towards the road. 'Does it matter?'

Ha, that's *so* Fake Fliss! What could the richest girl in school, the absolute epitome of white privilege, want when she has everything? I bet a million isn't that much by her family's standards. They're multimillionaires. For mine money is a matter of life and death.

'After what's happened, talking about money feels . . .' Her voice trails off.

My cheeks warm furiously. 'What's the view like from that moral high ground of yours?'

It's her turn to redden. 'Playing what-will-I-spend-my-imaginary-money-on isn't high up my priority list.' She touches her ribs.

'This explains why Silas was freaking out,' Kai says, cutting in. 'He must have thought we were trying to steal his fortune.'

Liam's eyebrows shoot upwards. 'What are the chances we'd do that?'

'Yeah, I know. Right?' Kai laughs hollowly. 'We're not thieves.'

I flinch at the word. That's exactly what Mrs C thinks I am. Maybe Fliss too. She flicks a fly off her hand and looks out to sea, refusing to meet my gaze.

'Silas must have been a thief,' I point out.

'You reckon?' Kai's gaze flickers back to the cash.

'How else did he get one million pounds? Drivers don't earn much. It *has* to be stolen.'

Fliss nods. 'It looks well dodgy. Only a criminal would keep this amount of cash in a crappy holdall.'

I swallow a snort. Even in a life-or-death situation, she notices labels – and the lack of them. I bet all her luggage is Louis Vuitton.

Liam rifles through Silas's *non-designer* bag, checking his guesstimate is correct. He hates being wrong and thinks 91 per cent in a maths test is a failure.

'Do we think the Audi driver knew about the cash?' Kai asks. 'Silas was worried about him when I got on the bus.'

I give a tiny shrug. 'It'd explain why he was chasing us.'

'And why Silas wanted to get rid of him over the cliff – he had to tie up a loose end to keep the money,' Kai adds.

'He'd probably have killed *us* if he'd made it off alive,' Liam says quietly.

'Seriously?' Sure, I'd overheard Silas threatening him and

65

Kai on the bus, but it's quite the leap to committing the cold-blooded murder of four teenagers.

I watch as Liam pulls out a dark shape from the holdall. It takes a few seconds for my brain to register that he's pointing a gun at Kai. My heart pounds furiously. My palms are slick with sweat.

Kai scrambles backwards on his heels.

'Liam!' I shout. 'What are you doing?'

He swings round.

Fliss shudders. 'Don't point that thing at me, you idiot!'

'Sorry. I'm not used to holding one.' Liam gestures in the air with the weapon. 'It's light. I think it's a fake. Silas probably kept it for show.'

He aims out to sea and pulls the trigger. A loud crack startles the seagulls. Their aggrieved chorus is deafening: a cacophony of long high-pitched notes.

'Holy moly.' His hand drops to his side.

'Jeez!' Kai exclaims. 'You could have shot me!'

'Put that thing down before you kill one of us.' My heart is beating a million, if not a trillion, times a minute.

Liam's hands shake as he carefully places the loaded gun on the grass. 'I don't know about any of you, but this is beginning to feel . . .'

'Unreal?' I suggest. 'Or plain crazy?'

Our classmates are having registration, but we've survived a high-speed crash. Two people are dead. We have a gun *and* one million pounds. Yeah, it's your average school day.

'Can everyone stop messing about?' Fliss snaps. 'I can barely walk. Someone has to flag down a car before one of us *does* end up dead. The police can work out what Silas was doing after we hand over the money.'

'Yes, of course that's what we should do.' Liam shivers, staring at the gun. 'We give the bag to the police. Let them deal with it.'

'Exactly!' she exclaims.

Kai runs his fingers over the loose notes inside the holdall. 'Yeah. I mean, it's not as if we could keep the cash, is it?'

The question hangs heavily in the air. The caws of the seagulls die down.

My heart skips a beat as I think of my sick brother:

Salih on his knees, throwing up repeatedly into the toilet.

Whimpering with pain on the sofa, tears streaming down his face.

Back in hospital, sunken-eyed and hooked up to tubes that keep him alive.

'We can't keep it,' Fliss insists. 'That would be theft!'

What the hell? Fake Fliss is the last person I'd expect to have scruples about . . . well, anything. Last term, she and

67

her friends ghosted Annie from my class, probably for the stupidly minor crime of not liking their Insta posts or TikTok videos fast enough. She's dropped out and moved to a new school.

But it literally *kills* me to admit that Fliss is right. I've been in pieces over that missing opal ring all weekend. I didn't steal it and her mum's false accusation continues to sting.

But . . . haven't I vowed to save Salih's life?

Family is everything, Baba used to say. *Nothing else matters as much.*

Isn't standing back and not trying to help Salih far worse than stealing from a psychotic dead bus driver? Silas can't claim the cash. Plus, there's no way he had that amount legally.

Salih is innocent, but Silas wasn't.

Kai can't stop touching the cash; it's like he's been hypnotised. 'What do you reckon the police will do with the money?'

'I read somewhere they incinerate illegal drugs from raids,' Liam replies. 'I'm not sure about stolen cash.'

Kai looks stricken. 'I don't want to think about burning one million pounds!'

'I guess they might keep it,' Liam says flatly.

'Lucky police!' Kai replies.

'Fascinating.' Fliss glowers at us. 'About flagging down that car?'

Liam's eyebrow twitches. He doesn't move. Neither does Kai. They both look deep in thought. I bite my lip until I taste blood in my mouth.

'Hypothetically speaking, what if we *did* keep the cash?'

Liam glances at me. 'Are you serious?'

A strange expression flits across Kai's face. Surprise? But isn't this exactly what he's thinking – Liam too?

Fliss shakes her head. 'Hypothetically speaking, we'd all go to jail.'

'Only if someone found out, but who would ever know?'

'*We* would!' Fliss's voice trembles. 'There are always repercussions. You have to live with what you've done . . .' Her voice trails off, her eyes shining.

'Fliss has a point,' Kai says. 'Maybe Silas had another accomplice.'

'That's not *exactly* what I was saying.' Fliss sighs. 'But yeah, one million pounds doesn't just go walkies. People will come after it.'

I try to keep my face neutral and not betray any flicker of worry. 'If that happens, wouldn't they assume the holdall went over the cliff with the bus? We'd have to be careful –

no flashing the cash on Insta or going on huge spending sprees.'

Kai inhales sharply. 'We couldn't tell anyone else – not even our closest friends or family. We'd have to keep it tight, to us four.'

I flash him a small smile. My heart beats faster as he grins back.

'This is crazy!' Fliss exclaims. 'I can't believe we're discussing this.'

I tear my gaze away from Kai's face. 'That's because we weren't born into money,' I say. 'You have no idea what life is like for *passengers on the Poverty Express*.'

'Yeah, sorry. I'd assumed you'd all know the difference between right and wrong. But I guess Mother was right about you, Layla.'

'You b—'

'Stop it, you two!' Liam steps between us, as I lurch towards her.

'I never stole that ring!' I yell. 'I was set up.'

'That makes two of us!' Kai exclaims. 'I didn't steal anything from your phone, Fliss.'

'The jury's out when you're both willing to steal now,' she hits back.

'This is different!' I shout.

'*Is* it? The money isn't ours.'

'It doesn't belong to anyone now, though,' I argue.

'Let's try to think about this logically,' Liam says.

Logically I'd like to thump Fliss – injured ribs or not. She doesn't get to judge me! Isn't it time my family had a break? We've experienced a run of terrible luck.

It was pure chance that the holdall didn't go over the cliff. And yes, I'm prepared to do something wrong. I'll become exactly what Fliss and her mum think I am: a thief. But it'll be worthwhile if it saves my brother. Wouldn't she do the same if she were in my shoes?

Wouldn't everyone take this chance?

There's no going back. I *have* to do this.

For Salih.

For Mum and Leon.

For Baba and Teta.

I take a deep breath. 'Let's split the cash four ways – a quarter of a million each. It'll be our secret.'

8

KAI

Two hundred and fifty thousand pounds.

I picture the four-bedroom house that Mum loves. Our future dream home. That's what she used to call Torside Lodge. Except the monthly rent was way beyond our budget, long before the village post office closed and she lost her job. She had to move away with my younger sister, Crystal, leaving me behind temporarily because of school. She's saving cash by living with her new boyfriend, Paul, and his daughter, Lucy, in Bristol. But it's only a short-term arrangement and she's promised to come back soon. I walked past Torside Lodge the other day – it's still empty. It has a massive kitchen, an outhouse for my bike and surfboards and a big back garden for Crystal. We wouldn't even have to share bedrooms if Paul and Lucy end up here too. Obviously, that's not ideal but I could try harder to get on with him for Mum's sake.

The beach is only a five-minute walk away. I could take the kids after school; we'd build sandcastles or look for seashells. Mum would bring a barbecue like old times, and we'd all stay until late, watching a firework display across the water at the Sea Haven. I close my eyes and can almost hear the laughter and smell the pungent charcoal and sizzling meat juices mixed with the salt air. My chest aches, an emptiness that grows and grows every day and can never be filled.

'I'm in,' I say loudly. 'Liam?'

He coughs uncomfortably. 'It's a tough one, morally and philosophically speaking—'

'An answer, not a lecture, please!' Layla says teasingly.

Liam shrugs. 'We should try to be non-judgemental. I'm guessing we each have a different rationale for wanting the cash. *Private* reasons.'

He fixes me with a hard look as if he's trying to read my mind. I glance away. I'm hardly likely to 'fess up to him about my makeshift living arrangements.

'I'm in,' he continues, 'but with the caveat we establish guidelines – rules about what we can and can't do.'

I giggle. 'Jeez. Do you want to draw up a spreadsheet?'

'I would if I thought you'd know how to read one, but I doubt they teach you that in sociology,' he hits back.

'Psychology actually.'

'Even worse!'

I mock stagger, clutching my chest as if wounded. Comedy is my best defence. It prevents anyone from realising the insinuations that I'm a dumb stoned surfer have hit home. I force the corners of my mouth to stay curled upwards.

'You've lost your minds.' Fliss winces as she slowly gets to her feet. 'I don't want to be a part of this. I'm outta here.' She sways before regaining her balance and limping away.

Layla's bottom lip trembles. 'We all have to be in this for it to work.'

'We could shoot her in the back,' I say, playing for laughs.

I swear Layla looks tempted, but Liam gives me a withering 'you are the stupidest person in the universe' glare before going after her.

'We're sorry,' he calls out. 'We're in the wrong, not you.'

She stops. No one could accuse *him* of being daft – flattery gets you everywhere with Fliss, along with money. *Usually.* She only mixes with the sons and daughters of property tycoons and millionaire farmers at school.

'You're right,' Liam says. 'You're in pain and we need to get help – that should be our priority. We don't have to decide *now.* We could discuss it later, after you've been checked over at the hospital.'

74

She turns round, her eyes narrowing.

'Don't rule it out,' he says quickly. 'Say you'll think about it.'

I hold my breath.

'Please, Fliss,' Liam adds. He shoots a pleading look at me.

I sigh – it kills me to beg for anything from Fliss. Her mates have been making Lou's life hell since the summer and she's done sweet eff all to stop them. I manage to get the words out without choking.

'We're sorry if you feel like we're ganging up on you. Aren't we, Layla?'

I don't know about her, but my family needs this money and I'll do pretty much anything to get it.

'Yes, sure,' Layla says through gritted teeth. 'We don't want to pressure you.'

Except that's exactly what we're trying to do.

I feel my dreams slip away, like sand between my fingers, as Fliss shakes her head. The house, Mum, Crystal. *My family together.*

'Please!' I cry. 'We'll all owe you.'

I regret those words as soon as they escape from my lips. Being indebted to Fliss is a terrible idea.

Her eyes narrow as if she's calculating something. 'Fine,'

she says at last. 'I'll think about it. But *that's all*. I'm not promising.'

My heart leaps as I dare to hope again.

Layla sways. 'Wow. I mean, thank you,' she says in a strangled tone.

'Like Kai said, you'll all owe me,' she replies sharply.

Something dark and frightening shifts behind her eyes. I blink and the strange expression has gone. I wonder if I imagined it.

'Sure . . .' Layla doesn't look happy, but at least we've bought more time.

I stare at the holdall and gun – we can't leave either lying around for the police to find.

'Why don't you two hide the bag?' Layla says. 'Fliss can stay here and rest while I head up to the road and find help.'

I beam at her. 'Brilliant idea!'

Liam swallows a snigger. Layla blushes, her gaze lowering. *Note to self: dial it back.*

We help Fliss sit down next to the holdall. Layla picks up the gun gingerly with her fingertips and opens the bag wider, placing it inside. A breeze catches the loose notes and scatters them across the grass.

'Dammit!' she exclaims.

Liam grabs the notes nearest to him. Layla heads in the

opposite direction and Fliss manages to stretch and grasp a few. I chase after the rest, scooping up a fistful. Carefully, as I hunch over, I slip a couple into my pocket to help tide me over. I can buy proper food instead of grabbing leftovers from the tables outside cafés. I turn round slowly, but the others are debating the best spot to look for a car and haven't noticed. I stuff the rest of the notes inside and zip up the holdall.

'Give us a shout if you see a motorist,' Liam says.

'Not sure you'll hear me if I have to walk to the junction, but I can try,' Layla replies.

As she makes her way up the hill, Liam examines the bus and car tyre marks. They've left deep gashes in the grass. Both sets trail up to the road, together with pieces of twisted metal and sharp pointed shards of glass.

'We need to find a hiding place away from here – the police mustn't accidentally come across it,' he says.

Why does he have to state the obvious? I'm not the village idiot!

I scan the bare hills, resisting the urge to react. The hedge isn't thick enough to camouflage the bright blue material, and we can't exactly dig a hole with our bare hands. The ground is parched after this summer's record temperatures.

'How about that?' Fliss points to an overturned cattle

77

trough, further along the slope. 'Could the holdall fit underneath?'

'I can't see a thing without my glasses,' Liam admits.

'It's worth a try,' I say. 'There's nothing else around here.'

I heave up the holdall, slinging it over my shoulder. My legs immediately buckle. My muscles scream with pain. I dump it down, exhaling heavily.

'Here, let me give you a hand.'

Normally I can easily lift weights, but I'm wasted. I used all my energy hanging on to the bus, and my kneecap burns.

We grab both ends and start moving, but Liam's arms are trembling.

'Can we do this?' he says, panting.

My words come out in staccato beats. 'Don't. Have a choice. If want. Money.'

A look of determination flickers across his face. 'Okay.'

We manage to stagger a couple of metres before putting the holdall down. We carry on like that – stopping and starting – for a few minutes as the pain builds in my kneecap.

'Let me get my breath,' I say.

We pause again. Liam rolls up his sleeves and stretches his arms over his head. Lou will probably appreciate a description of Hot Maths Geek's guns. They were flirting on WhatsApp before Tristram asked HMG out and the late-night messages abruptly stopped. What am I thinking? I can't tell Lou anything about this. Not a word. Even though Lou trusted me enough to tell me that they were non-binary before anyone else knew, I can't trust them – or anyone – with what's happened today.

We set off silently. Both of us are breathing heavily and concentrating on every step. I stumble as Liam drops his end. The bag slips from my grasp with a thud.

'Careful! The gun could have gone off.'

'Sorry. I felt a twinge in my back. Let's go.'

Clenching my jaw, we hoist up the bag and carry it across dead yellowing grass. The rusty cattle trough is a tetanus trap, but it's a good hiding place – no one will think to look under here. *Why would they?* Nobody knows the cash didn't go over the cliff except for the four of us. Liam carefully lifts it, avoiding the sharp edges, and I push the bag inside. He lets go, wiping his hands on his bloodstained trousers.

'It's not bad for a temporary hiding place,' he says begrudgingly, 'but it's risky leaving it out here for long. We'll need to move it later.'

'I can't cycle to . . . I mean, home, with the holdall. My knee's knackered.'

Liam touches his bloodied cheek. 'We're both banged up, but I doubt we'll be admitted to hospital. I might get a longer check-up given my medical history, but I don't think I've done any serious damage.' He touches his back and stretches.

I'm about to ask if he's got an old injury when he continues talking.

'We'll have to speak to the police, but they won't put us through hours of interviews. Not today anyway.'

I shiver. What were the chances *we* survived? I bet HMG, *Liam*, has calculated the odds in his incredible computer brain.

'I guess that means coming back tonight,' I say. 'But it doesn't solve the problem of how we shift the holdall. I don't fancy our chances walking.'

'I could borrow my mum's car and sneak out, say, three a.m.?' He pauses for a beat. 'I could pick you up if you can get away without your parents noticing?'

'Sure. Shouldn't be a problem. Meet me at the corner of Becket's Road and Boathouse Lane.'

'Affirmative. If one of us isn't there by three fifteen, it means it's off. My mum has sussed what I'm doing or you've been arrested.'

I bite my lip.

'I'm joking! The police don't have a clue the holdall exists.'

That's not what I'm worried about. What should I tell the

police when they ask about next of kin? And where will I sleep if I can't break into the holiday home?

'First sign of trouble here tonight – forensic teams or police guarding the site – we pull out. We shouldn't take unnecessary risks that could dramatically increase the percentage chance of being caught.' He stretches out his hand. 'Agreed?'

I manage to bite back a snarky remark about whether he's written a set of rules on another bloody spreadsheet. We shake on it.

'Thank you,' he says stiffly, as we walk back.

'For what?'

'You saved my life on the bus. If you hadn't pulled me out . . .' He shivers.

His mind must be taking him to dark places. Mine would. The agony of falling backwards over the cliff, knowing you'll die within seconds.

'No worries,' I say gruffly. 'You'd have done the same for me, right?'

He nods.

Hmmm. I wonder.

'How's Lou doing?' he asks.

I shoot him a sideways look at the sudden change of subject. Does HMG still care? He didn't seem to when he ghosted them, probably on Tristram's orders.

Before I can lie and tell him that Lou is doing great, two dark-clothed figures run down the slope. My heartbeat quickens.

'Who's that?' Liam says, squinting. 'Did Layla get help?'

'Maybe. They're police officers!'

'That's good, right?'

'Is it?'

Fliss calls out to the policeman and woman. Instead of trying to distract them, she points directly at us. They stare, before the policeman reaches for his radio.

Aargh! She isn't . . . Surely, she wouldn't . . .?

'What's happening?' Liam asks. 'Nothing's in focus.'

I shove my hand into my pocket. The fifty-pound notes crackle guiltily. My throat dries. A cold shiver runs down my spine.

'Kai?'

'Fliss has betrayed us!'

9

LIAM

'What are we going to do?' Kai looks around wildly.

He doesn't have many escape options unless he fancies leaping off the cliff. I'd put his chance of survival at 0.1 per cent.

'Calm down! We don't know what Fliss is saying.'

'That's what worries me,' he yelps, shoving his hands deep into his trouser pockets. 'She could have told them everything!'

'Or precisely zero.'

The fuzzy dark shape draws closer.

'Are you kids badly hurt?' a woman's voice calls out.

'Yes . . . no . . .' Kai coughs. 'We were keeping it safe,' he finishes lamely.

'Say again? I didn't catch that.'

'Stop talking!' I hiss before raising my voice. 'We're . . . walking wounded.'

The policewoman comes into focus. She's short with curly red hair. My gaze rests on the taser hanging from her belt.

'We've radioed for ambulances. Are there any other survivors?

'The two of us, plus Fliss and Layla,' I reply.

'Layla?'

'She flagged you down up there.' I nod towards the road.

'Not seen her yet. We were on our way to reports of a break-in and spotted the skid marks and debris. We followed the trail down here.' She pauses. 'If your friend is trying to get help, what are you two doing over here?'

'W-w-we split up,' Kai stammers. 'None of us has phones. We're t-t-trying to flag down a car.'

'Off road?'

'Look, I'm sorry—' Kai begins.

'We got confused,' I say, faking a stumble. 'I'm not sure where we're going. I can't see anything without my glasses.' This time I genuinely trip as my foot catches on a tuft of grass.

She eyes us carefully. 'You're both in shock. Come with me. We need to find your friend and make sure she's okay.'

Her voice is soft and kind, making my eyes well up.

'It was awful,' I blurt out. 'The other driver was killed and Silas . . .'

I start to weep. Kai puts his arm round my shoulders. That makes me feel worse about being vile to him. I automatically go into attack mode around surfers. They're usually the worst offenders at school for mocking my body. In return, I taunt their intellect – my brain is my only superpower.

'It's okay,' the policewoman says, as she leads us away. 'You're both safe.'

Are we? My heart beats rapidly. I've managed to hold it together until now because of the adrenaline coursing through my veins. I'd calculated the best way to evacuate the bus, according to my estimate of everyone's weight, and tried to organise the others. But Fliss was right. What are we doing, plotting to steal £1 million? It's the worst plan in the world. I must be the sensible one who puts an end to this before we get sucked any deeper into this black hole of madness. I glance back at the cattle trough.

'Have you dropped something?' the policewoman asks.

'His glasses.' Kai propels me forward. 'But they're smashed and no use.'

Her radio crackles as Kai frogmarches me away, whispering in my ear.

'Remember, we're not deciding now, we're . . .' His voice falters.

'What is it?'

'Layla's coming down the hill and the Lobster Bar boss is here.'

'Frankie?'

'Yeah, I think. Layla must have flagged her down. She's at the top of the slope, talking on her phone.'

Frankie and Mum are best friends – that's how I got my Saturday job waiting tables at her restaurant. She's the last person I want to see today but hopefully she's ringing Mum. I've never needed her more. Layla flings herself on the grass as we reach Fliss. The policewoman steps away to speak into her radio.

'So?' Kai blurts out. 'What did you tell them?'

'Shhh!'

Fliss jerks her head at a figure racing towards us. Long black hair streams over her shoulders. *Frankie.* Kai studies a patch of grass as we sit down. Even without my glasses, I can make out where we opened the holdall – the weight of the cash has flattened the sun-bleached blades and left a large, incriminating indentation. I shuffle along, sitting on the spot as Frankie throws her arms round me.

'Omigod, Liam. I can't believe what's happened. Are you hurt?'

My skin prickles with guilt at her kindness.

I'm a terrible person. The worst.

I push her away. 'Just a few cuts and bruises. Nothing serious.'

'I've left a message for your mum. When the ambulance gets here, I'll follow you to the hospital and wait until she arrives.'

'You don't have to,' I mumble.

'I know. I want to help. Are you sure you're okay? I mean, after your op—'

'I'm fine!'

Frankie flinches, but I can't bring myself to make eye contact. If I do, I just know I'll crumble and confess I've stolen from the Lobster Bar – two hundred pounds from her restaurant's takings so that I could buy Tristram's watch. I can't bear to see the hurt and betrayal in her eyes if she finds out. The awkward silence is broken as the policeman joins us. He checks our injuries and drapes foil blankets over our shoulders. It's only then I realise I'm trembling.

His colleague returns, fiddling with her radio. 'This is a crime scene. We need to close the road to stop cars from driving over the debris. Can you assist us, ma'am?' She nods at Frankie. 'That's if you kids are well enough to be left briefly? The ambulances are only a few minutes away.'

'Yes!' we say in unison.

'Holler if you need me,' Frankie says.

87

I still can't meet her gaze. She hesitates before joining the police officers. They follow the trail of detritus up the hill.

'I'm freezing,' Layla mutters.

Kai gently readjusts her blanket, which has slipped off.

'We need to get our stories straight before we're taken to hospital,' she says, shivering. 'We may not get another chance to be alone. Are you going to tell the police about the holdall or not, Fliss?'

My heart contracts as she keeps us in suspense. Is that deliberate? I'm sure there's a glint of satisfaction in her eyes.

'I've thought about it,' she says finally. 'I'm in.'

'Yes!' Kai's arm escapes from the blanket as he punches the air.

'Keep it down.' I glance up the hill, but Frankie and the policeman and woman have almost reached the top. 'What made you change your mind?'

'I think we've established we don't need to discover each other's motives,' she replies icily. '*I'm* certainly not interested in hearing them.'

Kai snorts. 'That's telling us!'

Fliss shoots him a glacial stare. 'I have one small condition.'

I try to stop a frown from settling on my forehead. 'Which is?'

'We agree not to touch our share, not a single note for six months.'

'W-w-w-why?' Kai stammers.

'Isn't it obvious? We can't get caught! It gives us enough time to lay low and make sure we're in the clear before we launder the cash.'

'You know about money laundering?' I gasp.

'Yeah,' she says, poker-faced.

Kai's mouth falls open.

She rolls her eyes. 'I've learnt as much as the next Netflix viewer from watching *Breaking Bad* and *Ozark*. Please tell me you've realised you can't go on a mega splurge with wads of cash – or pay it into your bank accounts?'

We exchange looks. I doubt any of us had thought further ahead than privately justifying our reasons for keeping it.

'Any amount over, say, ten thousand will flag an alert with a bank – particularly if it's checked in by a teenager,' she explains. 'The cashier will report it to the police immediately. The money must be passed through a legitimate business first – like the carwash on the way to Kingsborough.'

Layla bursts out laughing. 'Omigod. That's classic rich-girl speak. Walter White opened a carwash in *Breaking Bad* to recycle his meth cash, therefore you think all carwashes are laundering stolen money?'

'No. That's what our driver told me when I pointed out the carwash is always deserted. He says it's a front for a money-laundering business. Drivers meet lots of people. They know where dodgy stuff goes on.'

Emergency vehicles wail in the distance.

Layla shifts uneasily. 'Okay, but I don't see why we have to wait that long?'

Fliss's tone hardens. 'It's up to you. Six months or this isn't happening.'

Kai sighs deeply, biting his lip. 'I'm in.'

'I guess we should make a pact?' I suggest.

I'd prefer a written contract, which we all sign, but that's obviously out of the question.

Kai stretches out his hand. 'Sure.'

Layla hesitates, before placing hers on top. A tiny almost imperceptible shiver ripples through his body. Has she noticed the way he looks at her with those big puppy-dog eyes?

I'm next and Fliss is last. *Again.* I wonder if she holds a grudge for being left on the far side of the bus with Silas. It must have felt like a million years as she waited to escape.

Her hand is ice-cold on top of mine. I suppress a shudder as the sirens grow louder and louder.

'We're all in this together,' she says evenly.

'If you say so,' Layla replies.

'Of course,' Kai mutters.

'Together,' I repeat.

I try to remain completely poker-faced, the way Fliss did when she pretended to be a money-laundering expert.

No way can I wait six months. I've promised to pay Tristram the £500 skiing deposit. I also need £200 quickly before Frankie discovers my theft from the Lobster Bar's safe. Basically I have until this weekend to make things right.

Ambulances and more police cars pull up, lights flashing. I look from Layla to Kai and back to Fliss.

Who can I trust?

Their faces are blank canvases, giving nothing away.

I don't believe any of them will wait six months – not even Fliss who has unexpectedly discovered morals.

If I've learnt anything today, it's this: we're four good liars.

10

KAI

'Wait for me!' I lurch across the dark, deserted street towards the car, smacking my hand on the driver's window as it slowly pulls away from the kerb.

I hear a muffled scream. Liam almost bangs his head on the roof as he jumps. The car stalls.

I bite back a smile as I open the door and pull off the rucksack, flinging myself into the passenger seat. 'Sorry I'm late.'

'I was about to go! It's three sixteen and forty seconds.'

He's such a robot. Honestly I'd like to slice open his brain and see how it works. Not necessarily using anaesthetic. He's wearing a stiff blue shirt buttoned to his neck and tan chinos. If it weren't for the glasses held together with sticky tape and the large dressing on his cheek, he'd look like he's off to a job interview.

'Did you get delayed by your parents?' Liam's knuckles whiten as he grips the steering wheel.

'My dad did a runner when I was a kid and my mum's away . . . just for a bit.'

That's *one* truthful thing I've said in the last twenty-four hours, but I have no idea why I've blurted it out to Liam of all people. Having company feels comforting, even if it's with a pompous jerk. I haven't spoken to *anyone* since leaving the hospital. I knew if I headed over to Lou's I'd 'fess up and I can't involve them.

'Good.' Liam coughs awkwardly. 'I mean, well, that's awful. Sorry . . . about your dad.'

I wince inwardly. 'I was three when he walked out. I barely remember.'

'Well, I was twelve when my dad left and I remember *everything*. It was shortly after I'd had an op on my back.'

'For a sports injury?'

He swallows a laugh. 'Hardly. It was . . .' He wets his lips. 'Scoliosis – curvature of the spine. I had metal rods inserted.' He glances at me nervously.

'Sounds painful. Sorry.'

'It was at the time, but not now. You learn to live with it.' He takes a deep breath. 'Do you hear from your dad?'

I shake my head. Time for a change of subject. 'That was quite the grilling from the copper at the hospital.'

He grips the steering wheel tighter. 'Which police officer?'

'DC Walker. He said he's been assigned to the investigation.'

'Did you tell him about the cash?'

'What do you take me for?' I don't give him the chance to insult me. 'I told him the basics about the chase, but he kept pressing me about the other driver and Silas's reaction when I got on the bus. He obviously thought it was significant.'

'Sounds like he's figured out there could be a connection between them?'

'Maybe.' I pause. 'But the odd thing was, he asked about Bob.'

'Who?'

'Jeez. Have you forgotten him already? Our old school bus driver, the one who died!'

Liam stiffens. 'What does he have to do with any of this?'

'No idea, but DC Walker mentioned his hit-and-run. They're investigating fresh leads.'

The car veers towards the hedge.

'Eyes on the road, please.'

'Sorry! But do you mean he thinks Silas hit Bob and fled the scene? Or perhaps the other driver killed him?'

'He didn't give anything away – just fishing for info. He

asked if I'd seen anything suspicious in the village the day of Bob's death. Like I could remember that far back. I can barely remember what I was doing at the weekend.'

Liam's shoulders lower. 'I didn't get the third degree – my mum went into lioness mode and wouldn't let the police anywhere near me.'

I swallow a sigh. I'd watched from the next-door cubicle as she threw her arms round him. Frankie had stayed too. Layla's mum and stepdad had turned up, as well as Fliss's mum and her driver, who apparently knows the best place to launder money. I was the only one without a single visitor. No wonder DC Walker targeted me first. He'd quickly sussed I was the weakest link.

'Did you tell the others about tonight?' Liam asks.

'Only Fliss. I didn't have a chance to speak to Layla before I was discharged.'

The nurse gave me a form to fill in with contact details, which threw me. Mum's mobile has been disconnected – her bill must be unpaid – and I couldn't admit she's temporarily living in Bristol. I gave our old address and Lou's mobile number as I knew they would be in class with their phone turned off. They'll cover for me if the hospital calls later. After my knee was strapped up and I'd double-checked from a distance that Layla was being looked after, I'd sneaked off.

A car approaches in the opposite direction, flashing its lights.

'Oh God!' Liam exclaims. 'Do you think that's DC Walker? You *must* have let something slip! He's here to arrest us, you idiot.'

As the car passes, the driver mouths, '*Lights!*'

Liam flicks them on. 'Sorry. I'm being paranoid. I didn't mean—'

'Yes, you did, and you can bugger right off.'

I sink lower into my seat, shifting my body away from him. He nudges my arm, offering me a piece of chewing gum, but I shake my head. I'm tempted to shove it down his throat or button his shirt tighter until it strangles him.

Neither of us speaks until we reach the crash site. It's impossible to miss – yellow tape flutters by the verge in the bright beam of the headlights. Liam parks further along the road.

'It's creepy.' He shivers as he peers out at the all-consuming blackness. 'Did you bring a torch by any chance?'

And he thinks *I'm* stupid? I scoop up my rucksack. Earlier I'd managed to lever open the sash kitchen window and get into the holiday home. I'd found a heap of rucksacks and a couple of head torches in cupboards in the basement utility room. I toss one into Liam's lap and fix the other across my forehead.

'Thanks,' he says gruffly.

We climb out, adjusting the beams until we get the right

strength. The yellow ticker tape leads us down to the cliff edge. Waves roar dully. Something swoops low, almost brushing my face, and darts past Liam, making him squeal.

'W-w-what is that?'

'Bats!' I swing my beam, picking out the raggedy, tattered dark shapes.

We veer towards the lumpy-shaped hedge in the distance. Our torchlights focus on the trough. It's exactly where we left it.

'Let's get this over with,' Liam mutters. 'The bats are freaking me out.'

'They won't hurt you,' I drawl. 'They only want your blood.'

'Funny.' He streaks ahead.

I limp after him. We work quickly and in silence – I manage to heave up the trough while he kneels and feels for the holdall.

'It's still there, right?' My heart beats quicker.

'Affirmative.'

I help him pull out the familiar bright blue bag.

'Are you sure your back will be okay for this?' I ask.

'I'm just sore, same as you. It's nothing serious – if the rods had broken, I'd be in agony.' He pauses. 'But thanks for asking.'

I nod, then together we carry the holdall, synchronising our movements: me at the front and him behind. This time my knee doesn't give way and I have more energy. I broke into one of the fifties at the butcher's tonight and bought a fillet steak – the first substantial dinner I've had in ages.

'Hold on!' Liam exclaims. 'Turn your light off. Quickly!'

'What is it?'

I glance back. Liam is staring out to sea.

'Do it!'

He lets go of the bag and his light goes out. I fumble with my switch. Within seconds we're plunged into terrifying, suffocating darkness.

'Is this about the bats?' I hiss. 'You know they don't actually suck your veins?'

'Over there!' he whispers. 'By the edge of the cliff.'

A tiny light hovers like a firefly and dances in the air. It's joined by another.

'What *is* that?' he asks.

'No idea but it's definitely not bats.'

I hear a snatch of a voice, carried by the wind. *Am I imagining it?* The sea can play tricks with your mind, particularly in the dark. Sailors used to think they could hear mermaids singing to them.

'*Not far.*'

'*Okay.*'

I shudder. That's no hoax of the sea. Or mermaids.

'We have company!' I whisper.

'How's that possible unless they're scaling the cliff face?' Liam hisses.

I pause, thinking. 'I saw steps and an old handrail when I looked over the edge after the crash. It must be a disused route to the beach.'

'Holy moly. Let's get out of here.' Liam's footsteps pad away.

'Come back,' I say hoarsely.

'No!'

I lunge towards his voice, clamping a hand on his arm.

'Get off me,' he whispers loudly.

'Shut up! They're almost at the top.'

'Exactly my point!' He tries to shake me off.

'We can't outrun them. They'll pick us out with their torches before we get to the top of the hill.'

Liam catches his breath. 'What should we do?'

'Hide and wait for them to leave.'

Blindly we drag the holdall towards the trough. We duck down as the lights rise and hover in the air before lowering. They've made it to the top.

'Do you think it's the police? Maybe they're checking the wreckage.'

Liam's voice is tinged with hope, but this *can't* be the police. No way would accident investigators risk their lives going down rickety old cliff steps at night. Liam's fingers dig into my arm as voices drift towards us. The lights are stronger and about 50 metres away.

'Shall we report back that the cash went over with the bus?' a man's voice asks tentatively.

'All we know for sure is that Silas had it with him,' another man, with a Bristolian accent, replies. 'Schoolkids aren't likely to be carrying fifties. Doesn't mean it's all still down there, though.'

'What shall we do with these notes?' Guy Number One asks.

I hold my breath, remembering how I'd tried to grab a few fifties before they were swept over the edge.

'Do you want me to explain in graphic detail what they'll do to both of us if they find out we've kept a single note?'

Liam makes a choking noise.

'Should we check up here before we go?' The beam of light swings towards us. 'We might find more.'

We duck down, pressing ourselves into the ground.

'No point,' Guy Number Two replies. 'Coppers were combing the grass earlier. Finding some down there was pure chance. Forensics hasn't finished.'

I breathe out slowly.

'One or two notes might have got caught in that hedge.'

Liam takes a hoarse, ragged breath.

'What was that?'

Both lights are trained in our direction. Should we make a run for it? My palms are sticky. My heart is beating furiously. I'm sure they'll hear it.

'A badger or a fox, or whatever the hell lives out here in the sticks. Let's go.'

I let my breath out slowly as the dots move up the slope towards the road. Neither of us dares to speak or move, even when the lights disappear. We hear the roar of a motorbike a minute or two later.

'That was close,' Liam says.

'Yep. At least we're in the clear.' My voice wobbles.

'*Really?* I didn't get that impression.'

I hate to admit it, but Liam's right. Guy Number Two was far smarter than the first. I don't think we've fooled him.

We wait another ten minutes before we silently carry the holdall to the brow of the hill, not daring to turn on our head torches.

'Stay here with the bag and I'll get the car,' Liam says, panting. 'We can't carry it along the road. If they see us . . .'

He's probably thinking about that guy's terrifying warning: *Do you want me to explain in graphic detail what they'll do to both of us if they find out we've kept a single note?*

'Okay. And, Liam . . .'

'Yes?'

'I hate to sound like we're stuck in a bad movie, but be careful.'

'Ditto.'

As he walks away, my heartbeat quickens. What if this is a trap? What if those guys realised we're here and have turned off *their* torches? They could be waiting to pounce on me – or on Liam as he gets into the car. A couple of minutes later, something rustles nearby. Crap! I stagger on to the road, dragging the holdall, as a car speeds towards me, lights turned on full beam.

I'm blinded, paralysed to the spot. This is it.

I'm about to die. *For real.*

The car screeches to a halt and the passenger door flies open.

'Get in!' Liam shouts.

I manage to hoist the bag on to the back seat. Jumping into the front, the car pulls away before I've closed the door. I swear under my breath as I bang my good knee on the open glovebox. Liam grips the steering wheel, his shoulders rigid, wind rustling his hair. Glass is scattered around his seat.

'Oh God. Tell me this isn't what it looks like.'

'Someone broke in,' he replies in a strangled tone. 'They used a stone to smash the driver's window.'

Hairs prickle on the back of my neck and my hands are suddenly slick with sweat. I wipe them on my jeans. 'Maybe it wasn't those guys,' I murmur. 'Wouldn't they have waited for us?'

'They didn't need to.'

'Why not?'

Thorny brambles scratch my window, making me jump. Liam's face is ghostly white.

'They took my mum's ID badge from the glovebox. It has her full name, the hospital where she works . . .'

'Are you sure it's missing?'

'I saw it tonight when I was looking for chewing gum.'

'It might not . . . It doesn't mean—'

'Those thugs will put two and two together and track me down first.'

Neither of us spoke again on the way here. Now we're parking outside the holiday let. I couldn't face lugging the holdall up the hill to disguise where I'm dossing, and Liam's way too freaked out to take the bag home. Can't say I blame him. I climb out and heave the holdall from the seat. It lands with a dull thump on the pavement.

'Shall we meet later to split the cash?' I peer back into the car.

His face is all angles and lines. He's hanging on to the steering wheel like his life depends on it.

'Liam?'

He stares, unblinking, out of the windscreen.

'What do you want to do about the money?' I persist.

Finally he turns his head. He looks like he's aged by about a hundred years.

'I'm not sure I want to be a part of this. We survived the crash only to be hunted and killed for money?'

'But—'

He leans over and yanks the door shut. I jump back before my fingers get caught. The car pulls away without lights. There's no point jogging after him. The mood Liam's in, he'll probably mow me down. Then reverse over me.

I check the street is deserted and hoist up the holdall, heading round the back of the holiday home. I drop it and try again. It takes three or four attempts to reach the door. My knee's on fire. I pause to get my breath before pulling out my necklace – the spare key is hanging from a chain to prevent a repeat of yesterday. I let myself in and lock the door, ignoring the light switch. Using my head torch, I make my way to the dining room and find the cabinet storing the owner's private alcohol collection. I slurp together measures from three crystal decanters and knock it back. It tastes like battery fluid, but I chug the remainder of the glass and refill it.

Closing the curtains, I catch a glimpse of a helicopter landing on the helipad at the Sea Haven. The richest guests like to make an entrance by air. When I'm certain there's no incriminating gaps in the material, I flick on the lights. I'm way too wired to sleep and may as well divide the cash. Down in the basement, I hunt for more rucksacks. The only ones I can find have goofy designs.

Back upstairs in the kitchen, I unzip the holdall. Bricks and bricks of notes stare back. My breath quickens.

Holy shit! I still can't believe it.

I pull out a wad and count the notes: £5,000. The next bundle is the same amount. My heart pounds loudly as I empty all the wads of cash into a gigantic, glorious red heap. Carefully I pile ten blocks together: £50,000. Shuffling along the floor, I create stack after stack. Twenty in total. Only one looks slightly short – probably after the rubber band broke and some notes escaped. I sit back on my heels.

Liam was right! It's just shy of a million. With seven figures I could set up my own business – teaching surfing and launching my own merchandise line – in Hawaii. I could also invest in pop-up counselling sessions on the beach to improve men's mental health and buy a big house for Mum and Crystal in Hawaii, as well as in Sandstown. That may help win over Paul – he's not my biggest fan, but I could ignore his sarky digs and the constant baiting. We could *both* declare a truce. He'd love to treat his daughter Lucy to exotic holidays.

I shake my head, reminding myself this isn't all *my* money, and take another slurp of battery fluid. But I can't resist rearranging the stacks. If Liam doesn't want his £250,000 cut, that would make it more like £333,000 each between the three of us, which has a nice ring to it . . . And if Fliss changes her mind, it's a straight £500,000 for Layla and me: ten towers of cash each.

Even better.

I blink. No point going there.

I push the money back into place and divide it into four stacks. I pack each of the three rucksacks with £250,000. I have slightly less, which is only fair since I've skimmed from the stash. Resting on my heels, I remember something else. I stick my hand into the holdall and grope around the lining. I tip the bag upside down, but nothing falls out. I check beneath the table and chairs in case it slid out when I emptied the cash on to the floor. But it's not here.

I don't know how it's happened.

I can hardly believe it's true.

The gun is missing.

TEENAGERS ESCAPE HORROR DEATH CRASH!

Four teenagers yesterday survived a dramatic cliff-edge crash that claimed the lives of two people.

The Kingsborough High School bus was involved in a collision with a car on the coastal road, close to the village of Applemore, at around 8.20 a.m. yesterday. Both vehicles plunged into the sea, killing the drivers, following an apparent road-rage incident. The teenagers miraculously escaped, suffering only minor injuries.

The police have named the school bus driver as Silas Greenhill, who moved to Sandstown from Croydon, south London, around two months ago. He took over the bus route from Bob Swanson, who was killed in a hit-and-run accident. The second driver has been named as Ian White, also from Croydon. According to police sources, he was recently released from prison after serving a seven-year sentence for his role in a drug-dealing network.

Police are refusing to comment about any possible

connection between the two men or whether Mr Greenhill had previous convictions. They are investigating the deaths for the coroner. However, the Gazette *understands that DC Andy Walker from Devon and Cornwall's major crime team has been seconded to the case, though his role in the investigation has not yet been confirmed.*

Both vehicles have been removed from the sea, but divers are continuing to hunt for the bodies. The identities of the four teenagers have not been revealed.

Dave Gordon, head teacher of Kingsborough High School, said, 'Our thoughts and prayers are with their families. Counselling will be offered to the teenagers on their return to school next week.'

11

FLISS

I'm ready to confess.

The knocking on my door grows louder. I hobble across the room, wincing with pain. Thank God Mother's here. I shouldn't have let the Poverty Express passengers talk me into this. I'll tell her about the £1 million *and* the blackmail. Betraying the others will serve them right for what happened on the bus. No way am I made to go last. Like ever.

I throw open the door.

'Oh! It's you.'

'Sorry to disappoint, but I come bearing gifts.' Aaron holds a plate stacked high with chocolate chip cookies.

'I asked Chef to make a batch. They're warm, the way you like them.' He tilts his head sympathetically. 'I wanted to see how you're doing.'

'I'm great.' The lie catches in my throat as I open the door wider.

Inside, he places the plate on the table nearest the balcony, next to the framed photo of Daddy and me. The picture was taken shortly before he moved to California. My chest aches. Aaron gazes out of the window. 'You can see the whole bay from here. It's a better view than Mrs C's.'

Giving me the revamped executive suite was the least Mother could do after temporarily axing my monthly allowance and refusing to fork out for the gang's annual New Year ski trip to Verbier. She says we're asset rich but cash poor after the hotel refurb costs spiralled. I heard the word 'poor' and threw up a little in my mouth.

'Where is Mother?'

I didn't get a chance to chat to her in private yesterday. She was glued to her phone – arguing with someone in Spanish – while Aaron drove us back from the hospital. She had calls all evening, probably from her accountant and investors.

'She's busy with meetings. She'll try to pop in later.'

Try? How hard is it to come up a few floors in the lift? Aaron mistakes the choking noise in my throat for rib pain.

'Here, let's make you more comfortable.' He plumps cushions behind my back as I ease myself down.

'Mrs C says you're to rest today and not worry about anything.'

Not worry? The week started with blackmail. Now I've agreed to split a million with kids I can't trust. Layla's dying to get her own back after Mother wrongly accused her of theft and Kai and Liam have probably done a runner with the holdall.

I stretch forward, wincing. Aaron passes the bottle of painkillers, and a glass of water. Luckily my ribs were only bruised, not broken, but they still hurt like mad.

'Wow. Full service. I should *almost* fall over a cliff more often.'

'Please don't. You scared me to death.'

An unfamiliar warm feeling creeps into my heart before I remember that Aaron is only an employee. He's paid to care.

'Mrs C sent me shopping this morning. She wants you to have this.'

He passes me a small white box topped with a bow. Ripping off the ribbon, I lift the lid to reveal the latest iPhone in a sparkling Swarovski case. I blink rapidly to stop tears from forming. It's great – I mean, it's the latest model – but this probably means Mother won't bother to see me in person when she can message.

'Mrs C doesn't want you to feel cut off from your friends and told me to buy them phones as well.'

Weren't we supposed to be economising? I'd prefer money towards the ski trip than freebies for the gang.

'You should get refunds. My friends have the latest iPhones.'

'I meant the other teenagers on the bus.'

I cough. 'I wouldn't describe *them* as friends.'

'My apologies. I saw you talking to the girl and one of the boys in the hospital yesterday. You looked close and I assumed . . .'

'We were thrown together by the accident. We have *nothing* in common.'

'Understood. But Mrs C thought it might help to stay in touch with them if you need to talk about your trauma.'

As if! She's paying someone else to deal with my problems, like the psychiatrist she hired this summer.

'Wait, do you have mobile numbers for the . . . others?'

'I took the liberty of entering their new numbers when your data and previous contacts were transferred.'

I reward him with a smile as my co-conspirators' names pop up on the contact list.

Layla, Kai, Liam.

I'll set up a WhatsApp group and send an encrypted message, telling them I want to call this whole thing off before we get in any deeper.

'Have they got their phones yet?'

'I delivered them this morning – I managed to find addresses for Liam and Layla, but the other boy . . .'

'Kai?'

'He was more problematic, but Liam said he could get the phone to him.'

'Cool!'

I have four new messages, probably my friends checking in. My cheeks smart as I click on to them. Nothing from the gang! Haven't they heard what happened? I have one text from my network provider, outlining the terms of the deal. The other messages are from my partners in crime.

LIAM: *See you all at 2 p.m. We need to talk!*
LAYLA: *Sure. 2.*
KAI:👍

My brows knit together. What *are* they talking about?

'I'm guessing they accepted?' Aaron asks, scrutinising my face.

'Accepted what?'

'Mrs C's invite to a complimentary afternoon tea in the Ocean Lounge.'

My jaw drops. 'Mother did what?'

'She wants to support you. She thought you might need to talk about what you've been through with fellow survivors.'

Hardly! She's hired three babysitters to keep me out of her way. The Ocean Lounge is the last place we should discuss what to do with £1 million in stolen cash – guests mill around, and the waiters and waitresses eavesdrop.

'You don't look pleased,' Aaron observes. 'Should I cancel the invitations?'

'Tell Mother—'

I waver. Why should I tell her anything if she can't be bothered to see me? I almost died, FFS, and she can't make time for me. I stand and walk over to the window, shielding my eyes from the midday sun. This view always helps me think. The expanse of water glitters like diamonds. It looks calm, but it's deceptive and should never be underestimated. It has the power to trap and destroy most things.

My mind had been set on talking to the police when I thought I was going to die. But I'm less sure today. What if I don't tell the truth? What if I keep quiet about that night *and* hang on to the cash? The blackmailer might back off –

but if they don't, I can pay them. This amount of money gives me opportunities. I could start a new life in the States in six months' time, buying an apartment close to Daddy's new home. I'd be long gone by the time Mother ever found out.

'No, don't cancel,' I tell him.

It's good to keep my options open.

Taking my revenge on the others can wait – for now at least.

12

LAYLA

'Are you sure you're not dead?' Salih's fingers attempt to prise open my eyelids. 'Maybe you've come back as a zombie, and I'll need to stake you through the heart?'

'I'm sleeping, *habibi*,' I reply. 'Well, trying to anyway.'

Salih laughs, snuggling up closer. He's like my personal hot-water bottle. 'Why do you always call me "*habibi*"?'

'Because that's what Baba used to call you.'

He pauses. 'But no one else does now Dad's gone – apart from you and Grandma.'

'*Teta*,' I say gently. 'And that's why it's important I don't stop.'

'Whatever.' Salih yawns. 'Tell me again how you escaped from the bus. It's cool.'

My eyes fly open. I don't want to picture Silas's last moments. 'It wasn't!'

'But *you* were superhero cool – saving the others and holding on to the bus one-handed while Liam jumped out before you let go.'

'Erm, that's not what happened.'

'I'm bigging you up, dummy! That's what I'm telling my friends. They'll be dead impressed. You'll *finally* be able to get a boyfriend.'

Kai's face flashes into my brain. 'Thanks for the offer, but I don't want to go out with one of your ten-year-old mates.'

'No, I mean, an older boyfriend. A sixth-former. But someone who's completely brain dead obviously and can't find anyone better.'

'Thanks. I'd punch you, but you bruise easily and Mum would find out.'

Salih howls with laughter. No way would Mum find that joke funny.

'I'm glad you're alive,' he says. 'I don't want to lose you, even though you're annoying most of the time, MM.'

I screw my eyes tightly shut to stop tears from forming. *Right back at you.*

'But if you had died yesterday, I'd have got your bedroom,'

117

he adds. 'I wouldn't have been sad for long. It's much bigger than mine and I'd never have to tidy my Lego. I could leave it out overnight.'

'You do that anyway,' I point out. 'We all bear the puncture wounds. Anyway, I moved one of your old toy boxes in here last night to give you more space.'

I glance at the wicker basket in the corner, packed with soft toys. Baba's oud and kawala are next to it, along with my electric guitar, keyboard and camera tripod. They're all gathering dust. It's been months since I wrote new music or recorded a video; notes have stopped flooding into my head and lyrics no longer effortlessly flow. Maybe Salih *should* have the bigger room. I don't need space for choreography. I've withdrawn from ballet and modern dance classes, as well as piano, because I don't want Leon to worry about ferrying me on top of Salih's appointments.

He coughs, making my shoulders automatically tense. 'Are you catching a cold, *habibi*?'

'No, MM. I'm clearing my throat.' He rolls his eyes. 'When are you *ever* going to get a life of your own?'

Before I can think of a good comeback, Mum kicks open the door, carrying a tray. She's been in and out all morning, bringing snacks and drinks. I can't deny it – I'm enjoying the attention.

'Your sister needs her rest. Why don't you go downstairs, and we'll go through the maths paper your teacher emailed over?'

'I'd prefer to stay here and torment Layla.'

'I know you would, but scoot.'

Salih slowly scrambles off the bed, breathing heavily. Does his chest sound worse than usual? Mum's eyes narrow as she stares after him. She's thinking the same. Dammit. I *am* turning into her.

'Later, loser,' he says, sauntering out.

Mum smiles, shaking her head. 'Did he wake you? I wanted you to go back to sleep.'

'It doesn't matter. I need to get dressed.' I shuffle up in bed, as she passes a mug of cardamom tea.

'Are you sure you feel well enough to go out, love?'

'Yeah, I'm feeling much better.'

Obviously that's not true. I feel like death warmed up. Every inch of my body hurts, but I need to meet the others at the Sea Haven. I have to look each of them in the eye and make sure they're not having second thoughts about sharing the cash, particularly Fliss. It's impossible to tell by messaging on my new phone.

Mum frowns. 'DC Walker rang, asking when he could speak to you.'

I almost choke on my tea. 'What did you tell him?'

'The truth – you were asleep, and I wasn't sure when you'd feel up to talking.'

I stare into my mug. Mum isn't religious, but she's the most honest person I know. I wasn't allowed to grow up believing in Father Christmas, the tooth fairy or the Easter Bunny because she refused to lie about them. She told me from an early age they didn't exist but that I couldn't let on to my friends. I hated that secret. It made me feel different, the way I did when a kid at my old primary school refused to believe I was born in London and asked where I *really* came from. I felt worse when Baba had to tick my nationality as 'other' on the permission slip for a school trip. There was no space on the form to explain I'm proud to be British *and* Egyptian.

She eyes me suspiciously. 'What's wrong?'

I hesitate. I *want* to tell her about the cash, but if I do, she'll march me to the police station and make me confess to DC Walker. She can't bear dishonesty. I take after Baba – he once told me it's okay to tell fibs if it prevents someone you love from being hurt.

The truth isn't always helpful or welcome, habibti.

Family comes first, no matter what.

Wouldn't Baba do the same if he were still alive? He'd

keep the money to protect us, even if it meant telling bigger and bigger lies.

I *can't* tell Mum. Ever. Or Salih. Or Leon. Or Alvita and the rest of my friends. Mum scrutinises my face. Can she sense the secret growing between us, pushing us further and further apart?

'I'm still sore. But I reckon it would help to talk to the others.'

Kai is dead friendly, as well as crazy hot, and Liam is okay when he's not with Tristram. I'm sure they aren't sipping champagne in a first-class cabin on a one-way flight to South America. But who wouldn't be tempted to split £1 million 50/50 if they had the chance?

Mum stares at me. She could always catch me telling untruths when I was little. She used to claim the lie was written across my face. Is it now? I manage a small smile. I hope it's believable.

'Well, if you're sure, I'll ask Leon to drop you at the causeway. He'll be back from his shift soon.'

'Thanks, Mum. I appreciate it.'

She smooths the duvet cover before picking up the mobile from my bedside table. 'It was kind of Mrs C to buy you this – it looks better than mine.'

'It should! It probably cost at least eight hundred pounds.'

She snorts. I can tell she's mentally calculating how much the fundraising total would be boosted with an £800 donation.

'Yeah, it's way over the top, but Mrs C likes showing off.'

I take another slurp of tea. Mrs C had promised to fund the school's new ICT suite earlier this year in exchange for a name plaque. I overheard upper-sixth girls claiming she had threatened to pull the donation unless Fliss was made a choir soloist.

'Mrs C's been good to you,' Mum says.

I almost spit out my tea. Mum still doesn't know she unfairly sacked me. I'll have to suck up in return for her mega-extravagant present. I'd better take the receipt in case she accuses me of nicking it later.

'Have you forgotten how she treated Leon when we first got here?' I ask.

Mrs C had claimed no building work would be available *for the foreseeable future* when he'd asked shortly after we moved here. But the hotel was massively revamped earlier this year, with a huge infinity pool installed in the grounds.

'Maybe the bank approved a loan for the renovations,' she says.

'Sure. Or Mrs C was waiting until she found local *white* builders.'

Leon is a combination of cultures, like me and Salih. He's

Jamaican British and proud of his heritage – that was far less of a problem when he worked in construction in London. He'd met Mum while fixing a leaking roof at her old Tooting book shop.

'I hope that's not the reason she turned him down.' She sighs, lost in thought. 'But we should tap up everyone we can, whether we like them or not. We can't afford to be choosy. You could ask Mrs C to put flyers around the hotel, asking for donations to our JustGiving site?'

My eyes widen. 'I'm not sure . . .'

'The guests are rich. They won't miss a few hundred or thousand quid, but it'll make the world of difference to us.'

I can imagine Mrs C's face if I ask her to leave flyers in the foyer. She once ripped the head off a freelance landscape designer who put his business cards on display because they didn't look in keeping with the upmarket surroundings.

'How much do we have?'

'Two hundred and forty pounds, but the appeal's only been running twenty-four hours. It's mainly from family and friends in London.' She clears her throat. 'I'm ringing your grandma to tell her about the website. I doubt she can afford to give much. But imagine what we could raise from hotel guests or Mrs C herself?' She pointedly raises an eyebrow.

'No way, Mum! I *cannot* ask Mrs C for cash.'

'Why not? She's wealthy – look at that phone!'

'Because . . .'

I can't admit that: a, I don't want to beg from the racist cow who sacked me and, b, if I do get my share of the haul from Kai and Liam, I won't have to plead for cash from anyone. I'll have earned it myself. Well, not exactly earned it. *Stolen it.*

The words stick in my throat. I force down another swig of tea.

'We all have to contemplate doing things we don't want to.' Mum's gaze drifts to the corner of the room, her shoulders sagging. 'We must make sacrifices to raise the money.'

What does *that* mean?

'You're not plotting to rob a bank, are you?' I say jokingly.

Mum hasn't done anything illegal in her life – she doesn't have a single parking ticket. She was once undercharged in a shop and went back the next day to repay the money she owed.

'Of course not!'

'I'll try to bring it up if I see Mrs C, but she might not be there.'

Fingers crossed she's busy.

'Thank you.' Mum plants a kiss on my forehead. 'Your stepdad and I are prepared to beg, borrow – anything but steal – to get that cash for your brother.'

I fix another smile on my face as she scoops up the empty mugs and plates from the bedside table. Luckily for our family – or perhaps unluckily – I've got the stealing part of Operation Save Salih covered.

1.57 p.m.

Inside the Ocean Lounge, well-dressed couples sit at glass tables piled with towering plates of tiny exquisite sandwiches, pastries and scones. Chef's afternoon teas attract guests from all over Devon – the rich ones who can afford to fork out £150 for two. Glittering chandeliers drip from the ceiling; notes from the grand piano discreetly drone out the clatter of cutlery, as they would have done when the hotel reopened post Second World War following a massive rebuild. A few pensioners stare. Maybe it's due to my tie-dye sweatshirt, acid-wash jeans and Doc Martens, which breach the five-star dress code. But attitudes among some guests towards people of dual heritage probably haven't changed here since the 1950s.

I spot Fliss and Liam in the far corner. Frowns are fixed on their faces. A man in a suit stands close by, talking on his phone. One of the waiters will ask him to step out soon – mobiles aren't allowed. Fliss's face is bruised and cut, but her auburn hair is perfectly blow-dried and her cream blouse is obviously silk. Liam has a navy jacket, stiff white shirt and tie, but still looks out of place. His glasses are held together with tape and his cheek has a large dressing. Fliss spots me and shakes her head. Liam's eyes widen in horror, as he tugs at his too-tight lilac tie. I check my watch. What's their problem? I made it on time, despite the hotel being inaccessible by beach due to the high tide. The sea tractor slowly trundled across the causeway, waves smashing against its deep grip tyres. When we reached halfway, I spotted Kai in the distance, arriving at the pick-up point for the next service.

'Don't keep me in suspense,' I say, as I reach their table. 'Tell me what happened to the cash.'

The guy with the phone turns round, sliding it into his pocket.

My mouth drops open as I stare at the large man with the untidy beard and creased shirt. This is the police officer who was grilling Kai in the hospital yesterday.

He stretches out his hand and I numbly shake it.

'We haven't been introduced yet. I'm DC Walker from the major crime unit.' He pauses for a beat. 'What cash are you talking about?'

13

LIAM

The mathematical odds of us all getting arrested have increased by 95 per cent.

'It's a private joke,' I tell DC Walker, laughing nervously. 'I owe her twenty pounds and she won't let me forget!'

That's the fourth lie I've told today. I'd convinced Mum I had no idea what had happened to her car, saying someone must have broken in overnight, looking for cash or valuables. I'd also insisted I felt well enough to come here, and messaged Tristram to claim I wasn't up for visitors in case he dropped by after school. Not that he usually does, but I'd wanted to be careful. Prepare for all eventualities. It's a pity Layla didn't plan ahead. She's swallowing repeatedly. I think she's about to vomit or confess. Possibly both. I push a chair towards her, and she slumps into it.

'Tut, tut, you should always repay a debt.' DC Walker winks at me, as he leans on a spare chair.

He reminds me of a large grizzly bear with his straggly beard and rounded stomach. The buttons are straining on his crumpled shirt, which sports a few stains.

'Well?' he prompts. 'Are you going to give Layla the money you owe her?'

'Here you go.' I retrieve the last ten-pound note from my wallet.

'Anything bigger in there?' Fliss asks pointedly.

Does she really think I'd bring £1 million here?

'Sorry. I'll have to owe you the other ten.'

Layla nibbles on a nail as DC Walker studies us. His gaze settles on Fliss.

'Your mum isn't answering my calls about setting up an interview so I decided to call in. I've always wanted to bring my wife here. I thought I'd check out the menu.'

'If it's any consolation, my mother doesn't answer *my* calls,' she replies drily. 'But I could ask her to give you a special rate if you decide to book a table.'

DC Walker laughs. 'That's generous, thank you! I'll obviously need a test run first.' He pulls out the chair and sits down, helping himself to a pastry. 'How are you all doing?' he asks, biting into a cream horn.

We stare at him in horror.

'Don't worry – this isn't a formal interview. I'm here for the free food!'

'About making that booking for your wife . . .' Fliss is trying to get rid of him, but he doesn't take the hint.

'I can't believe my luck finding the three of you together. It saves me ringing around later.' He polishes off the pastry and takes another. 'I need to schedule interviews, with your parents present or an appropriate adult.' He pulls out three business cards from his pocket and pushes them across the table.

'Major crimes!' I try to keep my tone light as I read his job title. 'I know the crash was serious, but is it a major crime?'

DC Walker holds my gaze. 'I guess that's what I'm here to figure out.'

My heartbeat rockets. Can he tell I'm panicking? He looks away, wiping a blob of cream from his beard with a serviette.

'Have any of you heard from Kai?' he asks.

'I haven't seen him today,' Layla replies.

'Me neither.' I'd swung by earlier to give him the new phone, en route to taking Mum's car to the garage. I'd pushed the package through the letter box, with a note explaining it was a present from Mrs C.

'Nope,' Fliss says.

Her words are practically a bubble, hanging in the air, as I spot Kai limp into the lounge wearing an oversized green hoodie, ripped jeans and dirty trainers. He's weighed down by three bulging My Little Pony rucksacks. Is that what I think it is? I hadn't thought to drop off another note warning: DON'T BRING THE CASH TO THE HOTEL, YOU COMPLETE IDIOT!!

I look down, hoping he hasn't spotted me. *Too late.* A few well-dressed guests stop eating and watch as he comes over. Kai is delivering £750,000 to our table – straight to a detective from the major crime unit.

How can we stop him? Frantically I jab Fliss in the side. 'Ow!'

I cough, glancing towards the figure heading our way, but she ignores me, and Layla doesn't notice.

DC Walker swivels round. 'Hey!' he calls. 'We were just discussing you.'

Kai drops two rucksacks. He attempts a U-turn and clips the back of a woman's chair with another.

'Here, let me help.'

Kai resembles a rabbit caught in headlights as DC Walker strides towards him. The detective scoops up two rucksacks and returns to the table, mock staggering beneath the weight.

'What are you lugging about? Bricks?'

Layla squirms in her seat and Kai looks like he may projectile vomit.

'Well, this is quite the reunion!' DC Walker sits down.

Fliss glares furiously at Kai as he slides into the spare seat, clutching the third rucksack. His face is deathly pale – and that's before Fliss rips him apart limb by limb. How could he be so stupid? He's brought the cash to a public place. In My Little Pony rucksacks.

'You haven't answered my question,' DC Walker remarks.

'W-w-which is?' Kai stammers.

'What's in the rucksacks?'

Kai shoots an imploring look at me, but I have nothing. I button my lips. I can't breathe. I think I'm having a heart attack.

'It's schoolwork,' Layla says, improvising. 'We don't want to get behind.'

DC Walker gives a low whistle. 'Admittedly I went to school in the Middle Ages, but if I'd narrowly survived a clifftop crash, I'd have skived off for at least a week.'

'Well, it's not the Middle Ages,' Fliss says coolly.

'True!' He grins back.

Thankfully DC Walker isn't the brightest.

'I should leave you all to catch up – and recover.' He

stands. 'But before I forget, Kai, I need your home address. The one the hospital gave me was out of date.' For the first time there's a hint of steel in his voice.

I don't know what is going on in Kai's life, but I doubt that huge house he's staying in is his real address. I'm 99 per cent certain it's a vacant holiday home.

'It's Torside Lodge on Seadrift Lane,' he blurts out.

That's definitely a lie – 100 per cent. No way does he live on the poshest side of the village either, away from the scattering of council houses.

'I might drop by to arrange an interview.' DC Walker frowns. 'There's never any answer from your mum's number – the one you gave to the hospital.'

'She's busy at work, sorry, but I'll tell her to get in touch.'

'Great! I think we're done here.' He turns, almost colliding with a waiter. 'Thanks for the chat – and the free cakes.'

A collective sigh of relief ripples round our table as he walks away.

'Oh, one more thing.' He strides back, eyeing the cake stand. 'Do you mind if I take a few for my colleagues?'

'Be my guest,' Fliss says, her voice cracking.

DC Walker scoops the leftovers into serviettes before feeling inside his jacket's inner pocket. 'Last thing, I promise.

I don't suppose you guys found any more of these at the crash site yesterday, did you?'

He pulls out a plastic bag containing a bloodstained fifty-pound note.

14

KAI

'Whose blood was on the fifty?'

We've trooped up to Fliss's suite in silence, afraid to talk in case anyone overheard. Finally alone, I can't keep quiet any longer.

'Does it matter?' Liam throws a rucksack on to the cream carpet and loosens his tie. 'It could be my blood or yours or theirs.' He jerks his head at the girls. 'We're in trouble now we've lied to a police officer. In hindsight, we should have admitted we'd found a few notes.'

'Hindsight isn't helpful,' Layla points out. 'No one else spoke – I had to improvise. Anyway, if we'd confessed, he'd have told us to hand over the fifties. We couldn't exactly pull them out of our rucksacks. It was easier to deny everything.'

'But don't you see the problem? The police will try to lift fingerprints from the note and run checks on the blood!' Liam shoves the makeshift glasses up his nose. 'It'll belong to one of us – we were all bleeding. We all touched the notes.'

'It's a long shot, but the blood could belong to Silas,' I say.

Liam scowls. 'You think he cut himself shaving before he put the money in the holdall?'

'I don't know. He was clearly having the day from hell!'

He shoots me a contemptuous look before continuing. 'In all honesty, I'm not interested in anything you have to say when you've marched into the hotel carrying three quarters of a million pounds in kids' rucksacks. How could you be so dumb?'

Usually I play along with jibes like this, but irritation stirs inside me like a dragon waking from a deep sleep. 'Shut the hell up!'

'Why should I? It was an incredibly stupid thing to do.'

Heat crawls up my neck, mottling my skin. He's deliberately humiliating me in front of the others. Just because I love surfing, everyone assumes I'm brain dead.

'Do you and your friends think about anything apart from surfing and getting buff bodies?' Liam continues hotly. 'Or is that too much to ask for an idiot like you?'

Something inside me snaps. I shove him. *Hard*. He stumbles backwards, almost tripping over a chair.

'What would you prefer?' My fists are tight balls. 'That I kept the cash for myself?'

'Try it and see what happens!' Fliss pipes up.

Liam comes at me, but I easily dodge him, stepping aside.

'What do you think this is?' Fliss drawls. 'Shitstown Fight Club?'

Layla pushes us apart. 'We're all in this together, remember? We need a plan. We have to stick to the same story in the police interviews.'

Fliss walks slowly to the window and stares at the view as Liam glowers.

'Layla's right,' she says. 'We talk about the crash, nothing more. The police can't match any of us to that blood – they don't have our DNA. We're not suspects.'

'Not yet,' Liam stresses.

'They might check to see if the blood is a match against Silas's and the dead driver,' she says, turning round. 'Later, if we're forced to give our DNA, we can claim we were lying . . . or confused. We were in shock et cetera. It wasn't a formal interview.'

'You think that makes it all right?' Liam demands.

Fliss's expression is unreadable. 'I'm trying to make the best out of a bad situation,' she says calmly. 'You all talked me into doing this, remember? I said we shouldn't keep the money.'

'Well, I think you were right – we've made a terrible mistake,' Liam blurts out. 'We're in way over our heads. It's too dangerous.'

Layla gapes at him. 'What's happened? You were totally up for this before. *You agreed.*'

He shakes his head.

Fear twists in my gut. 'Was everything okay when you got home this morning?'

'Thanks for asking.' He rakes a hand through his hair. 'Luckily those psychos weren't waiting to perform a remake of *The Texas Chainsaw Massacre.*'

Layla gasps. 'Er, what?'

Liam looks away miserably.

'We weren't the only ones searching for the holdall,' I explain. 'Two guys were at the crash site. We overheard them talking. They found fifties at the bottom of the cliff.'

'Oh God!' Layla slumps into a chair.

I want to tell her everything will be okay, but I can't find the words.

Fliss walks over unsteadily and sits down. 'Go on.'

I sigh. 'One of them didn't sound convinced the holdall went over with the bus.'

'They were both afraid of whoever the money belongs to,' Liam adds hoarsely. 'They wouldn't keep a single note for fear of what would happen to them.'

'But we're safe, right?' Layla's voice rises in panic. 'They don't know *we* took the cash?'

Bright red spots appear on Liam's cheeks. 'My car was broken into while we were parked up, and my mum's hospital ID badge was stolen. "King" is a common surname around here, but those guys could still put two and two together and track me down.'

Layla holds her head in her hands.

'I guess someone else could have smashed the driver's window,' he finishes lamely.

'Big coincidence!' Fliss retorts. 'They just happened to be in the middle of nowhere at the same time?'

'We have another problem,' I chip in. 'One of us is a thief.'

My face burns fiercely as the others laugh.

'All four to be exact,' Fliss says.

I raise my voice to block out the titters. 'When I divided the money, I couldn't find the gun. It's not in the holdall.'

'You're kidding!' Fliss exclaims.

I shake my head.

'That's impossible!' Layla cries, almost falling out of her chair. 'I put it back on top of the notes.'

'I swear to God it wasn't there. I emptied everything out. It's gone.'

'Maybe it fell out when we shifted the holdall?' Liam suggests.

'How? It was zipped up and we'd have noticed. Plus, DC Walker would have mentioned they'd found it as well as the fifty.'

'Basically it means one of *us* took it.' Fliss frowns. Like me, she's trying to remember where we all stood before we parted ways.

Layla shoots her a hard look. 'You were alone with the holdall when the notes blew out.'

'You were too! And the boys had chances to take it. We were all distracted.'

'W-w-why would I want a gun?' Liam stammers.

'For protection,' I retort. 'You were freaking out.'

'We were all freaking out!' he counters.

No one can argue with that.

'One of us *has* to be lying.' Layla studies each of us in turn.

My face feels aflame, and the others' cheeks are also a guilty red colour.

'Let's face it, none of us can be trusted,' Fliss says flatly. 'We've deceived a major crime detective and we're planning to lie to our families and friends about stealing one million pounds.'

Liam groans, running his hands through his hair. 'No, no, no,' he mutters. 'I can't deal with this stress.'

'For God's sake!' I snap. 'Get it together!'

How dare he continually judge *me,* call me stupid, when he's too weak to see this through after twenty-four hours? I nudge a rucksack towards him with my foot.

'Take it and stop moaning – or agree to give up your share and we'll divide it between us.'

'Pardon?'

'You heard me. If you don't want it, we'll take three hundred and thirty-three thousand each. No hard feelings.'

'You—'

Bang, bang, bang!

We stare at the door.

I break out into a cold sweat. Liam freezes. Layla grips the side of her chair and Fliss turns ghostly pale.

DC Walker didn't buy our cover story about the schoolwork in the rucksacks.

He'll discover the stolen cash and arrest us.

We're screwed.

15

FLISS

'How do we get out? Is there another exit?'

Kai gazes at the patio doors. Does he think he's Spider-Man? I don't fancy his chances of surviving a jump from my balcony to escape DC Walker and his evidence bag. He'll split his head open on the rocks.

'How about we use the secret passageway down to the beach?' I drawl.

He gasps. 'Wow! Really?'

I roll my eyes.

'It's a reasonable reaction,' Layla says, leaping to his defence. 'Everyone claims the original Victorian building had a network of hidden corridors because the owner was a recluse. He'd wanted to avoid seeing people as he came and went.'

'They're just rumours!'

There's another sharp rap at the door.

'Fliss? Are you here?'

I breathe out. 'It's only my mother. Her timing is terrible as usual.'

'Great,' Layla mutters.

I ignore her. 'We need to hide the rucksacks.'

Liam peers down the side of one of the sofas. 'They should fit there.'

I head across the room, as the others work together, pushing them out of sight.

'I'm coming!'

Mother smiles warmly as I finally open the door. Her bobbed blonde hair is an immaculate helmet as usual, but her make-up doesn't disguise the violet shadows under her eyes. She pulled all-nighters during the renovations earlier this year and still can't be getting more than a few hours' sleep a night.

'There you are! I was looking for you downstairs, but the staff said you'd left.'

'We weren't hungry,' I mumble, as she pulls me in for a hug.

I inhale the familiar floral perfume – Chanel Nº 5. Daddy used to buy it for her every birthday. I disentangle myself and push her away.

'I wanted to speak to you earlier, but Aaron said you were busy.'

'I'm really sorry. Problems with contractors.'

'How awful! I had a problem when I almost fell off a cliff and died.'

She winces at my sarcasm. 'You survived thankfully! Are your friends still here? I want to meet the people who saved my little girl.'

'I doubt they feel up to company,' I say through gritted teeth. *And they're not my friends.*

'It's just a quick hello, sweetie.' She takes my arm and leads me inside, her cream Manolo Blahnik stilettos making small sharp indents in the carpet.

'There you are – my heroes!'

Mother embraces Liam but gives Layla a wide berth and doesn't make eye contact. Kai has gone AWOL – he must have slipped to the bathroom.

'Thank you for bringing Fliss safely home. If you hadn't managed to open the emergency window . . .' She shudders. 'Imagining life without my daughter is impossible.'

I blink back tears as Mother's voice cracks with emotion. Is she remembering how our family used to be inseparable? The three of us used to take coastal walks and explore rock pools at weekends. We'd all curl up on the sofa on Friday nights, with bags of chocolate and binge-watch Netflix shows. That was before she and Daddy started to fight, he left, and this hotel replaced me as her baby.

Kai looks sheepish as he emerges from the bedroom.

'You're just in time!' Mother says, beaming. 'I'd love to get a photo of the four of you together if that's okay?'

'Why?' Layla asks, wrinkling her nose.

'I want to put it on our staff noticeboard to showcase your bravery. It's where we highlight important events in the lives of our employees and family members – I recently put up a photo of our gardener who rescued a dog from the sea.'

I'm touched, particularly since Mother isn't usually interested in that board.

'I'd prefer not to – I look a sight.' Liam points to his dressing.

'Yeah, I'm not keen either,' Kai adds.

'It's for private use, I promise,' she insists. 'Not for socials or anything outside the hotel. Perhaps you'd all like to take photos today on your *new* phones?'

That's pretty pointed.

'Would you allow these flyers to be displayed at front reception if I agree?' Layla produces papers from her bag.

'Of course.' She takes the leaflets without glancing at them.

Liam and Kai shrug. I don't care either. No one looks at that noticeboard – the staff are too busy complaining about this summer's pay cuts. Mother slashed everyone's hourly rates despite all the rooms being booked out.

'Fabulous!' She drops the flyers on to the sofa, next to her handbag, and pulls out her mobile. 'Let's do this outside. It'll make a better pic.'

She herds us out to the balcony, removing Liam's broken glasses 'which might ruin the shot', and straightening Kai's sweatshirt. Tension still crackles between the pair, but Layla positions herself in between them. Mother takes three or four photos and examines them before saying goodbye.

'Give me a sec,' I tell the others.

I follow her into my suite, but she's already at the door. 'Hold on! We need to talk. And I mean properly.'

Mother glances back as the others troop into the room. She gestures for me to follow her into the hallway. 'We will later, I promise.'

'But—'

'I'm so sorry, but these contractors are a nightmare.' She rubs her furrowed brow. 'How about we catch up over a late supper? In the meantime, Aaron is at your full disposal.' She kisses me on the cheek before hurrying away, clutching her handbag.

That's all I get after what I've been through? Did she fake caring about me in front of the others?

She presses the button to call the lift and turns round. 'By the way, have you seen my rose-gold bracelet? I thought I left it in my office, but I can't find it anywhere.'

'I've barely seen you, let alone your jewellery!' I hit back.

'I'll make it up to you, I promise.' Her eyes narrow. 'But you should go back in there. You know Queen Latifah can't be trusted after that business with the opal ring.'

Before I can argue, her phone chimes. She answers it as she steps into the lift. The doors silently glide shut. Tears prick my eyes. Leaving here with £250,000 has never looked more tempting. Mother wouldn't even notice if I were gone! I can get £333,000 if Liam drops out. He sounds like he's three quarters of the way there; a small push and I could buy a bigger condo in Malibu. I kick the door behind me with my heel. Back inside, the others have retrieved the rucksacks.

'It's all there, before you ask,' Kai says miserably. 'I counted it out three times to make sure it was divided equally: two hundred and fifty thousand each. Well, I've got a little less. I reckon we lost a couple of hundred on the clifftop.'

Layla swings round with a pained expression on her face. 'I trust you. I'm not accusing you of stealing!'

'*You* aren't.' His tone hardens as he turns towards Liam. 'Have you made up your mind? Are you taking the money or not?'

Liam grabs a rucksack and walks out, slamming the door shut.

'I'll take that as a "yes".' Kai arches an eyebrow.

Dammit! Liam looked on the point of caving.

It's time to take a new tack. 'It's a "yes" for now, but Liam could change his mind again. I'm not sure we can trust him.'

'Me neither,' Kai says.

I reward him with a smile. I need to sew more seeds of distrust between them. It could take the heat off me later if everyone identifies Liam as the weakest link.

'Liam's fine,' Layla says shortly. 'He's worried, which is understandable after his mum's car was broken into.'

She'll be harder to manipulate than Kai. Layla's hands tremble as she scoops up her flyers from the sofa – Mother has forgotten them.

'I'll put them out in reception later,' I tell her, smiling.

Her face brightens. 'Thanks. That's kind!'

'No problem.'

That was almost too easy. I follow them to the door.

'I'll set up a WhatsApp group,' I say. 'It's encrypted and

we can keep in touch – make sure we're all on the same page; Liam in particular. We need to keep an eye on him.'

This time they both nod in agreement.

I count out the fifty-pound notes, arranging them into neat piles. It's the full £250,000. Kai hasn't 'accidentally' miscounted. I stuff the money into the rucksack and carry it into my bedroom. I stop in my tracks. A cabinet drawer is open, and the door to my walk-in wardrobe is ajar. This isn't how I left it. I grind my teeth. Kai! He pretended to go to the bathroom and had a nose around.

Heart thumping, I race into the dressing room and shove clothes out of the way, making silk blouses slither off their hangers. The wooden panel is intact, thank God! Kneeling down, I press the wood. It shifts and slides out into my hands. Like Layla, I'd heard rumours about secret passageways and studied architectural drawings dating back to 1895, as well as a blueprint of the 1950s plans when the hotel was revamped. Nothing showed up, not even the historic smugglers' tunnels that are supposed to run beneath the island. I'd found this false wall by accident after I'd tripped and damaged a panel. It wasn't hard to prise free.

I carefully move the small bulky object wrapped in a Sea Haven hand towel, and push the rucksack inside. If this hiding place is ever discovered by housekeeping, I'll be in serious trouble with Mother *and* the police.

Back in the sitting room, my gaze rests on Layla's flyers.

> *Please Donate to Salih's Cancer Treatment.*
> *Salih is ten years old. We need to raise $250,000 to*
> *fund pioneering treatment in the USA this month.*

I bite my lip hard. This is worrying – and not only for her family. I thought Liam was the weakest link, but it's Layla. If she tries to pay her share of the cash into this JustGiving appeal, she could land us *all* in prison. I drop her flyers into the bin and set up a new WhatsApp group: *WAITT*, short for *We're All In This Together*.

I fire off a friendly reminder of our pact:

Don't forget – 6 months!

A few minutes later, my phone pings with messages.

KAI: 👍
LIAM: *Yes!*
Layla is typing.

She changes her mind and doesn't post a reply.

I throw my phone on to the sofa and walk over to the window. I gaze down at the sea, clenching and unclenching my fists. The waves are battering the rocks, creating clouds of billowing cream foam. They're completely merciless. *Like me.*

Layla had better watch out. When DC Walker asked if we knew anything about that bloodstained fifty-pound note, only she replied. She could get into a lot of trouble for lying. I'd deliberately kept quiet as I hadn't wanted to incriminate myself. Mother has always taught me to have a fall guy lined up in case things go wrong.

If Layla crosses me, she'll lose everything.

16

KAI

'You almost died on the bus.' Lou's voice wobbles. 'I'd have lost everything. I wouldn't have anyone who . . .'

'You don't have to worry – I'm hard to kill, apparently!'

I shiver, remembering the guys on the clifftop.

'Are you cold?'

Lou fishes out a sweater from their wardrobe and throws it over. I'm lying on their bed, staring at the stick-on plastic stars on the ceiling, the way we used to when we were little. Rain patters loudly on the window.

'Thanks!'

Lou turns to the mirror, tying back their shoulder-length dark brown hair and applying eyeliner. They'd changed out of their school uniform and into black leggings and a cobalt blue sweater by the time I'd arrived here on my bike. My knee is still strapped up, but the swelling's going down and the painkillers are helping.

'Can you remember how many there are?' Lou asks.

'What?' I frown.

'The stars.'

I don't need to count. 'Thirty-three! You used to have thirty-four, but the adhesive wore off one star and it wouldn't stick. We buried it in the garden.'

Lou smiles at me in the reflection.

'Every fallen star must be mourned . . .' they begin.

'Because they burned so brightly,' I add.

We both grin. We've been best friends since nursery when Lou took me under their wing after another kid picked on me. I always loved coming here for play dates. It felt like a haven away from Mum's latest loser boyfriend. Lou's bedroom used to be plastered with pictures of Disney princesses and they wore Ariel and Cinderella dresses. After a few years, Lou's dad said it was time for them to grow up. Mr Tsang ripped down the posters and gave the dresses to a charity shop. Lou cried for weeks. Thankfully their dad never noticed how these stars light up in the dark otherwise he'd probably have got rid of them too.

'Did the blow to your head make you confused?' Lou asks.

'Come again?'

'You gave that detective my telephone number instead of your mum's. He's left a few messages on my mobile. A doctor at the hospital did the same.'

I look away, running a hand through my hair.

'Wait, that was deliberate?'

'It's a long story . . .'

'I love long stories! Only joking. Keep it short – you're boring me already.'

I laugh. 'The thing is, it's complicated. I swear I have my reasons, but do you mind texting back, saying I'll come in for an interview first thing tomorrow?'

Lou frowns. 'Why can't you ask your mum to message him?'

My cheeks sting. The truth is, I haven't been able to get hold of Mum for a couple of weeks. Lou is the least judgemental person I've ever met, but I don't want to risk embarrassing Mum. It's not her fault she's strapped for cash and can't pay her phone bill.

Lou sits down next to me on the bed. 'I thought we told each other everything? *No secrets.*'

I flinch, thinking of the rucksack stuffed with fifty-pound notes hidden in the holiday home and the reason I'm there in the first place.

'We did. I mean, we still do. I'll tell you everything

eventually. I promise . . .' I cough as the words catch in my throat.

Lou squeezes my hand. 'You know I'm here for you, right? Any time you need to talk – day or night. The way you were for me this summer.'

Tears prick my eyes. Lou knows the basics – Mum and Crystal had to go away temporarily – but I never admitted our old landlord threw me out and I've been dossing in a holiday home. Lou was going through enough without worrying about me. Their Mum and Dad took it badly when they announced they were non-binary. Mr Tsang said it was 'just a phase *he* was going through' and Lou 'should man up'. Things haven't got much better, and their dad still refuses to use the pronouns they/them. Now more time has passed, it's harder for me to talk about *my* family. If I say the words out loud, something will break inside me and I'm afraid it will never be repaired.

'Here goes as your mum.' Lou taps out a message on their mobile. '*Dear DC Walker. It's Heather here. I think you're hot.*' They glance up. 'Too much?'

I nod. 'He's not a Hot Maths Geek.'

Lou blushes. 'Don't!'

'Say I'll come alone at nine thirty tomorrow. Work won't give you time off.'

Lou raises an eyebrow. 'After my son – *you* – almost died? My boss must be a total dick. I should quit and sue for unfair dismissal. I don't sound appreciated.'

'Hmmm. If DC Walker's number rings, let it go to voicemail.'

Their eyebrows rise higher. 'Sure, I guess but . . .'

'Thanks, Lou.'

They sigh deeply. 'Tell me when you're ready.'

I nod. 'I will. You're a good mate.'

'I know. You don't deserve me.'

'True.'

'Despite the fact you're a rubbish best friend, can you stay for supper? Dad can talk to you about surfing, and it'll take his mind off the fact that I exist.'

'I can't, sorry. I've got to . . .' My voice trails off as thunder rumbles ominously in the distance.

'Another long story?'

'Even longer than the first.'

I manage a laugh as Lou pretends to fall asleep, rolling off the bed. But as I look up at the stars, the hairs on the back of my neck prickle with fear at the thought of where I'm heading next.

6.31 p.m.

A jagged bolt of lightning forks across the sky, illuminating the carwash forecourt. For a minute I thought it was a gunshot. I clench my fists, digging my nails into my palms as rain lashes my face.

Calm down.

This horror-movie weather is shredding my nerves. Suddenly the streetlight on the pavement goes out. Oh shit! That's just a coincidence, right? Not a warning to leave before I'm murdered? I hold my breath, but the huge tattooed guy doesn't move from reception; he's sifting through paperwork.

I glance at the security camera fixed on the outside wall. It follows me as I loop round the forecourt for the second time, past a couple of parked cars. Someone inside the building knows I'm here. They're watching me!

What should I do? I could come back in the morning, but I'm probably just as likely to be robbed and left for dead by money launderers in daylight. I move further away and check my mobile, under the shelter of a tree. Lou says DC Walker has texted back – he'll find an appropriate adult to sit with me during the interview tomorrow. I reply with a thumbs up and stare at the screensaver of me, Mum and Crystal on the beach. I go online and find the estate agent details for Torside

Lodge. It's a proper family home. The deposit is £1,300 and the monthly rent is over £1,150. I'll need about £8,000 to land it for six months – plus extra for living expenses. I could also buy a car ready for when I turn seventeen to help Mum and, possibly, Paul with errands.

You have to do this. Then we can all be together.

I set off at speed, throw my bike down on the ground and burst through the door before I change my mind. I stand, dripping wet, on the mat.

The tattooed guy folds his arms over his *huge* chest. 'We were wondering if you'd *finally* come in,' he growls. 'What do you want?'

We?

A larger man appears behind the counter. I hadn't noticed the door; it's covered with car posters and doesn't have a handle. I bite my lip before taking a deep breath.

'I wondered if I could discuss . . . your rates.' I shiver as water trickles from my anorak hood down my back.

'Sure thing.'

The first guy pulls out a sheet of paper and bangs it down. The smell of alcohol grows stronger as he leans closer.

'Would you like the wash and dry or full valet?'

His mate sidles round the counter, and walks over to the door, locking it.

'We're closing,' he says, as I spin round. 'Don't want any more customers.'

Panic spikes in my chest.

I'm trapped.

I lick my dry lips. 'Do you have anything off the books?'

The guy leans on the counter, flexing his fingers. 'Did you hear that, Tom?'

'Yeah, Gerry.'

Omigod. It's Tom and Jerry, like the old cartoon. The corners of my mouth twitch. It would be funny if it weren't for the fact that I'm probably about to be killed.

'It's Gerry with a G, not a J,' he barks.

I glance over my shoulder. Tom scowls. They're both built like brick shithouses. Punching one of them would probably break my fist, and I can't escape.

'I don't want any trouble! I want to make use of your other services.' I hold up my rucksack.

Tom is over in a flash. He rips it out of my hand and rifles inside.

'How much does he have?'

'Twenty-five to thirty grand.'

'Have Mummy and Daddy been generous with their pocket money?' Tom chortles.

'Look, are you able to help me launder this or not?' I'm

attempting to sound brave when I may have wet myself a little.

'Let's chat in private.' Tom grabs my arm and frogmarches me behind the counter. He shoves me through the handleless door. Now we're going downstairs.

'I'm sorry! I shouldn't have come. Let me go!'

I try to kick him, but Tom twists my arm tightly behind my back. My heart hammers against my ribcage. My armpits are wet with sweat. This is it. I survived the crash, only to be killed in a soundproof basement by money launderers named after cartoon characters. I stumble at the bottom of the stairs, but Gerry scoops me up as if I'm as light as a baby and flings me towards another door.

'Open it!' he orders.

My knees weaken. I do *not* want to see what's inside this room.

'I'm sorry. Coming here was a terrible mistake, but if you let me leave, I promise I'll never tell anyone about this place.'

Or make unfunny cartoon jokes.

'Too late,' Tom growls.

I hear a high-pitched scream as he opens the door and throws me inside. The noise is coming from my mouth. I'm expecting to see a torture chamber: chains hanging from the ceiling and gruesome surgical implements laid out in a neat line, gleaming under the harsh overhead light.

But what's inside is more shocking.

It's a modern office with a photocopier, water cooler and large desk, with red-plastic chairs arranged in front of it.

Liam is sat in one of the chairs, dressed in a suit. Layla is beside him.

Two rucksacks lie at their feet.

17

LIAM

'Layla? Liam?' Kai's face whitens. His gaze rests on me. 'What the hell are you both doing here?'

I can't reply. My throat has tightened and my heart feels as though it's trying to fly out of my ribcage. I tug at my tie, which is strangling me. Layla had arrived by taxi as I was parking Mum's car. I'm half expecting Fliss to turn up too – then we'll have a final thieves' reunion, or rather funeral. I close my eyes and count prime numbers backwards from twenty.

Nineteen, seventeen, thirteen, eleven . . .

Breathe . . .

'We figured you're all mates. Sit down.'

My eyes fly open as Kai lands in the chair next to me.

'How do you know what we do here?' Gerry asks.

Kai and Layla glance at me. I breathe in deeply. Obviously

we need to stick to the truth as far as possible – that's what I've learnt from movies: the bigger the lie, the more trouble you get into.

'We were talking about money laundering and someone, a local driver, mentioned this place,' I tell him. 'He said you'd give us good rates.'

Kai's eyes widen at my embellishment. Wait, does he think that money launderers work for free?

'What *are* your rates?' Layla asks in a small voice.

Tom shrugs. 'Depends on the risk and amount of cash involved.'

She picks up her rucksack. 'I have two hundred and fifty thousand pounds.'

'No!' I exclaim.

I've left most of the cash hidden under my bedroom floorboards, next to the collection of weights, after calculating the probability of us being robbed as 50 per cent. I'm currently scaling that up to 90 per cent.

Gerry gives a low whistle. 'How did you come by that, little lady?'

'That's none of your business,' she says, thrusting her chin in the air. 'And don't call me "little lady".'

'That's five thousand added to my rates – for rudeness.'

'You can't do that!'

'And another five thousand.'

'Layla, stop!' Kai cries.

She glares at him, but he's right. *They hold all the cards, not us.*

'You kids don't understand how money laundering works,' Gerry drawls, sitting back in his chair. 'There are no rules. We could empty out the cash from your rucksacks and lock it in the safe over there.' He jerks his head across the room. 'You can't call the police. You can't fight us – in truth, you can do diddly squat.'

Layla scrabbles about in her rucksack. My heart races. *Does she have the missing gun?* I breathe easier when she produces pieces of paper.

'What's this?' Gerry squints as she pushes a flyer across the desk.

'It's a fundraising appeal,' Layla explains. 'My little brother, Salih, is seriously ill with a rare type of cancer. If we can get him on to this medical trial in the States, he's got a good chance of fighting it. But if we don't . . .'

Kai reaches over and squeezes her arm as she wells up. 'I'm sorry,' he says softly. 'I had no idea.'

'Me neither,' I murmur.

'This is our best chance to save Salih.' Her voice falters but grows in strength. 'We have to get him on to this trial, but it costs two hundred and fifty thousand dollars – around two hundred thousand pounds. More for accommodation and flights to the US.'

Gerry makes another whistling sound. 'Pricey.'

'It's way beyond what we can afford. But I have this money.' She lifts the rucksack. 'I don't want to say how I got it, because it could land you both in trouble.' She grips the fabric tighter. 'You're right – I don't understand how money laundering works. What I *need* to happen is for this money to appear in my brother's JustGiving fundraising account. It must look as though an anonymous benefactor has helped us. Anything left over, I'll donate to other children's treatment.'

A lump grows in my throat. In my peripheral vision, I see Kai rub his eyes. Gerry and Tom – Gerry with a G, but it's still too ridiculous to say their names the other way round – examine the flyers. Have they been moved by her predicament?

'Nice speech, but we're not a charity,' Tom says, frowning.

He grabs the rucksack, emptying it out on to the table. They hold up notes to the light and tilt them. They're making sure the word changes between 'Fifty' and 'Pounds' in the hologram, and '50' and a '£' in the two gold foil squares. I've checked mine: they're real.

'She's not kidding. It's two hundred and fifty thousand.'

Gerry's eyes narrow. He taps at his computer. 'The Salih Abdullatif Fundraising Appeal looks legit.'

'It is!' Layla grips the side of her chair. 'Does this mean you'll do it?'

Gerry exchanges looks with Tom, who nods.

'We'll do you a special offer since we've both got kids,' Gerry says. 'We'll make a one-off payment through this business to the website. For an anonymous donation of two hundred thousand, we'll charge twenty per cent – fifty thousand.'

'But that wipes out all my money!' Layla exclaims.

'It's hot, which puts *us* in the firing line,' Tom retorts. 'We don't usually mess with a drug gang, but we're prepared to make an exception for this.' He jabs a large meaty finger at the flyer.

'How do you know this money is drugs-related?' I ask.

'Word is, that dead bus driver on the news stole it from *dangerous people*.'

Silas! That sounds about right.

'We don't want to get on the wrong side of them – and neither should you,' Tom continues.

Kai shudders.

'What guarantees do I have that you won't keep the money?' Layla persists.

Gerry bursts out laughing. 'You don't! But that's the risk you take. It's up to you – you're free to leave.' He nods to the door. 'Or stay and gamble.'

Holy moly. This is such a bad idea. Should we try to grab our rucksacks and make a break for it? Layla stretches out her hand. Gerry reaches over the desk and gives her a handshake – a bone-crunching one, judging by her wince.

'When will it go into the account?'

'Within forty-eight to seventy-two hours. Keep checking but remember we don't like customer complaints!' He winks but his grey eyes are as hard as granite.

'Thank you. I trust you'll do the right thing for my brother.'

The pair stare back impassively.

'What about the boys?' she asks.

The surgery scar that snakes up my spine prickles uncomfortably as their gaze switches to us. I shift in my seat.

Kai opens his rucksack. 'I have thirty thousand.' He hands it over.

'And you?' Tom jerks his head at me.

'Forty thousand pounds.'

I cling on to my rucksack as Kai inhales sharply. He was sensible and brought the least amount of cash.

'This will be trickier – no one-off payments to charities, I'm guessing?' Tom asks.

We shake our heads.

'How many bank accounts do you each have?'

'Only one,' I say.

Kai nods. 'Same.'

'You'll need to set up multiple – four or five each – and we'll give you a rate of fifty per cent.'

'Fifty?!' Kai exclaims. 'Why can't we have the same rate as Layla?'

'This is more difficult and time-consuming,' Gerry chips in.

I'll only get £20,000 back – that's if they don't take everything.

'How long will it take to get the cash?' My voice is tiny.

'Same as your friend.' He nods at Layla. 'Give us the account numbers and sort codes in person on Thursday morning – not by email or phone – and we'll transfer the funds: fifty per cent spread across all accounts by the evening. Friday morning at the latest.'

That's doable. I'm supposed to give a statement to the police tomorrow morning before Mum starts her shift. After that, I can catch the bus into Plymouth and visit the banks. I could pick up new glasses. The spare pair I've resorted to wearing are held together with tape after breaking months ago.

'Okay.' I exhale slowly. At this point I'll be grateful to walk out of here with my life.

'It's great doing business with the three of you!' Gerry scrapes back his chair. 'We'll keep all the rucksacks under lock and key tonight. You won't need much cash to set up the bank accounts – pay in the minimum to open them.'

'But—'

Kai stops when he sees the look on Gerry's face.

'Thank you for your investments.' Tom's eyes crinkle with laughter.

Investments? We're in the process of being robbed.

Tom opens the door and stands aside. 'Let yourselves out upstairs.'

I lurch towards the exit, my knees trembling. I feel Layla's hand slip beneath my right elbow and Kai's at my left as we climb the stairs.

'They're polite for muggers,' Kai mutters.

'Don't say that!' Layla cries. 'I have to believe I'll get that money.'

'I hope you do.'

'Me too,' I say forcefully.

For once, we're all telling the truth. We reach the reception and Kai's hands shake as he unlocks the front door. Relief floods over me when he lets us out. Cold air hits my face; it's stopped raining.

Kai wanders over to his bike. 'You should get your car washed before you leave, Liam. It's only gonna cost you forty thousand.'

'Funny.'

He turns round. 'Talking of funny – what triggered your change of heart about keeping the cash? Or was that a performance in Fliss's room? You pretended to be spooked by the car break-in, so we'd never suspect you'd turn up here?'

'I was . . . I *am* still frightened about those men.' I try to keep my voice steady. 'I changed my mind about the money after I left the hotel.'

Kai lets out a low, sarcastic whistle. 'Gotcha. You're a spur-of-the-moment type of guy. Not someone who likes planning and spreadsheets at all.'

My cheeks burn. 'I don't remember either of you mentioning this earlier!'

'Can you both please stop?' Layla's voice trembles. 'Let's get out of here while we can. I need to call a taxi.' She pulls out her phone, almost dropping it.

'I'll give you a lift. You too, Kai. I can fit your bike in the back.'

It's time for a peace offering. I'm not proud of the way I

169

goaded him in Fliss's suite, and he's suspicious about my motives. He's dangerously close to the truth.

'Thanks, but my knee's much better and I need to clear my head.'

He climbs on his bike, wincing, and slowly cycles across the forecourt. He pauses by one of the parked cars, and stares into the driver's window, before checking the passenger side.

'What are you doing?' Layla calls over.

'Nothing.'

He cycles past, missing me by inches.

'This has to be our secret,' I call after him. 'We can never tell Fliss.'

He loops back. 'Of course not! Jeez. She'll kill us if she finds out one of us is lying, let alone all three.'

His tone is provocative. I can't look at him.

'Well, she'll definitely be peed off,' Layla admits.

Kai shakes his head. 'She has the gun, not us. Imagine what she could do if she realises we've turned her over?'

'We don't know that for sure,' I say shakily.

'If one of *us* had taken the gun from the holdall, don't you think we'd have brought it tonight for protection?' he asks.

Chills ripple through my body. Kai's right.

We've double-crossed Fliss and she has a loaded weapon.

WhatsApp group: WAITT

FLISS: *Police interview went okay this morning. No mention of £££. Stuck 2 talking about crash. Anyone else?*

LIAM: *Same. DC Watkins completely in dark!*

KAI: 👍

LAYLA: *Ditto. We got away with it!* ☺

FLISS: *Anything else?*

LAYLA: *No*

KAI: 🙈

LIAM: I bought new glasses in Plymouth!

FLISS: 👻

LAYLA: *Thinking of u 2day. Keep safe.*
15:06

KAI: *U2 x*
15:07

LAYLA: 🙂
15:09

18

LAYLA

A loud bang rings out, followed by a scream. I tumble out of bed, crashing to the floor as my foot becomes tangled in the duvet. My mind races to dark places. Is Fliss exacting revenge after we double-crossed her on Tuesday night? Or have the dodgy guys from the carwash broken in, looking for more cash?

'Mum!' I shout.

As I reach the landing, Salih appears, rubbing his eyes. 'What's going on?'

'Go back to your bedroom, *habibi*, and don't come out until I say it's safe.'

'Why?' His forehead crinkles.

'I'll explain later.' I steer him towards the door. 'Wedge a chair beneath the handle.'

'You're weird.' Salih saunters inside. 'Why can't I have

173

a non-tragic sister, instead of you, MM?' He takes a flying leap on to his bed.

'Omigod!' Mum cries.

'I'm coming!' I holler back, closing Salih's door.

I run down the stairs, grabbing my hockey stick from the hallway and fly into the kitchen. I glance about wildly, brandishing the weapon. Mum and Leon are hugging each other, standing among fragments of crockery.

'What's going on?'

'Why are you waving that thing around?' Mum asks over Leon's shoulder.

I prop the hockey stick against the chair, my hands shaking. 'I thought you were being attacked.' I stare at the broken china at her feet. It's Mum's favourite teapot. At least it's not Baba's espresso cup and saucer.

'That's my fault!' She grins back. 'I dropped it in shock. I was shouting with joy!'

My heart beats rapidly. Could the guys from the carwash . . .? Have they . . .?

'The most amazing thing's happened!' Leon waltzes Mum round the table.

'What?'

'You have to dance first!' Leon says, laughing.

He grabs my hand and the three of us do a clumsy routine,

rippling our arms up and down. It's the first time I've seen them both looking happy, *properly* happy, for months.

'Okay, enough. Tell me!'

'Mrs C has come up trumps!' Mum gasps. 'She's donated a huge amount to the JustGiving page!'

'Let me see!'

Leon shoves the laptop across the table. Heart thumping, I check out the latest donation, which landed at 6.02 a.m.

£210,000.

'I don't believe it!' I slump into a chair. Tom and Gerry have laundered the cash. They've helped Salih – and deposited £10,000 more than they said they would, leaving extra money to cover our flights and expenses. Maybe they're softies at heart?

I breathe out heavily, my eyes brimming with tears.

'Don't cry, love,' Mum says. 'This is a day to be happy!'

'I am.' I wipe my face with the pyjama sleeve. 'I can't believe it . . .'

Mum holds me tightly. 'It's all thanks to Mrs C,' she points out.

I tense beneath her arms. 'I thought it was an anonymous donation?'

'But think about it – shortly after you gave the flyers to Mrs C, this is paid into the fundraising account.'

I cough. 'Yeah, true.'

'Who else could it be? We haven't had any publicity. The appeal has only just got off the ground and your grandma hasn't called me back, so she won't have asked extended family or friends in Egypt yet.'

'Maybe one of the guests at the hotel?' I'd taken the leaflets to please her – but I'd also needed a plausible cover story in case I did successfully launder the money.

'I should ring Mrs C later, to thank her for putting them out. Or I could get the sea tractor over there and do it in person.'

'I wouldn't do that,' I say hastily. 'She was dead busy on Tuesday.'

'But we have to do something,' Mum insists. 'Anyway, we need to celebrate! Is Salih awake?'

'Yes.' I head into the hall. 'Saliiiiiihhh! Come down!'

He doesn't reply.

'Go and fetch him!' Leon shouts after me. 'He has to hear the news.'

I head up the stairs, my heart beating with excitement. I've pulled off the impossible. Baba would be proud I'm helping my brother, wouldn't he? Even though I'm a thief. I try not to think about that part.

Salih will get his treatment and recover.

A heavy weight lifts from my shoulders. We came here

for a fresh start – Leon had planned to renovate holiday homes while Mum opened a bookshop. But that dream ended when Leon fell from his ladder shortly after we moved and Salih became ill. Now Salih can get the treatment he needs, and maybe Leon could get regular physio too. Everything is finally within our grasp.

I nip into my bedroom to grab my phone and set up another WhatsApp group for me, Kai and Liam. Group name: *Cartoons.*

ME: *I have it!*
Liam is typing.
LIAM: *Congrats! Me too – late last night!*
ME: *Fab! Kai?*

I stare at the screen, willing him to wake up and check his messages. I message him privately:

££££

'Salih? Didn't you hear us calling?' He's staring out of the window as I walk into his bedroom. 'Ow!' I pull off the Lego piece attached to my big toe and pick my way through the shattered space shuttle.

'Hey! What are you looking at?'

'A guy on a motorbike.'

Typical! Salih loves motorbikes almost as much as football. I join him at the window. The street is deserted. 'Where? I can't see anyone.'

'He's gone. He was right there.' He points across the road.

'What was he doing?'

'Standing by his bike, watching our house. He took photos with his camera.'

My heart beats quicker. 'What did he look like?'

'He had a helmet on, dummy! Do you think we should tell Mum?'

'Why would we do that?'

'He could be a burglar, casing the joint. Ooh, wait. He might be a stalker or a serial killer. We should call the police.'

My heart thumps loudly. 'No, I'm sure it's nothing. Come on. Mum has something to tell you.'

'Good or bad news?'

'It's great news, *habibi*!'

I lead him downstairs, my palms sticky with sweat. It's a coincidence, right? Tom and Gerry won't turn up here and the scary guys from the cliff can't have tracked me down. That newspaper story never named us. Maybe it was an estate agent, looking at next-door's house. Didn't Mum mention the neighbours are moving?

It's nothing! We took a massive gamble and it paid off.

I try to ignore the doubt that's flickering in the corners of my brain. As we reach the bottom of the stairs, Salih stops.

'You should put your dressing gown on, MM.'

'Why?'

'You're shivering.'

19

FLISS

I'm shivering violently, crawling across the floor. Glass stabs my hands and knees. I must make it to the back of the bus, but I can barely breathe. The pain in my ribs is unbearable. Layla, Kai and Liam are laughing and pointing.

Help me!

They do nothing. The faster I move, the further they drift away.

The floor softens beneath my touch. I'm lying on carpet, close to a bed. My face feels like it's exploding. I taste blood in my mouth. A gold watch and black-leather wallet lie on the table far above my head, next to two drinks. Is that my phone? I reach up, but it's beyond my grasp. I have to get out. I hear a man talking in the background. He's on the phone. I crawl towards the door. Suddenly a hand grabs my ankle. I scream and kick, but he's dragging

*me back. His hand clamps over my mouth, muffling my
cries for help.*

The room tilts backwards and I'm falling, falling, falling.

I sit up, panting. My forehead is beaded with sweat, my
ribcage throbs dully. I look around, taking in the dresser and
the photo of Daddy on my bedside table. I snatch up the
picture frame and clutch it to my heart, sinking back into the
pillows.

You're not on the bus.

You're not in that suite.

You're in your bedroom.

You're safe.

No one can hurt you.

I breathe out the way Liam showed me, willing my heart
rate to slow. I don't want to think about the crash – or that
summer night. I ease myself on to my side, groping for
my phone. I feel another sharp, stabbing pain in my chest
as I check my messages. Still nothing from my so-called
friends! Not a single text since the crash. Don't they
remember what happened to Annie after she forgot to invite
me to her party? I made her life a misery until she moved
schools.

It's time to remind them who's boss. I add Tristram, Lisa,
Spencer and the numbers for the rest of the gang to a new

WhatsApp group: *Am Back Bitches*. It's a nod to one of my favourite lines in *Pretty Little Liars*.

I type out an invitation.

Come and celebrate my survival at the Lobster Bar 2M, 7.30 p.m. PS I'm paying!

I stare at the picture of Daddy as I wait for their replies. I try to picture the beachside apartment I'll buy in six months' time. I can't be away from the water – that's literally the only thing I'll miss about my life here, apart from Aaron. I push away my happy childhood memories of Mother; they're long gone.

My heart leaps as the phone vibrates. Has Tristram RSVP'd first? Or Lisa? She lives in fear of becoming the next 'Annie'.

I click on the message from an unknown number:

Price has doubled to £10,000 – but u can afford it, right?

My heart beats louder and louder. My blackmailer is back! They must know we've stolen the cash. No, I'm being paranoid. They would have asked for more money regardless. My phone pings again. No message this time – only a photo.

I heave over the side of my bed, vomit spattering on to my Prada slippers.

It's one of this summer's incriminating pictures, stolen from my hacked phone.

I'm half dressed and kissing Robert Brody, a drunk VIP guest.

I took the selfie in his room a few hours before he fell to his death from the cliff behind the hotel.

20

KAI

I open my eyes and stare at the unfamiliar cream ceiling. The walls are light blue. Where am I? *Torside Lodge*. I've rented somewhere at last – Mum's dream home! My heart contracts as I spot the framed picture of me, Mum and Crystal on the bedside table. It's from my sister's seventh birthday party last year. I plant a kiss on the photo and check my phone. Layla and Liam have their cash too! It won't be long now before Mum and Crystal come back.

I send a thumbs-up emoji to our secret WhatsApp group, before switching to my private exchange with Layla yesterday.

GR8! Xx

My heart skips a beat as she sends a love heart back! It's the best day *ever.* Her brother can get his treatment in

184

the States and I'm sorted. Tom and Gerry had transferred the cash into my new Plymouth bank accounts by 5 p.m. last night. Afterwards I'd cycled to the estate agent's before it closed and claimed Mum was too ill to come. I paid the deposit and six months' rent upfront for this house by bank transfer. I slipped them £200 in fifties to waive our references. Business is slow – most locals can't afford rentals around here any more.

I need a good hiding place for the holdall and my rucksack, which are lying on the polished wooden floorboards. For now, it's the loft. I head out on to the landing and poke open the hatch door with a stick, pulling down the ladder. Once up there, I cough, pushing aside dusty old boxes the previous tenant left behind. I stuff the holdall and rucksack inside one and close up.

On the way downstairs I picture hanging framed family photos on the walls. We could display Crystal's attempts at pottery in the hallway.

I pass the sitting room – it's light and airy with a large red sofa, where we'll fight over the remote control before watching TV together. The kitchen is *huge*. We'll spend loads of time in here; I'll rustle up a mean spag bol while Crystal and Lucy draw at the table. Mum used to complain she had nowhere to put her saucepans in our poky old flat;

she'll love the floor-to-ceiling cupboards. We even have an ice dispenser. I imagine her laughing as Paul calls it 'dead fancy'. My stomach growls, but there's no point checking inside the large stainless-steel fridge – it's empty.

Grabbing my coat, I put on the alarm and lock the front door, whistling one of Crystal's favourite songs from a musical – I always forget the name. For the first time in weeks the tight knot in my chest that keeps me awake at night is loosening.

A motorbike roars down the road. As it passes, the driver looks back briefly, before accelerating. I try ringing Mum's mobile to tell her the good news, but it's still disconnected. She hasn't managed to pay the balance yet, but I can sort that, along with her other outstanding bills.

As I reach the supermarket, I notice the guy in black leathers and helmet. He's sat astride his motorbike on the opposite side of the road. A camera hangs from his neck. Maybe he's a tourist. I duck inside and pick up a couple of sausage rolls, a chocolate bar and a coffee. Mum wouldn't approve of this breakfast, but I can stock the cupboards when she tells me what date they'll be back.

As I pass the newspapers, I freeze. The food slips from my hands. The coffee spills on the floor. The guy behind the till shouts something, but the buzzing in my ears drowns out his words.

I stare at the photograph on the front of the *Kingsborough Gazette*.

A voice in my head screams, 'Run!'

21

LIAM

'What's the big surprise? Why did I have to pretend I had a dental appointment?'

Tristram wriggles as I cover his eyes with my hands. Tucked beneath his right armpit is a copy of the *Kingsborough Gazette*. I'd never pegged him as a fan of local news. His broad back feels solid and comforting against my chest. My stomach flips with excitement as I take in his familiar citrus aftershave.

'Well? Tell me, babe!'

Half of me wants to stay like this for ever, my arms wrapped round him in the street, but I'm dying to share this moment.

'It's a late birthday present – something you've always wanted.'

I lift my fingers, holding my breath. Tristram gasps as he takes in the black Jeep Renegade parked outside my house. It's second-hand but ex-demo with low mileage. Anthony the salesman hadn't blinked when I'd asked last night if he'd accept £20,000 in cash. It was a calculated risk – one I'd figured was worth taking. I'd guessed Anthony would skim off a few thousand without telling his boss. No one else will find out. This way we both win – I don't touch the laundered money in my new bank accounts and Anthony tops up his commission. He'll never report me to the police. I'm safe.

'Are you kidding me?'

Tristram spins round, staring at me wide-eyed as a motorbike pulls up and parks across the road. He flashes one of his dazzling Hollywood smiles that lands him the lead in school shows. My heart flutters.

'It's no joke – it's yours.' I pass him the keys.

'But how . . .?'

His voice trails off as he glances at our small rented terraced house. I wince as I see it through his eyes: blistering paint bubbles from the rotting windowsills. The front garden is concreted over, with weeds growing through the gaps. Mum keeps talking about fixing the gate. Tristram's gardener does odd jobs like that around their property – a Georgian farmhouse set in five acres.

'I had a win on the scratchcards.'

'Omigod. I don't believe it! That's so funny.'

I frown as he throws his arms round me, laughing. Why is that amusing? I thought this would be the most logical explanation – he wouldn't believe I'd stolen it from a dead bus driver – not that I'd ever have told him that.

'It's not implausible. The odds of winning are about one in 2.76 million.' There's a defensive note in my voice.

Tristram laughs. '*Of course* you'd know that stat. Congratulations!' He twirls the keys round his fingers. 'I've never thought to try my luck. How much did you win?'

'W-w-what?'

'On the scratchcards?'

'Two hundred and fifty thousand pounds.' The words escape from my lips before I have a chance to think. I'm never able to refuse Tristram, but cold dread sweeps over my body. The hairs on my arms prickle uncomfortably as he walks round the Jeep, gazing admiringly at the paintwork. As he unlocks it, I notice the guy on the motorbike staring at us. Hasn't he seen a gay couple before?

I slide into the passenger seat alongside Tristram, pulling the door shut. 'Here's something else – the deposit for the ski trip.'

I hand him an envelope stuffed with fifties, but his face doesn't light up.

'Whooaa! Your neighbours will think this is a drug deal. You should have done a bank transfer.'

'Sorry.' I wince as he puts the envelope in his pocket. 'Will you book the holiday today?'

'I'll speak to the others later. Check they're still up for it.'

I feel a pang of disappointment that he's not more excited about our New Year plans.

'You mustn't tell them about my win – or put anything on social media. Promise?'

'Why not? We should celebrate your success.'

It's time to improvise, the way he does in drama classes. 'I don't feel the need to document my life for everyone else to pass comment on.'

A frown mark snakes between his eyes. Has he taken that the wrong way? He posts on Instagram and TikTok most days.

'People could ask me for money,' I finish lamely.

'Yeah, I guess your old friends might, but it's not like any of *us* would.' He squeezes my knee. 'But, I mean, it's great for someone like you!'

A knot tightens in my stomach. *Someone like you.*

When Tristram unexpectedly asked me out in the canteen queue two months ago, I stopped hanging out with Mohammed and Aisha from my maths class. Now I spend every break time and lunch with his circle of friends, even though we're worlds apart.

They're not like us, Aisha had warned. *You'll never fit in.*

She was right. His group can easily afford the ski deposit – their allowances are probably larger than my mum's monthly pay cheque.

Tristram presses my hand to his lips and kisses it. 'It'll be our secret.'

'Thanks.' I clear my throat. 'The insurance is sorted – you can start driving straight away. The theft didn't affect your premium badly.'

I'd expected the insurance to be sky-high after his dad's stolen Merc was found burnt out five miles away. But I've managed to get it covered for less than £1,000 on my new credit card.

Tristram's eyes cloud over. 'You didn't tell the salesman the truth, babe? My dad will go nuts if he knows I screwed up over the keys. He won't let me drive this, let alone Mum's car. And it would definitely affect the insurance.'

'Of course not!'

'I knew I could rely on you.'

I melt as he strokes the side of my face. His dad's car was stolen the same week as Bob's hit-and-run. It sounds like DC Walker suspects Silas or the Audi driver killed Bob.

Maybe the detective will get to the bottom of the Merc theft too.

'You're the best boyfriend ever!' Tristram pulls me into his arms. His mouth finds mine, his tongue gently probing. My troubles – the police interview, setting up new bank accounts in Plymouth and worrying the carwash duo would beat me when I returned alone – all disappear. Tristram, the sexiest boy in school, fancies *me*.

Nothing else matters.

His fingers stroke the back of my neck. I feel myself shrinking smaller and smaller as he snatches his hand back.

'What's wrong?' I ask.

'I thought I'd hurt you,' he says quickly.

'It's okay. I don't feel the scar.'

Why did I wear an old T-shirt on an important day like this? I forgot to put on a short-sleeved shirt, buttoned to the collar, which he prefers. He thinks it makes me look preppy and 'hot'.

'Do you have to get that?' Tristram asks, as my phone vibrates. 'It might be the police.'

'Why would the police want to speak to me?'

'Because you survived a clifftop crash, genius?'

'Oh, of course.' I pull the mobile out of my pocket. Kai

again! Does he think I'll crack and confess if he grills me about when I decided to launder the money?

'Who is it?' he asks, frowning.

'No one. No one that matters anyway.'

His eyes narrow as he grabs my phone and reads the name of my missed caller. 'Should I be jealous?'

'What? No!'

My throat dries. What would Tristram say if he knew we'd been spending time together because of our pact? I want to be completely honest about seeing Kai twice since the accident, but I can't tell Tristram about the cash beneath my bedroom floorboards or the new bank accounts. It's too risky.

'Kai's a colossal loser, right? Always looks like he's dossed on the beach. And he's friends with Lou. What a fricking joke! They're both beyond tragic.'

Something shifts uncomfortably in the pit of my stomach. Lou took time out from revision when I was ill with food poisoning last term and checked on me every day. Lou loves the same movies, and never makes fun of me being nerdy, the way Tristram sometimes does. I open my mouth to defend them both, but it's easier to stay quiet and ignore the red flag. I can't confess my feelings for Lou. My *old* feelings. Because I don't think about Lou any more. Not really.

'Shall we find a movie on Netflix later?' I ask. 'We could

go vintage – *Halloween* or the first *Saw*? You can't beat a corpse rising from the dead.'

'Eeeugh, I hate horror.'

'We can watch anything you want. You promised you'd come over.'

'I'd love to, but I can't tonight.' He squeezes my hand. 'Coach has organised a last-minute training session.'

'What about tomorrow?'

'I have drama club, sorry.'

'Saturday evening? No wait, I'm working. What about—'

'We'll spend quality time together soon, I promise.'

He leans across and kisses me on the lips, but it's disappointingly fleeting. As I shuffle closer, he turns the key in the ignition, revving the engine.

'I'd better head into school.' He taps the steering wheel. 'Like I said – best boyfriend ever!'

Slowly I climb out.

Tristram winds the window down and leans out. 'Look sharp, babe!' He tosses the newspaper to me. Predictably I drop it.

'You'll never make the rugby team, but you look dead hot in the picture!' he shouts, as I chase after the fluttering pages.

'What picture?' I spin round.

He toots the horn and drives off. My phone is vibrating

like mad in my pocket. I collect the escaped pages, slotting them back inside. My gaze rests on the front-page story.

My vision swims, my neck is slick with sweat.

The menacing growl of a motorbike engine grows louder.

Staring back at me is a photo of the four of us on the balcony of the Sea Haven.

BRAVE TEENAGERS BATTLED TO SAVE DRIVER!

Four teenagers attempted to help their driver escape from the school bus before it plunged off a cliff on Monday morning. The Kingsborough High School pupils caught up in the tragedy have been named as Fliss Cavendish, 17, Kai Marsden, 16, Liam King, 17, and Layla Abdullatif, 16. The students managed to escape through an emergency window as the bus hung over the cliff edge. But despite their rescue attempt, the driver, Silas Greenhill, was unable to exit before the vehicle plunged into the sea.

Mrs Sophia Cavendish, owner of the Sea Haven hotel, said, 'Fliss told me how she put her own life at risk, attempting to save Silas. She also made sure Layla escaped from the bus first. They are as well as can be expected after their ordeal and I've made it my personal mission to make sure they are supported. I have gifted iPhones to each of the teenagers to enable them to keep in touch – I feel it is the least I can do under the circumstances.'

The Sea Haven was hit by tragedy this summer when businessman Robert Brody, 25, from Kensington, south-west London, fell 100 metres to his death from cliffs behind the hotel's tennis courts on the private island. An inquest found that his blood alcohol level would have made him four times over the drink-driving limit. Mr Brody had been drinking cocktails in the hotel bar, before continuing to down shots alone in his room. The coroner has ruled his death was accidental.

WhatsApp group: WAITT

LAYLA: *WTAF, Fliss? Yr mum stitched us up!!*

FLISS: *Sorry! No idea she was planning this!!! Am as angry as u!*

LIAM: *What are we going to do?*

FLISS: *Will talk 2 her. Make paper print retraction.*

LAYLA: *2 late! Our names and faces r out there. We're all in danger!*

FLISS: *They know our names – nothing else. This doesn't prove ANYTHING!!!*

KAI: 🏍 *following me!!*

FLISS: *WTF?!*

LAYLA: 🏍 *here 2. Brother said guy was staring at our house.*

LIAM: *Ditto outside my house. Think he was watching me and Tristram.*

FLISS: *Probably a coincidence. Lots of* 🏍️ 🏍️ 🏍️ *around!! Don't panic and don't draw attention to yrselves. Will sort Mother.*

22

FLISS

'How could you?'

I ignore Maura, the PA who keeps the world's lamest collection of cockapoo ornaments next to her computer, and storm into Mother's office. I fling the *Kingsborough Gazette* on to her desk. 'You deliberately tricked us! Tricked *me!*'

'I'm sorry, Nick. I'll have to call you back. My daughter needs me.' She puts the phone down and stands up. Her face is drawn and pale, her mascara smudged as if she's been crying. I ignore her dishevelled appearance and launch into my tirade.

'You never had any intention of using that photo on the staff noticeboard! You wanted to show off about giving away free phones to make yourself look good, but you didn't stop to think about the harm it could cause me and the others.'

Mother wipes her eyes. 'What harm? You're all heroes!

201

Everyone gets to hear about your bravery.' Her heels make gentle clicking noises as she walks round the desk. She smooths the wrinkles from her cream Chanel skirt. 'I don't see the problem, unless there's something you're not telling me?'

I bite my lip. This is my chance to explain about the blackmail, the £1 million *and* the guy on the motorbike who might be stalking the others. But anger bubbles furiously inside me. I clench my fists. I want to shake her, not make a confession.

'You had no right to make our names public.'

'I'm sorry you're upset, but I thought it was a smart move. We need good publicity after what happened this summer.'

Her words are like a punch to the stomach. My knees weaken. I lean against the filing cabinet, winded. Mother picks up the paper and doesn't notice I'm attempting to catch my breath.

'It's a pity the reporter ruined the piece we agreed by mentioning that event,' she says, sighing. 'It draws attention to the Sea Haven in the worst possible way.'

That event. The death of Robert Brody. I shudder. To her it's something else that must be managed and dealt with. Like me.

'All you care about is your reputation,' I say, trembling. 'Above everything! Above me. What I've been through.'

'How can you think that? I'm protecting *you*. I'm lying for *you*.'

'Well don't!'

'What do you mean?'

I hesitate. 'When I was trapped on the bus, I vowed to go to the police if I survived and explain my side of the story – exactly what we discussed that night.'

The vein in Mother's forehead throbs. 'Thankfully you came to your senses,' she says briskly. 'This is behind us, sweetie. It's our secret and must stay between the two of us.'

That's the problem. A third person knows: my blackmailer. I could tell her without letting on about Silas's holdall. I open my mouth, but she's distracted, shuffling bank statements and invoices with red 'reminder' stamps on her desk.

'You were never implicated – your name didn't come out in relation to Robert's death at the opening of the inquest,' she says without glancing up. 'We need to keep it like that unless you want to risk being charged with murder and me as your accessory?'

I take a sharp intake of breath. 'It wasn't my fault,' I say, my voice cracking.

'I know, sweetie!'

'But if you'd reported what happened in his room, none of this would have happened.'

'I couldn't call the police.' Mother's vein twitches.

'Why not?' I whisper.

She sighs deeply. 'It would have been your word against his – a rich, powerful man. The police might not have believed your account. You went to his room voluntarily to drink alcohol, while underage, remember? He'd have paid the best barrister in the country to paint you in the worst possible light in the eyes of the jury. I couldn't put you through that ordeal. It would have been traumatic.'

Her words stab my chest. I'm momentarily speechless. She should have had my back that night, regardless. She should have *made* the police believe me. I stare at her, but she won't meet my gaze. She's holding something back.

'Really? Or was it just that you didn't want the bad publicity of *him* being arrested and led away in handcuffs in front of the other guests?' I can't bring myself to say his name. 'It would have been bad for business, right?'

She fiddles with the waistband of her skirt. 'Robert Brody was a douche bag who accidentally fell to his death on hotel property. Consider it karma. But no good can come from either of us talking to the police now. All this could be taken away like that.' As she clicks her fingers, I notice a few of her red nails are broken.

'I don't care!'

'That's not true. You were upset when I put the brakes on your Verbier trip, and I had to temporarily suspend your monthly allowance.'

I glower at her.

'You enjoy our lifestyle, and I'm working hard to keep it. I'm growing the business and creating a legacy. You'll have all the things I never had growing up.'

'All I ever wanted was for you and Daddy . . .' The word almost chokes me. 'For us to be a proper family. Together.'

'He left me, remember? He walked out on our business, on both of *us*. For another woman.'

'You drove him away.'

'He did a runner, leaving me to deal with all the debts he'd stacked up!'

'I don't blame him for leaving. I wish he'd taken me with him!'

'Fliss!'

I stumble blindly out of her office, my vision swimming.

'Are you okay?' Maura knocks the desk, making her china dogs rattle. 'Can I get you anything?'

I ignore her and run into the corridor.

I'm not waiting six months. I'm getting the hell out of here, even if it means packing the money into my suitcase and getting on a plane.

My phone vibrates in my pocket. My heart thuds painfully as I check my messages. It's the unknown caller again:

8 p.m. tomorrow. The Lobster Bar. Bring the cash.

My mouth falls open. That's when I've organised my *I Survived* party! Has my blackmailer found out that Maura booked a table at the restaurant this morning or is this a horrible coincidence?

As my finger hovers over the 'reply' button, a second message lands – another stolen photo of me and Robert Brody. This *cannot* go viral. If it does, it'll haunt me for the rest of my life.

I was going to pay before I left for the States. But blackmailers don't stop – they always come back for more money. That's what I've learnt from Netflix.

I'll find out the identity of my blackmailer and get rid of them for good.

It's time to set a trap.

23

KAI

'Can we talk about traps?' Mrs Gibson throws open the door to her garden shed. She smooths escaping white tendrils of hair into the tight bun at the back of her neck as she peers down. I'm on my hands and knees, putting the last floorboards back into place. I've dug a hole beneath them to conceal my cash. It's sealed into toolboxes to keep out the damp and buried in the soft earth along with the empty blue holdall.

I scramble to my feet. Mrs Gibson never usually ventures to the east side of her grounds, away from her favourite flower beds and lawns. This is the smallest of her three sheds and only used for storing bags of fertiliser. It should be the perfect hiding place. I have the keys to here and the gardens and can come and go whenever I want. Mrs Gibson will never see me from the house during the day or night.

'You have mice?' I kick away incriminating soil with the heel of my trainer as her gaze flickers around the shed.

'The little blighters have got into the kitchen. I want to catch them humanely.'

'I can bring a few traps next week. The hardware store near school sells them.'

'Perfect! Now come and have a slice of my home-made cherry cake – unless you have more to do?'

'No – just checking you have enough bags.'

I brush the soil from my jeans, sling the empty rucksack over my shoulder, and follow her out. I lock the door behind me and pocket the key. I'll move the sacks back later.

'Your near-death experience has got me thinking about my own mortality,' Mrs Gibson says, as we walk slowly towards the house.

I suppress a shiver. 'I was lucky, I guess.'

'At eighty-nine my luck has all but run out. I'm living on borrowed time.' She places a hand on my arm. 'I've guessed you're in trouble, Kai.'

I open and shut my mouth like a goldfish, but no words come out.

'I'm no one's fool. I haven't seen your mother or sister in the village for some time.'

I feel a tiny hand clutch my heart and squeeze it tight. 'I d-d-don't—'

She links her arm through mine. 'If you need anything, you must ask. It may help to know your part-time job will *always* be safe. When my son inherits all this, he'll continue to employ you. I've included these wishes in my will, along with the stipulation that this property remains in the family. It can't be sold to developers. Charles will respect my wishes. He knows how much I despise second homeowners forcing up house prices and driving out locals.'

'You're kind,' I say, my voice cracking.

She squeezes my arm. 'Families are funny things, aren't they? They give you so much pleasure *and* the most pain.'

1.20 p.m.

I message Layla as I turn on to my new street, asking if she's free. I need to tell her who I suspect *really* smashed the window of Liam's car the night we retrieved the holdall. I also want to hear her voice. I check over my shoulder, but there's no sign of the motorbike. Fliss was probably right – it was a coincidence and had no connection to that newspaper article. I brush past the wheelie bins outside Torside Lodge and head through the open gate into our garden. I must have forgotten to lock it. My mouth dries and my heart rattles in my ribcage as I spot the shattered glass on the ground. The back door is ajar, a panel smashed. This must be an opportunist break-in, right? No one knows I've moved in except for Lou. I'm pretty sure the motorcyclist didn't see me leaving yesterday when I popped to the supermarket.

I hold my breath as I step inside the kitchen. Cupboards and drawers hang open. Whoever ransacked it, must have been disappointed. I have virtually no belongings. I should get the hell out, but I *want* to interrupt a junkie searching for the odd ten-pound note or something valuable to flog. That's a far better scenario than the one whirring around inside my head. I clutch my mobile, ready to dial 999. It vibrates, making me jump. Layla's messaged back, saying to call her in ten mins.

As I step into the hallway, pain explodes in the back of my head. My knees buckle. I fall forward, my head slamming on to the tiles. My phone skitters away. I see a pair of black motorbike boots walking towards me.

I hear a bang at the front door. And another.

The boots freeze as a voice calls through the letter box.

'It's me! I'm here for the grand tour. Are your mum and Crystal back? I can't believe you all live here now!'

Lou.

The letter box rattles.

'I thought we could watch *Hereditary* or *Midsommar*? I'm desperate to get out of a family dinner at the Lobster Bar.'

I open my mouth to cry for help.

Nothing comes out.

'Kai? Are you in?' Lou raps harder.

The boots remain motionless until Lou gives up and leaves. Then they back away.

My eyelids flutter.

Everything goes black.

WHATSAPP GROUP: WAITT

FLISS: *Any 🏍 sightings?*

LAYLA: *Nothing so far. Am being careful tho.*

LIAM: *All quiet here. But am staying in.*

FLISS: *Okay. BTW yr all invited to a party tonight, 7.30 p.m., the Lobster Bar.*

LAYLA: *What r u celebrating?!*

FLISS: *My survival.*

Fliss is typing.

I mean our survival.

LAYLA: *Thanks for late invite. Did someone cancel? LOL*

FLISS: 😣

LIAM: *Am working there tonight*

LAYLA: *Me 2! New job. Guess we can serve you?* 😬

FLISS: *Kai?*

LAYLA: *Just about to speak 2 him.*
FLISS: *Tell him about tonight. U all must come.*

24

LAYLA

'Are you writing a song in your head? You've barely touched your sandwich and you're distracted.'

I stop scanning the street and focus on Mum. She's treating me to a girly lunch, but the café was rammed when we arrived. We're sat on full display by the window. My mouth is horribly dry. The only lyric that springs to mind is the chorus:

I'm too young to die.

On repeat.

I take a swig of water and force down another bite of my cheese sandwich. My gaze is drawn back to the road. *Were we followed here?* Leon has taken Salih to his hospital appointment. I can't remember the last time we had mum and daughter time, but I'm desperate to leave. I check my phone. Kai still hasn't rung.

'Well, are you going to let me hear it?'

'What?'

I message Kai again. *Am freaking out. Can u call?*

'Your new song.'

'Oh, sure. When it's finished.' I place my mobile on the table.

'Fantastic!' She beams back. 'You have such a talent. You take after your dad, of course. I don't have a musical bone in my body.'

I manage a small smile. Baba was head chef at a London hotel and loved to cook, but his true passion was music. He composed songs on his oud and kawala, inspired by Egyptian folk tales. He told me the music found him, not the other way round. It's a talent that has run through the Abdullatif family for generations. What would Mum say if she knew I no longer hear snatches of melody in my head, the way Baba did, and can't come up with a single lyric? That I've stopped trying to compose anything because all I hear is a blur of tuneless white noise that obliterates everything? When was the last time I was totally honest with her?

Definitely not since Salih became ill. I haven't admitted I barely get more than a few hours' sleep each night, my school grades are rubbish, I was sacked from the Sea Haven and could be kicked out of choir.

Probably not since Baba died.

I haven't told her how much I miss the sound of his laughter, listening to his music and the taste of his cooking. There's no chance of eating any of his dishes around here. I miss the smell of walnuts toasting on my birthday as he prepared my favourite meal, Sharkaseya; drinking Mirinda on the soft white beaches at Sharm el-Sheikh, and the loud family get-togethers in Cairo, where he was the life and soul of the party. I used to watch him giggling and chatting to everyone, while I ate sweet, sticky baklava until I felt sick.

How much I miss everything about him. How I miss seeing Teta.

'You've been preoccupied the last few days,' Mum persists. 'Are you having second thoughts about being left on your own? You could stay with Alvita. I'm sure her parents won't mind.'

'I'll be fine,' I say quickly. I can't drag her into this.

Salih's place on the medical trial has been confirmed and the flights to the US and accommodation in Florida are all booked. Mum, Leon and Salih leave tomorrow afternoon. I'm thrilled for Salih's sake, but a tiny part of me doesn't want them to go. What if that motorcyclist outside our house and Liam's wasn't a random guy? What if he's connected to the stolen cash?

Mum reaches over the table and takes my hand. 'It's been

tough recently. But you can talk to me, the way you used to. Being married to Leon doesn't change how I feel about you and Salih. You're both my top priority.'

I bite my lip, glancing away. That's not what's worrying me. Leon will never replace Baba, but he's always been kind and supportive.

'I'm a good listener, remember?' she says. 'We used to be able to discuss anything before . . .' Her voice trails off.

I wish I could turn the clock back to those days – before I helped steal £1 million, before Salih got sick, before Baba died.

Before, before, before.

'Don't fuss, Mum. I'm not a kid any more.'

As I snatch my hand away, I see a flash of pain in her eyes. I bite the inside of my mouth.

I can't tell her anything. *Anything at all.*

2.03 p.m.

'Did you forget to shut the front door?' Mum asks.

'W-what?' I drag my gaze away from the parked cars.

'No matter. Leon's back.'

He appears in the hallway, deep grooves furrowed between his eyes.

'Is it Salih?' Mum gasps.

She sprints down the path. I run after her.

Leon falls back a step. 'No, he's upstairs.'

I follow Mum through the hall and into the sitting room, my heart beating rapidly. Omigod!

Mum stops in her tracks. Sofa cushions are slashed open, the stuffing scattered across the carpet. Pictures are ripped off walls, drawers emptied.

'Who would do this?' she cries.

Leon shakes his head numbly, enveloping her into his arms. 'I've rung the police – they're on their way.'

'And the rest of the house?' she asks.

Before he can reply, I head out of the room and up the stairs. Salih is sitting on his bedroom floor, weeping, surrounded by smashed Lego models and upturned drawers.

'I hate whoever did this!' He roughly wipes away a tear.

I crouch beside him and put my arm round his shoulders, but he shakes me off as if it's my fault. *Is it?*

He scrambles to his feet and bolts out. I follow him but pause on the landing as he charges downstairs. In my bedroom, Salih's old toy box is untouched, but boxes of school files are turned upside down, books have been swept off shelves and cupboards emptied. My chest tightens painfully at the sight of my keyboard and electric guitar: knocked over and broken. Baba's oud and kawala are gone.

I search beneath mounds of clothes and my Arabic dictionaries; the spines are broken, and pages ripped. I run out and check Mum and Leon's bedroom. They're not there either. I'm half devastated, half hopeful. This *must* be a random burglary. The oud would sell for at least £500 on eBay. I can't see my laptop either.

I run downstairs and burst into the sitting room. Mum is slumped on the base of the sofa.

'They took Baba's oud and my laptop! *And* I can't find his kawala.'

'Leon's got your laptop, but your dad's instruments . . .' She stops, her face paling. 'Well, they were already gone.'

'W-what do you mean?'

Mum takes a deep breath. 'I'm sorry, Layla, but I pawned them on Tuesday afternoon, while you were at the hotel.'

'You didn't!'

I close my eyes and see Baba.

Playing his oud on stage with other Egyptian musicians at WOMAD Festival. I'm sitting on Mum's shoulders, bursting with pride as I watch him perform.

Teaching the kawala in a workshop for festival-goers, patiently explaining how to play it.

Sitting in our old bedroom in London, composing melodies for Salih and me on the oud to help us sleep.

'I warned you we'd all have to make sacrifices for Salih's treatment,' she says. 'That's what your dad would have done. He loved those instruments, but he'd have given them up in a flash for either of you.'

My eyelids fly open. 'But we have the money! We don't have to lose *everything* of his.'

'We haven't. This was because—'

'You've taken down his photos from the mantlepiece. You've got rid of his instruments. You want to scrub him out of our lives!'

'Layla!' Leon frowns. 'Stop shouting. It's not helping.'

'This was before I knew about the donation,' Mum explains. 'The bank wouldn't approve an overdraft and your grandma hasn't returned my calls. I was desperate. I had to do something, and they were gathering dust in your bedroom.'

My mind is whirling. The stabbing pain in my chest is sharper. I can scarcely process what she's saying.

'That's no excuse!' I say, sobbing. 'How could you? When you know how much they mean to me? They're all I have left of him apart from old photos.'

'I didn't have a choice.' She stands up, reaching for me, but I shrink away.

'We all have choices!'

'It's probably a lucky break they weren't in the house

during the burglary,' Leon points out. 'You can buy them back next week now we've got the plane tickets. They could have been lost for good if they'd still been here today.'

I can't reply. A painful lump has formed in my throat. I sink to my heels as Leon picks up the *Kingsborough Gazette* from the table.

How hadn't I noticed Baba's instruments were missing?

But I know the answer: I was wrapped up in stealing the money. That almost feels like a worse betrayal of Baba's memory than pawning the oud and kawala. I never knew they were gone until it was too late.

'Do you think this has anything to do with the news story?' Mum asks.

'Maybe,' Leon replies. 'Whoever broke in, could have thought we had spare cash lying around.' He studies one of the newspaper pages.

'As if!' Mum exclaims. 'How can people read what our family has been through and do this?' She lifts her hands helplessly.

I stare from one to the other. 'Read what exactly?'

Leon passes the paper, open on a centre page. My eyes rest on a photo of Salih. My head pounds as I take in the headline:

MYSTERY DONOR STEPS UP FOR LOCAL BOY'S CANCER FUNDRAISER

An anonymous benefactor has donated £210,000 to a fundraising appeal for a ten-year-old's cancer treatment.

Days after a horror bus crash almost claimed the life of 16-year-old Layla Abdullatif, a mystery donor funded the amount needed for her brother Salih's trip to the USA for pioneering treatment. His mother, Sandy Abdullatif-Johnston said, 'We're grateful to whoever helped our family. We'll never be able to thank them enough.'

My vision blurs. I blink repeatedly but the words swirl around the page. The newspaper falls through my fingers.

'Omigod.' I stare at Mum in horror. 'What have you done?'

She flinches. 'I rang the editor to complain about using your photo from the Sea Haven without permission and mentioned our good luck. She suggested writing a story to thank whoever helped us.'

I stagger to my feet. 'How could you be so stupid?'

'Layla!'

Leon cuts in. 'Don't talk to your mum like that. This isn't her fault. She had no idea this would happen. Plus, we thought Salih would get a kick out of seeing his picture in the paper.'

'Well, we've all got a kicking. Great idea!'

'Why are you being so horrid? What's got into you?' Her tone softens as she steps closer. 'You've been acting oddly since the crash. You can talk to us, love. Why don't you—'

'Why don't *you* leave me alone and stop trying to pretend Baba never existed!'

I flee the room and head out of the front door, slamming it shut. I keep running until the stitch in my side feels like it will split my body in two. It's what I deserve.

Mum and Leon don't understand. Whoever read this article has slotted the clues together – the bus crash, the missing money, my full name in the previous newspaper article and this mystery £210,000 donation.

They *know* I've helped steal £1 million and they're trying to find it.

SATURDAY, 28 SEPTEMBER, 2.35 P.M.

LAYLA: *Pls call me!!! Something terrible happened! x*
14:35
KAI: *Last seen today at 13:20*
LAYLA: *Kai????I need u!!!! xx*
14:36

2.38 p.m.
WHATSAPP GROUP: WAITT

LAYLA: *We've been burgled!*
FLISS: *Shit!!!*
LIAM: *Are you okay?*
LAYLA: *No!!!! Am terrified.*

FLISS: *Cd be coincidence . . .?*

LIAM: *Another one? They're coming for us!*

FLISS: *U don't know that. But safer to bring*
pets here?

LIAM: *Can take care of £££ myself, thanks.*

FLISS: *FFS! Need to use *pets* code.*

LIAM: *This is encrypted, you said so yourself.*

LAYLA: *Am worried about Kai. Still not replying.*

LIAM: *Surfing?*

LAYLA: *No!!!!!*

FLISS: *Try 2 keep calm. Let's speak properly*
tonight.

25

LIAM

'Are you sure you should be here?'

A hand clamps on to my shoulder as I check my phone for the millionth time. I let out a high-pitched squeal and spin round.

'Sorry! I didn't mean to scare you.' Frankie pulls her long black hair into a ponytail. 'I wanted to check you're well enough to work a shift.'

Mum had said the same thing before I'd set off tonight. I'd lied and said I felt fine, even though I've thrown up twice since hearing about Layla's burglary. But it's important to keep to my usual routine in case I'm being watched. Plus, I had to get my stash out of the house – the motorcyclist knows where I live. I've stuffed the rucksack in my staff locker until

I can figure out somewhere safer. Only I have the padlock and outsiders can't tell which compartment is mine. There's another crucial reason why I had to turn up. Frankie will go to the bank on Monday morning with the last fortnight's takings. Tonight is my last chance to make things right.

'I want to get back to normal.' I manage a smile despite the taste of bile in my mouth. 'Plus, you won't find anyone to cover at short notice.'

'That's exactly what Layla said. She refused to call in sick. I'd struggle without you kids. We're booked out – it'll be a busy one.'

I turn away to hide my surprise. I hadn't expected to see Layla but she must want to get away from her house and the police.

'It's her first shift. Do you mind showing her the ropes?'

'No problem.'

I jump as the door widens and Carla sticks her head through the gap. 'Chef's going nuts. She says the fish delivery is short.'

'Dammit!' Frankie pulls out a pile of receipts from her desk drawer. 'Can you make a start on this while I sort out the kitchens?'

'Affirmative.'

'You're a star. I don't know what I'd do without you.'

I manage a weak smile as I feel yet another stab of guilt. When the door closes behind her, I grab the key from the top left-hand drawer and kneel by the safe. I enter the combination and pull the lever. The last fortnight's takings are arranged in note order. I grab four fifties from my pocket, wrap them in an elastic band and sneak them in. I'd *borrowed* £200 in twenties to buy Tristram's watch, but Frankie won't notice she has more fifties than usual. I've also exchanged notes in the till to get rid of a couple of hundred.

'There you are!' The door bangs open.

I fall back on my heels, my heart hammering. Layla stands in the doorway, clutching the local paper.

'You almost gave me a heart attack.' I put a hand on the floor to steady myself. 'How are you doing?'

Layla rubs her eyes; they're puffy and bloodshot. 'Terrible. I had to get out of the house – Mum's distraught and Salih's crying. Leon's beating himself up that he couldn't prevent the break-in, and it's *all my fault.*'

I suppress a shiver. 'What did the police say? Did they mention—'

'They don't know about the money,' she says, cutting in. 'It was different police officers anyway, not DC Walker. They think it was opportunistic – we're the only house on the street without a burglar alarm.'

'They could be right?' I'm clinging on to the smallest grain of hope.

'Whoever broke in was looking for the cash, I'm sure of it.' She stares at the piles of notes on the floor, distracted. 'What *are* you doing?'

'I'm not stealing, if that's what you think!'

'Why would I think that?' Her nose crinkles as she frowns.

'Sorry. I'm getting ready for the stock take.' I put the cash back in the safe, lock up and return the key to the drawer.

'I need to show you this before the others get here.' She pulls out the newspaper from beneath her arm.

'We've discussed this – the front-page story and picture of us doesn't mean anything. Like Fliss said, we should stay calm.'

'This is something new. We need to work out how to handle her.'

'Why?'

Layla flicks through the pages and shoves the paper towards me. My eyes rest on the headline:

MYSTERY DONOR STEPS UP FOR LOCAL BOY'S CANCER FUNDRAISER

Cold shivers ripple down my spine. I only manage to read a

few sentences of the story before the words swirl around the page. This is exponentially bad.

'Liam? Talk to me.'

I shake my head. I can't formulate a sentence.

'We were burgled the same day this story appears. It can't be a coincidence. Someone read it and thought I'd kept *all* the money.' She chews on a ragged nail, waiting for me to correct her.

I can't. It's the most logical conclusion. I massage my temples. My head is pounding.

'We're both in their firing line,' she says quietly.

'H-h-how do you mean?' I stutter.

'Well, your mum's ID badge was nicked. That means you're the next easiest to find. No one knows where Kai is, and I doubt they can get to Fliss since she lives in a hotel on a private island.'

I lower my gaze as she nibbles her nails. Guilt burrows into my chest, almost taking my breath away, but I can't admit the truth.

'We have to confess to Fliss before she sees this story and works out we've double-crossed her,' she says. 'That means coming clean about money laundering.'

'She'll be angry, avenging and armed with a gun. Not a pleasant thought.'

'What choice do we have, Liam? She'll know I've broken our six-month rule as soon as she reads this.'

We fall into a worried silence, punctuated by the beating of my heart that sounds horrifically loud.

'I still can't get hold of Kai to warn him,' she says. 'What if . . .?'

I wince. I can't let my overactive imagination go there.

'Look, I'm sure he's all right. He's—'

'Please don't say he's probably surfing. That's not all he does. He's not the walking cliché you think he is.'

There's no point arguing. I grab my mobile as it vibrates.

Blood drains out of my cheeks as I check my notifications.

'Noooooo!'

'What's up?'

I almost drop my phone. Tristram's tagged me into his Instagram post. He's posing in front of the Jeep.

Best boyfriend in the world bought me a £20,000 SUV after winning £250,000 on the scratchcards! Celebrations on him @LobsterBar tonight!!!

'What is it? Has something happened to Kai?'

I stumble backwards.

'Liam! You're scaring the shit out of me!'

I try to speak, but my throat is tightening painfully. Fliss is about to discover that two of us have broken our spending pact – but that's the least of our problems.

Those guys from the clifftop know our names from the local paper. They're probably monitoring our social media as well as our friends' accounts and where we work. They'll realise that two bus survivors have both come into *a lot* of money this week.

Layla's speaking. Her words echo distantly in my head as I ring Tristram.

Pick up!

Predictably it goes to voicemail. He never answers his phone. I message him.

Please delete your post! You promised not to tell.

Layla grabs my arm. 'Tell me! I'm thinking the worst. Is it Kai?'

I can't speak. I can't breathe.

My heart is beating a million times a minute. I try to count forwards and backwards through my panic.

Two, three, five, seven, eleven.

Eleven, seven, five, three, two.

Nothing works.

I close my eyes and attempt to remember what life was like before the crash.

I worried about silly things like staying top in maths, physics and chemistry, the Cambridge interview, my A-level exams and making Tristram happy. Now I'm terrified I won't make it until the end of my shift.

Layla's right.

Whoever targeted her will be coming for me next – and now they know exactly where I'll be tonight.

26

FLISS

My blackmailer had better watch out. I'm coming for him or her.

I scroll through my phone as I sit in the back of Aaron's Range Rover. No new messages from the WAITT WhatsApp group – and still nothing from Kai. I guess everyone's keeping their heads down after Layla's burglary.

'Are you sure you're well enough to go out?' Aaron looks in his mirror. 'Mrs C thinks you should stay in your room and rest.'

I swallow a snort. I doubt Mother has noticed I've left the hotel.

'My ribs feel better.'

The painkillers have dulled the spasms. I flick open my compact mirror and inspect my make-up. I can't call off tonight.

My blackmailer doesn't care I'm popping pills. I touch my Louis Vuitton backpack. Inside is a plastic bag containing £10,000 in marked notes. I've coated each fifty with a spray of ultraviolet paint. Mother keeps a bottle in her office to check up on staff using the tills after the spate of thefts.

I've made sure that Kai, Layla and Liam will be here. I can't rule any of them out as my blackmailer. Kai had the chance to hack my phone at the surf school. He helped the full-time gardener at the hotel over the summer and may have picked up gossip about Robert Brody, along with Layla who was working in housekeeping. Liam could have heard rumours about my involvement from Frankie at the Lobster Bar – she knows most people on the Sea Haven's staff rota.

I'll find out tonight. Whoever touches the notes will have ink on their fingers for weeks. It's invisible to the eye, but an ultraviolet torch will reveal the incriminating fluorescent yellow. I'll invent a reason to inspect everyone's hands and take my revenge. I reapply my lipstick – war paint is essential.

'Your friends will be pleased to see you.' Aaron glances back. 'They must have been worried sick.'

I snap my compact shut and stare out of the window. Were they? I doubt any of them care. Perhaps one of them is the blackmailer.

Tristram? Lisa? Spencer? Whoever it is, they'll regret crossing me.

We pull up behind the Lobster Bar. Aaron drives around the car park a few times before finding a space. I hug the backpack to my chest. Why can't I be in bed, watching reruns of *Killing Eve*? I check my watch. I have around thirty minutes until the drop-off.

'I'll wait here in case you want to go home early,' Aaron says, noticing my hesitation.

That's a relief. I might need a quick getaway.

A glass shatters loudly as I step through the door. A waitress with a long dark brown ponytail picks up the pieces. She stands, holding a broken tumbler.

Layla! She gives me a deliberate hard stare, forcing my gaze to follow hers.

Shiiit! DC Walker is sat in the corner, with a woman who has a sleek black bob. He takes her hand across the table. This is a horrible coincidence, right? He looks like he's having supper with his wife, not keeping us under surveillance. Layla disappears behind the counter. I breathe out slowly. Thank God she tipped me off before I did something stupid like deliver my money to the table next to him.

I shiver, glancing around. My blackmailer is probably already here. I spot Lou having what looks like a miserable family meal. Nearby, Tristram and Lisa are holding court, next to my reserved seat at the head of the table. Callum and Spencer are locked in a heated discussion. My eyes narrow as I scan my guests. Fifteen in total. Who would cross me by declaring war? At least half of them probably hate me. Are they here to party or to pick up the money? Or is it someone else?

I scan the restaurant. There are no single diners who would ring alarm bells. Each table has at least a couple, which means my blackmailer has arranged the perfect cover. Why aren't I surprised? Liam strides past, his face ashen. He must have clocked DC Walker. He stops and speaks to Lou, as Lisa jeers and aims pieces of bread at them. I head to the bathroom to splash cold water on my wrists.

Stay calm.

DC Walker has no idea what's in my backpack. I *must* pull this off otherwise I'll be wearing handcuffs by the end of the evening.

'It's the heroine of the hour!' Tristram knocks over a glass of water as he stands.

'Welcome back, Flish,' he slurs, clapping his hands.

Seriously? He's drunk.

Thank God he isn't driving tonight. His dad has refused to let him near his new company car. At least one person in his family has sense.

'How about we do a round of "For She's A Jolly Good Fellow"?' Tristram cries, as another table joins in with the applause.

'How about you sit down and shut the fuck up?'

I gaze across the restaurant, my heart pounding. A few tables cheer. DC Walker smiles and waves.

Great! I may as well have a spotlight shining on my face. If my blackmailer hadn't spotted me walk in, they'll sure as hell know I'm here now.

'Why's everyone boring and touchy tonight?' Tristram slips back into his seat. 'We need drinks. Where did that boyfriend of mine get to?'

'Which one?' Callum winks. 'The Limpet's over there.' He points at Liam behind the bar.

Titters ripple round the table. Tristram takes a swig from a hip flask before banging on the table loudly.

'We need service!'

Why did I invite him?

Liam exchanges a few words with Layla before coming over. Tristram grabs his wrist and pulls him closer.

'There you are! We'd love a round of beers to get this party started, babe.'

'Sorry, I can't,' he replies, attempting to keep his tone light.

'Is this because of the Insta post?' He rolls his eyes dramatically. 'No need to get pissy. I've deleted it.'

'What Insta post?' I ask.

Liam crumbles beneath my hard stare.

'A piccy of my new Jeep,' Tristram explains. 'I wanted to thank my lovely boyfriend for his gener-o-geneross-sity.' He finally manages to get the word out.

'You. Bought. Tristram. A Jeep?'

My blood pressure rises to boiling point. I grip the sides of the chair tightly to prevent myself from flying out and throttling Liam. He's supposed to be the brainy one!

How could he be so stupid? Didn't we agree to wait six months?

I'm breaking our pact tonight out of necessity, but I'm not advertising it to the whole fricking world.

'He had a lottery win,' Lisa shouts across the table. 'Two hundred and fifty thousand.'

'Woooo-hoo!' Callum hollers. 'Drinks on him tonight.'

More clapping. I'm grinding my teeth so hard at least one is in danger of snapping. Liam looks like he's about to throw up. I feel a scorching stare on my back. Did DC Walker hear? I daren't check. Hot tears prick my eyes. I feel my plans – the escape to Malibu, the apartment by the beach – disintegrate. I can barely contain my fury. I want to smash every single glass on the table.

'About those beers for everyone,' Tristram wheedles, holding on to Liam's wrist.

'How about mocktails?' he replies shakily. 'Frankie has added more varieties to the menu.'

'Pretty please? You could sneak them over. For me.' His grip tightens.

'How do you fancy getting us arrested? Do you see that guy over there?' I nod towards DC Walker. 'He's a policeman. He knows my age and Liam's. He'll have clocked that we're mostly an underage table. Stop being a dick and let him go.'

I will murder him later.

Tristram laughs. 'Well, it was worth a try.'

Liam's eyes shine. A vivid redness lingers on his wrist as he stiltedly takes our order. Tristram drapes an arm over Callum's shoulder, stroking the nape of his neck as soon as Liam walks away. I slump in my chair. Liam has jeopardised everything for this douche bag. I can't bear it.

'You're a first-class jerk *and* a slut,' I snarl. 'We should stage an intervention over your drinking. It's getting out of control, don't you think? And why are you going out with Liam – and inviting him to Verbier – when you don't give a shit about him?'

'I'm getting a cab home *obviously*. I'll drink whatever I want and go out with whomever I choose. I don't need to justify my life to you.' He snatches up his phone and taps out a message. 'FYI, you're a first-class bitch, but it's too late to stage an intervention. It's a terminal condition.'

Laughter ripples round the table. Callum and Lisa are holding up their mobiles. They're probably filming us to share on TikTok. I've never hated my frenemies more. I'm about to tell Tristram – all of them – where to go, when my phone vibrates. Shakily I check the message:

Drop the money in the bin in the accessible toilet and go back to yr friends. If it's not there in 5, yr pix will go viral. Ditto if anyone follows.

I look up. Tristram is still glued to his phone. His dad might be the head of a multimillion-pound property development company, but all the money in the world won't protect him if I discover *he's* my blackmailer.

'Do you seriously want to pick a fight with me?'

He rolls his eyes. 'Okay, my mistake. You're only a bitch *some of the time.*'

I fix him with my best ice-queen stare until he lowers his gaze. It isn't him. He backed down too quickly. I glance around. Everyone has their phones out. I shove my chair back and scour the restaurant. It's impossible to pick out the culprit – most people have mobiles lying on their tables. Layla and Liam are hunched over one at the counter. DC Walker is checking his messages, along with Frankie behind the bar.

Where are you? I know you're here.

'I need to powder my nose,' I say tersely.

'Shall I come with you?' Lisa asks.

She's attempting to claw her way back into my good books. I throw her a dirty look and she sinks into her seat.

This is it! My heart pounds frantically as I manoeuvre round the tables. Nothing feels out of the ordinary until I reach the emergency exit. The door's propped open with a fire extinguisher even though it's cold tonight. An OUT OF USE sign is stuck on the accessible toilet door.

I push open the door a few centimetres, afraid that someone might jump out. But this isn't a scary movie. The room is empty. I pull out the bag of cash from the backpack. I'm about to place it in the large empty bin when I hear a creak. I spin round as the door slowly opens.

WTAF?

I hold my breath as a familiar figure ducks inside.

I wrap my arms tighter round the money as I stare at my blackmailer. It all makes perfect sense.

This isn't about money. It's revenge.

27

LAYLA

'It's you!' Fliss jabs a long, manicured fingernail at me.

'Sorry to barge in.' I shiver as I shut the door. I don't think anyone's noticed me slip in, but the restaurant's rammed with unfamiliar faces. One of these strangers could have ransacked my house earlier. 'I had to catch you on your own. We need to talk.'

'You bitch!'

'Excuse me?'

'This isn't about the money because you sure as hell don't need it any more.'

'W-what?'

Fliss barely draws a breath. 'It's about the ring, right? I know you didn't steal it, and I don't give a shit about it anyway. You're making a huge mistake getting on the wrong side of me.'

My eyes widen. This isn't the way I expected this conversation to go. We've gone off track, down an unexpected, off-piste potentially dangerous route. 'Erm, you could have told your mum I was innocent before she fired me?'

She eyes me strangely. 'As if she'd listen to me! It wasn't personal but blackmail is.' She takes a step closer. 'You'll regret this, Layla. You have no idea what I'm capable of. No one does. Not my psychiatrist. Not even my mother.'

I blink. *Blackmail?* Fake Fliss is even more of a psycho than usual, but I need to focus. I don't have much time before Frankie notices I'm AWOL.

'I'm not blackmailing you. I'm here to warn—' I pause as she tightens her hold on the bag. Bulky red shapes press against the plastic. 'Is that what I think it is?'

Fliss stares at me hard. 'You mean those messages weren't from . . . You need to go.'

'Why? What are *you* doing?'

I spin round as the door creaks open.

'Get out, Layla!' Fliss shouts. 'I mean it!'

Her shoulders lower as Liam slips inside, pushing gold-rimmed glasses up his nose. He locks the door.

'Has Layla told you?' he asks, frowning hard. 'We're sorry.'

Fliss glares back darkly. 'You're sorry the whole world

knows you've won a stack of cash?' She slow claps sarcastically. 'Bravo! We're all safe now you've apologised.'

'What?' I gasp.

Fliss switches her death stare to me. 'Wait, there's more?'

I open my mouth, but the words die in my throat. She looks like she wants to rip off my head.

'Tell me later,' she hisses. 'You both need to get out. You're messing up everything.'

'Messing up what?' Liam's voice wobbles.

She shakes her head.

I point to her bag. 'Something involving her stash.'

'What about your six-month rule?' Liam asks.

'Hilarious! You mean, the rule you conveniently ignored so you could buy your boyfriend a Jeep, you bloody hypocrite? You'll land us all in prison!'

Before I can ask what she's talking about, a huge explosion rings out from beyond the door, followed by muffled cries and shouts. We stare at each other in stunned silence.

'What was that?' Liam gasps.

He fumbles with the lock, throwing open the door. People are flooding out of the emergency exit. I check over my shoulder as I follow them. Fliss is behind me, but empty-handed – she's left the bag. She stares back at me murderously. She's right – whoever's blackmailing her has made a huge mistake.

Outside, the car park flickers with strange orange shapes and an acrid smell fills the air. Flames shoot into the sky from a vehicle. DC Walker runs past people filming on their phones, his mobile rammed to his ear.

'My Jeep!' Tristram yells, pushing through the crowd.

Flames shoot through the windows, smashing the glass.

I'm about to step closer, when Liam grabs my arm, pulling me back.

'What is going on?' I demand. 'Why did you look like you'd seen a ghost in Frankie's office? And what's this about a Jeep?'

He takes a deep breath. 'I'm sorry. I bought it for Tristram. He was supposed to keep it a secret, but he posted on Instagram. This . . . I think it's a warning.' He nods at the burning Jeep.

My knees buckle. Everything is spinning.

'How can you be so clever yet so stupid? You always have a go at Kai, but you've done the dumbest thing ever!'

'I know! I got carried away. I'm sorry.'

I can't hold back the tears.

'Please don't cry! I feel bad enough. You see—'

'Hey, over there!' Fliss calls out.

Kai is lurching across the car park. My heart leaps until I spot the bandage wrapped round his forehead. Lou reaches him first but he brushes them off. The hurt look in Lou's eyes is unmistakable even from here. Kai stumbles as he reaches us and falls into my arms. He smells of disinfectant and surgical dressing instead of the usual suntan lotion and salty water. I hug him tightly.

'What happened?' I mumble into his shoulder.

'I was attacked.' He disentangles himself. 'You're all in danger. They know about us.'

'No shit, Sherlock!' Fliss's eyes glitter with anger as she jerks her head at the blazing Jeep.

I wrap my arms round my body. I can't stop shivering.

'Correct me if I'm wrong,' she continues in a low voice. 'But Liam fucked up and this happened. Layla somehow fucked up today and her house was burgled.'

'W-what?!' Kai exclaims.

She jabs a manicured nail at him. 'What did *you* do?'

I glance at DC Walker. He's 25 metres away on his phone. If he turns round, he'll see us arguing.

'Let's not do this here,' I urge.

'Why not? What haven't you told me?' Fliss's voice rises an octave. 'We're all in this together, remember?'

Her phone vibrates.

'Great. Time for *my* bad news. Maybe the hotel's on fire?'

Her face pales as she checks her mobile.

'What is it?' I ask.

Before she can reply, my phone pings, followed by Liam's and Kai's.

My knees turn to jelly as I pull up the message from a new WhatsApp group called *Thieves*.

Enjoying your early Bonfire Night? We know you have the cash. Return million £££ in full or we'll kill you one by one. Want to place a bet on who dies first?

28

LIAM

Flames glitter in my peripheral vision, burning stronger. Oxygen is squeezed from my lungs and black dots swarm before my eyes. The sound of shouts wash over me. What am I going to do? The question hammers, drill-like, into my temples.

I know the atomic weight of every substance in the periodic table and can calculate the gravitational force on the International Space Station as it orbits the Earth. But I have no answer to this terrifying conundrum. I resort to my safety net. *Numbers.* I attempt to work out the figures in my head.

Layla has spent her entire £250,000.

Kai lost £15,000 to the money launderers. He could have spent the remaining £15,000 in his bank accounts by now, plus hundreds or thousands in cash.

I have just under £203,000 left after buying Tristram's Jeep and insurance, paying the ski deposit and transferring £5,500 into Mum's bank account to help with rent and bills.

How much has Fliss spent? She had £10–15,000 in that bag in the accessible toilet. That means we could be short by at least a third of the cash.

Sure, I can tell Mum I've made a mistake with my bank transfer and ask Tristram to return the deposit, but my £20,000 money-laundering fee is lost for ever and the Jeep has gone up in flames.

Will returning two thirds of the haul be enough to save our lives? The mathematical odds don't give me much comfort. I estimate they're two to one that any of us get out of this situation alive.

Sounds become sharper, lights brighter as the figures fade away in my head. The others are still arguing.

'Well, we give them what they want obviously!' *Fliss.*

'Except we can't.' *Kai.*

'Why the hell not?'

Layla's mumbling. I catch the words 'money laundering' and 'carwash'.

'You did what?' Fliss yells. 'All three of you?'

Kai is trying – and failing – to calm her down.

Fliss. 'Why should I die because of you idiots?'

'We're sorry!' *Layla.* 'But we can't do this here. They're watching us!'

Her words are like an electric shock. The realisation dawns on me.

The gang is here. So is my cash.

Should I leave it? But if someone breaks into the lockers, I lose my leverage. I scan the unfamiliar faces in the crowd. Everyone's focused on the blazing Jeep, apart from two people. Lou is attempting to make eye contact with Kai, but he turns his back on them. The wounded look in their eyes makes my chest tighten, even though Kai is obviously trying to protect them. DC Walker's gaze flickers over. He's talking to Tristram and jotting notes in a pad. That's not good. Tristram has probably admitted I bought the Jeep, but DC Walker can't know I stupidly paid for it in cash – not yet.

Should I give him the rucksack and try to strike a deal that doesn't involve jail time? Or should I hand it over to the drug gang and beg them to spare my life? They might show leniency. Alternatively I could do what is colloquially known as a runner . . .

My heartbeat quickens, the way it used to whenever the bell rang for break at primary school. My tormentors were always waiting for me in the playground, ready to pounce because my body didn't look the same as theirs – one shoulder and hip was higher than the other and it became more noticeable as I grew. I knew the rules of the game back then – I didn't have to run the fastest. I just had to be quicker than at least one of the other bullied kids they chased.

We'll kill you one by one.

Don't get caught first.

'Who has the gun?' Fliss asks. 'We need it for protection.'

'We thought you had it,' Kai mumbles.

Fliss shakes her head.

'*No one* should think about using a gun,' Layla says, her voice shaking. 'We're in enough trouble. We should leave here while we still can.'

Does *she* have the gun? Or is Fliss double-bluffing? I'm not waiting to find out.

'Layla's right. I have to fetch something before we go.'

'I'm coming,' Fliss says.

We return inside the restaurant as a fire engine arrives, sirens flashing. Fliss darts into the accessible toilet while I make for the lockers. It could be a scene from a zombie apocalypse movie – half-eaten food lies on tables; coats are draped on the backs of seats. Goose bumps spring up on my arms as I wrestle with the lock. I yank out the rucksack and run to the door, looking left and right. The hairs on the back of my neck prickle. The restaurant appears empty, but I can't shake the feeling that someone else is here, watching me.

When I get outside, Fliss has returned to the others. She's fumbling with a torch, trying to switch it on.

'How is that possible? It's literally been two or three minutes tops!'

'Since what?' Kai asks.

I sling the rucksack behind my feet.

Fliss takes a deep breath. 'Since I dropped off ten thousand pounds in the accessible toilet. Someone took it while we were distracted by the fire.'

'Why would you leave cash in the toilet?' Kai looks bewildered.

'She's being blackmailed,' Layla pipes up.

'About what?' he asks.

Fliss shakes her head. 'Does it matter? That person has my money.' She glowers at us.

'Well, it's not me.' I nudge the rucksack further behind my ankles.

'Me neither,' Kai chips in. 'I doubt your blackmailer's hanging about. He's probably long gone.'

'Or *her*.' Fliss stares pointedly at Layla.

'Touché.' She glares back.

'Sorry, but unless you[...]
all four of us, we have [...]
out.

Fliss's torch flickers on. [...]
before aiming the beam at [...]

'What *are* you doing?' T[...]

'I could ask you the sam[...]
that?'

'How about you don't?' I[...]

'Why not?' Kai demands. [...]
because I know—'

'Are you all right?' a famil[...]

We spin round. It's DC Wa[...]

Holy moly!

Fight or flight kicks in. I w[...]
run. But I force myself to rem[...]

'Everything's great,' Kai blust[...]
his head at the Jeep. Two firefigh[...]

DC Walker's eyes narrow. 'C[...]
his tongue. 'That's not the word[...]
place like this to have a sudden s[...]
you think?'

We remain frozen to the spot[...]

'Is there anything you want t[...]

I shake m[...]
what you me[...]

'That I be[...]
how a teena[...]
one, even se[...]
or twenty-fi[...]

'It was a[...]
DC Wal[...]
Such a lov[...]
been thrille[...]
eighteen to[...]
I'm sw[...]
Layla. 'An[...]
hitting its[...]
sizeable d[...]

'We we[...]
'Less l[...]
article abo[...]
her face c[...]

'We're[...]
die in her[...]
DC Wa[...]
points to l[...]
Kai av[...]

head. 'We didn't set fire to the Jeep if that's
an?'

ieve.' DC Walker pauses. 'What puzzles me is
er from a modest background can afford to buy
ond-hand. It must have set you back, say, twenty
e grand?'

l-l-lottery win,' I stutter.

er's face remains impassive. 'So I've been told.
ly surprise after the bus crash. You must have
. Strange though – I thought you had to be over
buy a ticket and claim a prize.'

ating profusely as he switches his attention to
congratulations on your JustGiving fundraising
target. It's incredible that a benefactor made a
nation days after the accident.'

e lucky,' Layla splutters.

cky to be burgled the same day the newspaper
ut your mystery donor was published.' He studies
osely.

the only house on our street witho—' The words
throat.

ker swings towards Kai. 'What happened to you?' He
s bandaged forehead. 'That looks like a fresh injury.'
ids his gaze. 'I fell over.'

'Bad luck. Was that in the lovely new house you're renting? You've paid upfront for six months at Torside Lodge, right? That's a tidy nest egg you've got stashed away.'

Kai's chest heaves up and down. He's hyperventilating. Either that or he's about to 'fess up to everything we've done.

'Look—' I begin, stepping in front of him.

'Are you interviewing us?' Fliss says sharply. 'Because we don't have appropriate adults present.'

He raises his hands in the air. 'This isn't formal. I'm trying to be helpful.'

'We don't need help, thank you,' she says tightly.

That's one of the biggest lies she's told to date.

'Are you sure about that?' DC Walker glances at the Jeep.

The firefighters have brought the blaze under control. Smoke billows from the charred remains, leaving a pungent smell.

DC Walker turns back to us. 'Did I ever explain why my unit is involved with this case?' Before anyone can reply, he continues. 'We had a tipoff a county-lines gang was using your school bus service as a front for drug-running after your old driver was *conveniently* killed in a hit-and-run. Shortly after we launched an undercover operation, Silas died, along with the other driver. Both men had previous drugs convictions.'

'Are you allowed to talk about this?' Fliss sniffs. 'Either way, I can't see what this has to do with any of us?'

'I hope to God it hasn't! I'm praying you've steered clear. But my gut tells me you're in way over your heads. Something, perhaps, to do with that bloodstained fifty-pound note we found at the scene. I suspect there were a lot more fifties where that came from – we think Silas got wind we were on to the gang, panicked and did a runner with his boss's cash.'

'Sounds foolish,' Fliss says coolly.

'It would also be extremely foolish for anyone who's come across the money to spend it. We'll check to see if more fifties are in circulation.' DC Walker nods at the Lobster Bar. 'It would be unusual to see large numbers of a high-denomination note in use locally.'

I freeze, thinking of the fifties I've put in Frankie's takings and the till tonight. But that's nothing compared with paying for the Jeep in cash. Why was I so stupid?

Layla sways. She's laundered the most cash, even though it was for a good cause. Kai's cheeks are a guilty red. I bet he's slipped fifties into plenty of local shops. They'll have CCTV cameras catching him in the act. Me too.

Fliss stands ramrod straight. She holds DC Walker's gaze.

'Are you sure you didn't find more notes after the crash?' he asks. 'I understand the temptation, but the money belongs to dangerous people. If you tell me the truth, I can protect you from them.'

We all stare back silently.

Will one of us crumble?

We're all in this together.

DC Walker's tone hardens. 'We've tested the blood on the note – it's not a match for Silas or the other driver. You four were the only other people at the scene. It would be helpful if you would all agree to DNA tests.'

Fliss arches an eyebrow. 'Are we under arrest?'

'Not at this stage.'

'But we could be arrested?' Kai pipes up.

'It depends if we suspect you've done anything illegal.' DC Walker raises a hand as Fliss tries to interrupt. 'I genuinely want to help you all. Now's the time to tell me what's going on. Because, believe me, things will get worse if you've got on the wrong side of these people.' He gestures to the blackened skeleton of the Jeep.

A mixture of fear and uncertainty flits across Kai's face. Layla's biting her lip hard, until a pinprick of blood appears. I look at them pleadingly.

We have to tell him the truth.

I bend down to pick up my rucksack. Handing it over will save our lives.

'We have nothing to say.' Fliss's voice is steel and ice. 'If you want to question us again, it will be with our lawyers. And you're not getting our DNA until we've taken legal advice. We're victims, not suspects, and if you continue with this harassment, my mother will lodge an official complaint.'

I gulp, forcing down the bile that's rising in my throat.

DC Walker sighs deeply 'Have it your own way. But this isn't over, far from it.' He pauses. 'Here's my chance to sound like a cop in a movie: I'll be watching you all. Don't think about skipping town.'

29

KAI

'Where are you going? And why do you smell so bad?'

I step out of Torside Lodge's front door and collide with Lou. I was too afraid to sleep here last night and bunked down behind dustbins in a car park. I've briefly returned to the rental to grab a change of clothes and the framed picture of me, Mum and Crystal. I don't have time to say goodbye to Lou or Layla.

I readjust my rucksack. 'Sorry, can't stop.'

My train leaves in an hour – I mustn't miss the bus to the station. I try to edge past Lou, but they block my path.

'You're never up this early on a Sunday. Neither am I, incidentally, and I haven't had a coffee yet. If you try to insult my intelligence by claiming you're off to church, I'll happily throttle you.'

I check my watch as they walk into the hallway. Skipping

town is the only option. We can't negotiate with the people we've crossed (Layla's suggestion). The drug gang will kill us *one by one*. But if we come clean with the police (Liam's plan), at least three of us could go to jail for money laundering and theft. It's a question of who gets us first – DC Walker or the gang. I don't fancy our chances either way.

Game over.

'Omigod!' Lou stares at the dried blood spots on the floor and follows them into the kitchen. When I finally regained consciousness yesterday, I'd staggered out of the back door and called for a taxi to take me to A & E.

Dammit.

I haven't had time to call someone to fix the damage. I've taped an old cardboard box over the missing panel. Lou takes in the shattered glass, lying on the tiles.

'You've had a break-in?'

I decide to tell the truth – there's no point trying to claim I got locked out.

'I disturbed a burglar yesterday.'

Well, a half-truth.

'Jesus.' Lou points to my bandage. 'And they gave you that?'

'I only needed a few stitches. Luckily I've got a thick skull!' I tap my forehead, playing for laughs.

Lou shudders. 'Don't do that!'

'What?'

'Put yourself down. I hate it. You do it all the time. It's your self-preservation tactic, but you don't need to put on an act with me.'

I bite my lip. Mocking myself has become an automatic reflex.

'Why didn't you call me? I'd have come with you to the hospital.'

I hear the hurt in their voice but brush it off. 'I thought you might be busy.'

That's not true, but I couldn't risk anyone seeing us together. I can't drag Lou down with me.

They arch an eyebrow disbelievingly. 'I messaged you a few times yesterday and called round here, but no one was in.'

I stoop down to pick up a shard of glass. No way can I admit that while they stood at the front door, I was lying in the hallway thinking I was about to die.

'I guess that explains why you had such an intense conversation with that police officer last night. Dad pointed him out. Said he's been asking questions in the village about the school bus.'

'DC Walker?'

I immediately regret uttering his name.

'That's the guy you got me to message about the interview?'

I gulp. 'Yeah.'

Lou studies me closely. 'About your mum . . .'

'Can I call you later? Like I said, I need to be somewhere.'

Lou folds their arms. 'Where? Meeting your new friends? You all looked pretty tight outside the Lobster Bar. Did you tell *them* what happened here?'

Heat radiates from my cheeks.

Lou's bottom lip trembles. 'I'm supposed to be your best friend, but you can't talk to me?'

'You *are* my best friend!'

I edge towards the door, but Lou grabs my sleeve.

'You blanked me last night because you wanted to speak to HMG, Layla and Fliss.' They almost spit out her name. 'You were with them for ages, *and* you left together. How could you spend time with Fliss? You know what she and her friends are like. Lisa and Spencer threw food at me in the restaurant.'

I hold up my hands. 'I didn't want to, but they spoke to me.'

'You made a choice.'

I bite the inside of my mouth.

'Is Fliss your friend? Everyone says her mum gave you a new iPhone.'

'It was a present,' I say stiltedly.

'Why would you accept it? You must have heard how badly she treats staff at the hotel. *Like mother, like daughter*.'

I'm racking my brains to think of a plausible excuse.

'I get that you shared a terrible experience, but Fliss hasn't changed. This isn't a clichéd teen movie where the high-school mean girl learns the error of her ways and turns good by the closing credits. You've seen how she and her friends treat me and yet –' their voice trembles – 'you chose *her* over *me*.'

'I swear I didn't.'

'Well, that's how you made me feel. Are you embarrassed to be with me in public?'

'Of course not!'

'It's the *only* explanation that makes any sense.'

'That's not it, I promise.'

Lou taps their foot on the floor, waiting for me to spill the beans.

'I'm sorry I hurt your feelings. I promise I'll make it up to you. Soon.'

'Great! You can start by telling me why you look like you've slept in your clothes. Why did I have to impersonate your mum to DC Walker?' They look around. 'And why are you alone in this big empty house she could never afford?

265

Heather and Crystal have been gone for ages. When are they coming back?'

'Soon!'

'You keep saying that. I'm worried, Kai.'

'Well, don't be! Everything's good. Mum gave me the deposit for here.'

'I don't believe you! Why do you keep lying about *everything*?'

Escape is my only option.

'I can't do this.' I head to the door.

'Don't walk away from me! This is important.'

They follow me into the hallway, but I'm already setting the rental's burglar alarm. Lou reluctantly steps out. I close the door behind us and lock up.

'Where are you going? Tell me that one simple thing and don't lie.'

I shake my head. I can't tell anyone, least of all Lou.

'Are you going to see Fliss? Please tell me the two of you aren't a couple. My mum said she saw you with her, Layla and HMG at the Sea Haven on Tuesday. What was that about? You never mentioned it when you came over afterwards.'

I hesitate. Lou has never let me down. They're the only family I have here, along with Mrs Gibson. If I tell them what I've done, they'll stick by me. But that's what frightens me most. I *must* protect them. By driving them away.

'You're right.' I force my chin up. 'The crash brought us together. Fliss is my girlfriend.' I inhale deeply. 'Give her a chance. For me. She's different, *nicer*.'

Lou falls back a step, stunned. 'I don't believe it!'

They stare at me, eyes wide open in horror.

'It's true. I'm off to the Sea Haven to hang out with her.'

Their voice trembles horribly. *'How could you?'*

I want to put my arms round Lou and tell them it's not true, that I would never betray them. Particularly not with Fake Fliss. But I force myself to walk away as Lou sobs.

With every step I tell myself I'm doing the right thing. Putting distance between us is probably saving their life.

But that doesn't stop tears from rolling down my face.

30

FLISS

I brush the tears from my cheeks as Daddy finally picks up.

'I have to get away for a while. Can I come and visit?'

I drum my fingers on the bedside table, waiting for his reply. There's a fumbling noise as he grabs his glasses or Cartier watch.

'What time is it?' His voice is hoarse and cracked. I catch another indistinct voice in the background – Amanda is probably bitching about being woken up.

It must be around 2.30 a.m. in Malibu. Who cares? My life is on the line.

'I don't know. I haven't got used to the time difference since you left me.'

He inhales sharply as my carefully aimed barb finds its target.

'Can we discuss this later, Flicky?' he asks quietly.

My heart aches whenever he uses my old nickname. I want to wrap it round myself like the comforter I had as a kid. I loved that blanket, but Mother threw it away when it became threadbare.

'I need to speak to you *now.*' Fresh tears well in my eyes. 'Things are bad, Daddy.' The last sentence comes out as a whimper.

'What's happened? Are you still in pain?' His voice is tinged with sympathy, which gives me a warm glow inside. We've chatted just once since the accident – he's only had time to check in with a few texts like Mother, but I'm sure he had more important reasons than her.

I sniff. 'Sure, my ribs still hurt.'

'Poor pet, you must rest.'

'I *need* to see you. I could fly out first thing tomorrow. I've been looking at flights and there's one at—'

'Flying is the last thing you should be doing if you're in pain.'

Dammit.

'Actually my ribs feel much better.' I keep my voice light and breezy as I attempt the largest U-turn in history. 'I'm practically back to normal. I think, I mean, I *know* I'm okay to fly.'

'I'm not happy about you travelling in your state and I'm sure your mother has said "no".' He pauses. 'Wait, have you mentioned this to her?'

'She has nothing to do with this!'

'Have you two fallen out again?'

I swallow a bitter laugh. Can he even remember the last time we got on? It was long before he left.

'Sure,' I say through gritted teeth. 'That's why I want to get away. I don't care about my ribs. Or the meds. I want to see *you*. You're the only person in the world who matters to me.'

A painful silence lengthens.

'Daddy? Are you still there?'

'The truth is, Flicky, I'm taking Amanda away for a break this week.'

'I could come with you!'

My lips twitch. Amanda will have a heart attack at the thought of me ruining their romantic getaway.

'Not this time.'

'Will it ever be *my* time? When will you or Mother put me first? I always come second, after the hotel, after Amanda . . .'

'Let's discuss this when you've calmed down.'

'What's the point? It'll probably be too late!'

'For what?'

'Like you care!'

I throw my mobile across the room.

Now what? I can't run or hide on this island for ever. I can't rely on Mother. Or Daddy. The rest of the Sea Haven Survivors – *that's what people are calling us* – are probably planning their escapes.

I retrieve my phone from beneath a chair. I need to persuade them to stay, to buy me more time.

If they leave, I'll be in far more danger.

One of *them* must be picked off first.

31

LIAM

'Is this supposed to be a joke? We fly to Barbados tomorrow on an open-ended ticket?'

Mum stares at my spreadsheet suspiciously as if she's discovered a strange species of insect in the Amazonian rainforest. 'Where on earth do you think we'd find the money for a trip like this? And how would I get time off work?'

I ignore my vibrating phone. It's probably another message from Fliss demanding we meet later to discuss a plan.

Not getting killed is my one and only aim today.

I force my lips to curl into a smile. 'It's an early birthday present – along with the money I've transferred into your bank account to help with the rent and bills.'

Mum frowns and runs a hand through her short ash-blonde hair.

272

'And you could treat yourself to a haircut,' I add, glancing at the dark roots.

'What are you talking about? Where's all this money come from?'

'Surprise!' The word feels hollow on my lips, but I persevere with the story I've rehearsed. 'I've won thirty thousand pounds on the scratchcards. I want to splash out on a holiday – we can book straight away!'

Her face doesn't light up. Instead, it folds in on itself like a fragile piece of origami. Guilt pricks my conscience. She can't know about the full £250,000. I'd figured £30,000 was a safer figure if she checks my bank accounts *and* finds out about Tristram's Jeep.

'You never buy scratchcards – especially not after Tristram claimed they were only for common people.'

Her words are like a sharp slap. I'd forgotten he'd once said that. 'He meant it as a joke!'

She raises an eyebrow. 'Really?'

'I don't always agree with him.'

'I can't remember the last time you expressed an opinion that was your own.'

I sigh heavily. Mum was supportive of me coming out and has no problem with me being gay, but we clash repeatedly over Tristram. She doesn't understand what a big deal it is that he chose *me*, how special that makes me feel.

'You never talk about your old friends,' she continues. 'They don't drop by any more. You talk and dress differently. You act differently.' She holds up my spreadsheet of flight details and five-star hotels. 'Did he put you up to this?'

'No!'

'What about the hair appointment? I bet he's mentioned my roots! He makes a point of staring at them whenever he comes over.'

My cheeks flush. 'That's only because he's used to his mum looking immaculate.'

'Oh, thanks! And I resemble the inside of a dustbin?'

'I meant she gets her hair coloured every month. But you could pamper yourself with my money. You'll have plenty left after paying this month's rent.'

'I'm saving every penny in case there are redundancies. I'm sorry if that makes you ashamed of me in front of Tristram.'

I feel my face turn a brighter scarlet. 'Why are you turning this into a discussion about him? Can't I do something nice for you without an interrogation?'

Mum crosses her arms. 'Tristram's family might be wealthy enough to drop everything, but I can't abandon my patients. You have school. We both have responsibilities.'

'I thought this would make us both happy!'

She frowns. 'Did you? Honestly?'

I swallow the vomit that's rising in my throat. 'Please, Mum. *We* need this.'

'No, love, we don't. Running off, the way your dad did, never helps anyone.'

I wince. He's the last person I want to think about. His birthday cards stopped arriving when I was fourteen.

'Dad left because of me.' My voice cracks. 'Because I'm not perfect.'

'That's not true! Don't ever think that.' She reaches over and squeezes my hand. 'You are perfect. In every single way.'

I shake my head. 'You're just saying that because you're my mum.'

'The reasons he left had nothing to do with you – his drinking, the other women . . .'

I glance away miserably.

'Face your problems head on. Stay here and work them out. I'll help you.'

That's out of the question. I can't win this battle. If I hang around here, it'll end with a funeral – and there's a high chance it will be mine, followed by hers.

'Why don't I make us a cup of tea? We can talk this through together.' She turns round to fill the kettle. 'You don't look like you're getting much sleep. Are you worried about your back flaring up? Or are you having flashbacks about the crash? We could ask the GP to arrange counselling. There's no shame in that.'

'I don't need bloody counselling! I need a holiday. Is that too much to ask after I almost died? After everything I've been through over the years?'

She spins round. 'You never swear. Why are you acting like this?' Her eyes plead with me to tell the truth.

I can't. I must protect her.

'Fine! I'll ask Tristram to go with me.'

Mum snorts. 'You're not bunking off school to go to Barbados with *him.*'

'I'm seventeen. I can do whatever I want.'

'This is my house, my rules.'

'Well, maybe I don't want to live here with you any longer.'

'Liam!' Her lower lip wobbles.

'I thought you'd be grateful I'm putting you first for a change, but instead . . .' I pause, calculating how to inflict the biggest blow. 'You're being a first-class bitch. I'm not surprised Dad left!'

The hurt look in her eyes almost breaks me in two as I storm out. My bags are packed, and I've taken her car keys. I'd prepared for the worst-case scenario: that Mum wouldn't go along with my plan. In the hallway I grab my rucksack stuffed with stolen cash, and another with schoolbooks and an overnight bag.

'Where are you going? To Tristram's, I suppose?'

'What do you care?' I throw open the front door.

'Of course I care! Stay and we can talk about this. *Please.*'

'Forget it!'

I stride out, unlocking Mum's car with the zapper. I throw my bags inside. As she comes down the path towards me, I start up the engine and pull away, almost colliding with another car. The motorist hammers on their horn.

I keep driving until my vision swims with tears.

I pull over and rest my head on the steering wheel.

I've no idea where to go next, but that doesn't matter.

There's no going back.

I must lead the gang away from my home.

Away from Mum.

32

KAI

I've been careful and haven't accidentally led anyone here.

I look up and down the street as the taxi pulls away. I made the driver take a roundabout route in case that guy in the blue anorak *was* following me at Bristol Temple Meads station earlier. I could have been mistaken. Anyway, there's no sign of anyone dodgy hanging about and I haven't heard the ominous revving of a motorbike.

I stare at the house, my heart beating rapidly. It's a semi with a tiny front garden, nothing special. The one I'm renting is far bigger and nicer. I ring the doorbell and hold my breath as I hear the light tapping of footsteps. A woman with spiky dark brown hair and a nose ring opens the door. My chest tightens painfully and my eyes swim with tears.

Her eyes widen. 'Kai?'

'Mum!' I fall into her arms. 'I've missed you so much.'

278

All my worries slip away: the stolen money, the drug gang, hurting Lou, abandoning Layla. Nothing else matters. *I'm here.*

'What on earth?' She pushes me away, examining my cut and bruised face. 'What happened? How did you get that?'

I touch my forehead. 'It's a long story . . .'

I'm about to explain about the crash, but she steps backwards. She pulls at her baggy purple jumper, touching her stomach.

'What are you doing here?'

'Visiting you! I couldn't call. Your phone's been cut off. Are you okay?'

'Everything's fine, love.'

An awkward silence grows as she grips the door frame tighter.

'Erm, can I come in?'

'Paul's taken the girls swimming. He'll be back soon, and I think—'

'Please, Mum!'

She hesitates, but that's probably because she hates being taken by surprise.

'Sure. Excuse the mess.'

The hallway is a bland cream colour – this must be Paul's choice. Mum opts for bright hues and upset our old landlord by painting the kitchen sunshine yellow.

'This is nice. I'm happy for you.'

A sharp pain pierces my heart as I notice the shoes lined up neatly on a rack: Mum's, Paul's, Lucy's and Crystal's. There's no space for my trainers. I pause beside a framed photo of the four of them hanging on the wall. When I turn round, Mum's gone.

'How's everything?' I ask, following her into the kitchen. 'Have you managed to find any work?'

She's pouring boiling water into two mugs and doesn't glance back.

'It's going well. Paul's contract's been renewed and I've found a part-time position in a jewellery shop. It doesn't pay much, but it's better than nothing. I'm managing to save a little.'

'That's great! And Crystal?'

'She loves it here! She gets on with Paul like a house on fire and has settled in well at her new school with Lucy. They're best mates.'

I flinch. It still wounds that Mum found a temporary new school for Crystal and not me, but I guess she didn't want to disrupt my A levels. It's harder to move high schools mid sixth form.

'Look, Mum, I know we agreed we'd wait for you to get on your feet before you came back, but there's a change of plan. I need to stay here for a while until things calm down in Sandstown. I hope that's okay?'

Her shoulders tense as she brings over mugs of strong tea. I stare into mine. She's forgotten I like it milky. She takes a long, slow sip of her drink.

'I get it – Paul's worried about an extra mouth to feed when things have been tight, but I'll pay for my food and rent . . . your mobile bill and anything else you owe. I'll cover it all. You don't have to rely on him. *I* can take care of you and Crystal.'

I grab a thick envelope of fifties from my rucksack and push it across the table. I've left the rest beneath Mrs Gibson's shed – it's safer there.

Mum examines the wad of money. 'Where did you get this? Wait, don't tell me. I can't get caught up in funny business.' She shoves the envelope towards me. 'Keep this. That way I won't worry about you making ends meet back home.'

Anger flares inside me. 'What *home* are you talking about?'

'Well, where you've been living in Sandstown.'

'Where is that exactly? How the hell would you know?'

She stares back impassively. 'There's no need to raise your voice.'

'Isn't there?' I almost choke on the words. 'Have you been worried about me at all since you left?'

I don't give her a chance to answer.

'I *have* struggled. The money you left to cover the rent ran out sharpish. The landlord kicked me out. I didn't have enough to buy proper food until recently. I was hungry and homeless. I was hurt in an accident.' I take a deep breath. '*No one* came to see me in hospital. No one cares about me, especially not you!'

Mum reaches for my hand. 'Of course I do, love. I didn't know you were injured. I'm sorry.'

I shake her off, my eyes stinging with tears. 'It's your job to know, but I couldn't get hold of you! You haven't called me and your phone's dead. I have no idea when you're coming back.'

She inhales sharply, glancing away. 'That's the thing . . . I've been putting off telling you . . . I've decided to stay. I'm building a life here with Paul.'

My mouth falls open. 'W-w-what?'

'There's no work for either of us in Sandstown and Paul's job is stable.'

'But what about me?' I blurt out. 'I've been waiting for you.'

Mum still won't meet my gaze. 'Paul says you're old enough to stand on your own two feet, the way he did. He left home at sixteen and found a nice flat and an apprenticeship that paid well. He didn't have to rely on his parents. He says it was the making of him!'

I stare at her, aghast. 'But I'm not bloody Paul, am I? And I don't want to be anything like that moron!'

'That's exactly the kind of talk that puts his back up! You rub each other the wrong way, always have since day one.'

'Because he wants to drive a wedge between us – and it's working!' I wipe my wet cheeks with the back of my hand. 'Why can't you see what he's doing? I don't care what Paul says – this has nothing to do with him. I want my old life back with you and Crystal. *Together.* The way you promised.'

'That can't happen.'

I pretend I haven't heard and rummage in my rucksack.

'Look at me, Kai.'

I shake my head. I'm searching for the estate agent details about Torside Lodge. This will change *everything*. Mum won't be able to resist our fantastic new rental. She could pick up waitressing shifts at the Lobster Bar and Crystal can re-enrol at her old primary school.

'Please!'

Slowly I raise my gaze, my heart thumping uncomfortably loud.

'I'm pregnant.' She leans back in the chair, cradling her

stomach. 'I have to plan ahead and think of what's best for our baby and the girls – Crystal and Lucy are still little. I must put them first.'

It takes several seconds for her words to register.

'Where do I fit into this?' My voice sounds strange and faraway, like someone else is speaking.

'Paul's right,' she says, sighing heavily. 'You're almost seventeen and practically a grown-up. You have your whole life ahead of you.'

My brain's whirring with panic and I can't think straight. I try to breathe in and out slowly.

'I don't understand what you're telling me.'

'You can't stay here, love – we don't have the space,' she says gently. 'There's no spare bedroom and Paul won't let you kip on the couch. The pair of you will be at each other's throats within hours. Go back to Sandstown. You obviously have enough money to rent – you won't be homeless. Finish your A levels and go to uni or get a job. This will work out the best for everyone in the long run, you'll see.'

I grip the table as the room spins.

I feel my world collapse around me.

Everything I care about slips from my grasp.

'B-b-but . . .' The words jam in my throat. I can scarcely believe what she's saying.

'Admittedly I could have handled this better. I should have been straight with you sooner, but I was a coward. You know how much I hate confrontation and Paul thought you'd probably get the message when I changed mobile providers.'

An invisible weapon drives deeper and deeper into my chest, causing fresh wounds.

Her phone wasn't disconnected. It had nothing to do with money. She deliberately cut *me* off.

'Paul made you choose between us . . . and you picked *him*?' I practically spit out the word.

She doesn't reply and scrapes away a dried Cheerio that is glued to the table.

'You're treating me like shit but I'm your son!' My voice cracks. 'I'll always be part of this family, even with a baby on the way. They're my half-brother or sister.'

'Of course! I'll message you my new number, and I promise I'll do better at keeping in touch. You can come for visits and see the new baby . . . and everything.'

I hang on to the table tighter. I'm not above begging.

'Don't do this, *please*.'

I wait for her to admit she's made a horrible mistake, that she's choosing *me*, but she's silent. I stumble blindly to my feet, knocking over a chair.

She passes me the rucksack. 'Take care of yourself, love.

Whatever's happened in Sandstown, running away isn't the answer. You must face things.'

'Like you have?' Tears roll down my cheeks. 'By abandoning me?'

I rip the bag from her hands. The pain in my chest is crippling. I *am* stupid. I deflected my teachers' questions about parents' evening to avoid her getting into trouble, and never admitted my worries to Lou. I stuck to her cover story, but it was built on a web of lies. She probably never had any intention of returning for me.

I can barely breathe as I reach the hallway and steady myself against the wall. Glancing up, I see the photo of the four of them together. I rip it down.

'What are you doing?' She touches her stomach. 'Stop!'

I toss the framed picture on the floorboards and stamp on it, shattering the glass.

'Kai!'

I kick the shoes from the rack before wrenching open the front door.

I stagger down the path and on to the street.

I'm totally alone in the world.

33

LAYLA

'Are you worried about being left alone?' Mum is inspecting the suitcase labels by the front door. 'We've changed the locks and installed a burglar alarm. It's perfectly safe, I promise.'

She checks the to-do list on her mobile for about the millionth time.

'It's not that.'

'Hold on a minute, love.' She hollers up the stairs for Leon. 'Can you check the bathroom cabinet? I think I've forgotten the thermometer.'

I try again. 'I'm looking forward to having the place to myself – watching whatever I want on TV and having wild parties. You know, inviting upper-sixth boys to stay overnight, drink alcohol, experiment with drugs and have sex.'

Mum turns round, frowning. Ha! I have her full and undivided attention.

'I want to be there for Salih,' I persist. 'He needs me while he's in hospital.'

I check my mobile. Yet another message from Fliss arrives, suggesting we meet to discuss a battle plan. Well, this is *my* escape route.

Salih breezes past. 'I don't need you, MM.'

'He doesn't mean that,' I say hastily, as he disappears into the kitchen.

'Yeah, I do, loser,' he shouts. 'Mum said we'll have treats like visiting Universal Studios. Guess you've got school and detentions to look forward to!'

Mum sighs. 'I said "maybe" a trip to a theme park if the doctors allow it. We have a day or two to recover from jet lag before we need to check in at the hospital.'

I want to shake her and scream, '*I don't give a flying crap about Universal Studios! If I don't come with you, I could be killed.*'

'Have we got everything?' Leon clutches the thermometer as he runs down the stairs. 'Passports, medicine, doctors' forms, all the papers we need?'

'Packed, packed and packed. We're good.' Mum gently moves me out of the way, as she stuffs the thermometer into the suitcase.

'Mum? I mean it.' I follow them into the sitting room as

they do a last-minute check. 'I want to come. We could book a plane ticket online. I won't be on the same flight as the three of you obviously, but I could fly out later. We'd still be together, *eventually*.'

'It's natural for you to be anxious about your brother.' Mum walks over and puts an arm round my shoulders. 'But Salih will be in great hands. They're a fantastic medical team – the best in the world.'

I shrug her off. 'That's not it. We should be together, as a family.'

'It's too late,' Leon points out. 'The taxi will be here in forty minutes.'

'Give me your credit card details and I'll book a flight while you're in the taxi. We could meet at the airport here, or I can make my way to your hotel in Florida.'

Mum frowns. 'You have school, remember? You can't miss two or three weeks of lessons. We want to keep things as normal as possible.'

Anger, but mainly fear, bubbles up. It spills out of me in a torrent. 'Since when have things been normal for any of us? I don't remember what that is any more. Apparently normal is you flogging Baba's oud and kawala to a total stranger.'

Mum flinches. 'That's beneath you, Layla. I've given you

the pawnbroker's ticket. You can claim them after school tomorrow.'

'Great! I have to decide between rescuing Baba's instruments or going with Salih?'

'No,' she says gently. 'We've made that decision. I wish you could come, but there's only enough money for the three of us, and Leon will drive the hire car to and from hospital. I promise we'll ring every day and keep you updated.'

My gaze rests on Leon's wallet next to the sofa, but he notices and shakes his head. 'Your mum's right. We can't afford another flight. We'll need the remainder of the cash from the fund for living expenses while we're there.'

Hot, shameful tears spill down my cheeks as my chance of escape slips away.

'Layla? Please don't cry! Everything will be all right.'

I run out. Up in my bedroom, I bury my face into the duvet.

A few minutes later, I hear the door click open and the pad of footsteps. The mattress dips next to me.

'Hey! Sorry I called you a loser.'

I turn over, wiping the tears away. Salih stares down at me. He'll probably scream loudly in protest, but I sit up and throw my arms round him. This could be the last time we see each other.

'You're squashing me,' he says breathlessly. 'And you forgot to put on deodorant.'

I let go quickly.

'I was joking about the last part. You smell okayish.' He bites his lip. 'If it's any consolation, I don't actually want to go with Mum and Leon.'

'You don't fancy a trip to Universal Studios, *habibi*?' I wink, but he doesn't crack a smile.

'I'm not talking about the theme park.'

'Then what?'

He looks away.

'The injections and stuff are sucky, but this is a good thing. The best thing that's happened to us in a long time.'

'That's what everyone keeps saying.' Salih breathes out slowly, lying down next to me. 'Also "you should never give up". I get that a lot. But is giving up so bad? I read online that sometimes the bravest people know when to stop fighting.'

I stare at him, horrified. 'Don't say that. Don't ever say that.'

'Why not? I'm tired of being prodded and poked and told what to think. I'm tired of *trying*. Sometimes I want it all to stop.' He hesitates. 'To do nothing. Be *me*. Not a sick kid in hospital who people feel sorry for. Just Salih. The old Salih.'

'But you have to try. For Mum. For Leon. *For me*.' The words almost choke me. '*For Baba*.'

'Don't hate me, Layla, but . . .'

'What?'

'I don't remember him.'

My heart contracts. 'That's okay because I can remember him for both of us.' I take a breath, lacing my fingers between his. 'He used to call you *habibi* or *my little batata*.'

Salih frowns.

'*Batata* is Arabic for sweet potato. You wanted to eat them for every meal, including breakfast! Baba used to roast trays and trays of sweet potatoes.'

Salih shakes his head sadly.

'He read you bedtime stories about animals and played his kawala whenever you had a nightmare to soothe you back to sleep.' I turn on to my side to face him. 'Whenever we visited Teta, we went to Mandarine Koueider in Zamalek, which has the *best* Egyptian sweets and desserts. You used to eat a Nutella and pistachio ice-cream cone sitting on Baba's shoulders. Once the ice cream dripped into his ear!'

A smile lights up Salih's face. 'I *think* I remember that.'

'We used to stare for ages at the trays of baklava, konafa and basbousa while Baba and Teta chatted to friends and waited for their orders to be boxed and tied with lilac ribbon.

Everything looked and tasted amazing. We never wanted to leave.'

'I remember the smell of sugar! And syrup.'

'Baba used to make us balah el sham – syrupy fritters – even when he became too ill to go to work. He still cooked our favourite food at home. He tried to keep going. He didn't want to give up for all our sakes.' My voice breaks. 'He wanted to be with us for as long as possible.'

Salih disentangles himself from me and covers his eyes with his hands.

'I know it's tough.' I pause. 'Actually I have no idea, because I'm not going through this. *You* are. But I think you want more than this – being hooked up to tubes and feeling awful. You want to play football with your friends. *You want to live.*'

He's silent.

Please, please, please say you want to live.

I brush away a tear from the corner of my eye and clear my throat. 'That means you have to be brave, braver than you've ever been before, *habibi*.'

'That sounds like a line from a soppy movie.'

'It happens to be true.'

He stares at me solemnly. 'What would you do if you were me?'

I think about what's waiting for me outside the front door when everyone leaves today. It truly terrifies me.

But I remind myself what I've got to lose: Salih, Mum and Leon. Alvita and the rest of my friends. Kai. My fellow survivors from the crash – none of them deserve to be hunted down and murdered.

'If it were me . . .' I swallow hard. 'I'd fight to the end, the way Baba did, however bad it gets.'

SUNDAY, 29 SEPTEMBER, 4.16 P.M.

WHATSAPP GROUP: WAITT

FLISS: *Stop ignoring me! This isn't going away. We need to meet. Today.*
LIAM: *Where?*
FLISS: *7 p.m. here. U can stay. Plenty of spare rooms. It's safe for *PETS**
LIAM: *Yes please.*
LAYLA: *Is yr mum around?*
FLISS: *She's never around!!!*
LAYLA: *Okay, I guess . . .*
FLISS: *Kai? R u coming? Safety in numbers!*
KAI: *No way. Am long gone.*
FLISS: *WTF?! We have 2 return all ££££! ONLY WAY to live.*
KAI: *Can't u see we're dead already?*
LIAM: *You'll get us all killed!*

FLISS: *Come back!!*

LAYLA: *Pls, Kai.*

KAI: *Go while u can. Sandstown isn't safe.*

LAYLA: 😢 🖤
16:19

KAI: *Sorry xxx* 🖤🖤
16:20

34

FLISS

We have the £££. How do we return it?

I tap out the message in my suite and post it on the *Thieves* WhatsApp group. 'Done! We can't change our minds.'

'Now what?' Liam slumps back in one of my chairs.

Layla swallows hard. 'We wait for them to make a move.'

She nibbles a ragged nail. My palms are moist and my throat is horribly dry. Can we pull this off? Inviting them to the Sea Haven tonight gave me a chance to search Liam's bags while they both nipped to the bathroom. I'd lied and said my facilities were out of order and sent them down a floor; I couldn't risk them ransacking my bedroom, like Kai. Unfortunately Liam didn't bring his cash, but I've ensured it can't remain hidden long.

I've kept him busy doing what he loves most – creating a spreadsheet, with help from Layla. I ordered room service while they calculated how much money we have between us (just under £670,000 with Kai's share, and £443,000 without). We've come up with a high-stakes plan. Stage one: pretend we have £762,000 left (my human calculators have worked out all the expenditure that's public, like Kai's rental, but we're banking on the gang not knowing about the money laundering). I shudder as Liam's warning rings in my ears:

Anything less than three quarters remaining, and there's a high statistical risk they'll kill us one by one.

I focus on stage two, which is where things get interesting: I've persuaded Liam and Layla we should ditch the stolen cash that incriminates us. We set up a meet and tip off DC Walker, who catches the gang red-handed. I haven't divulged my secret scheme to get my blackmailer arrested at the same time. And there's no way either of them can find out about my grand finale. I rub my mouth, concealing a smile. I honestly think I've surpassed myself.

Liam gasps. 'Look! Someone's replying.'

We peer over my phone, which is next to the tray of drinks and uneaten sandwiches on the table. I hold my breath while the mystery person writes a message. Liam clutches Layla's arm as it lands.

Is Kai with you? Do you have his ££££?

'Holy moly,' Liam mutters.

Layla clamps a hand to her mouth. 'Should we lie and claim we have it?'

'Definitely,' I reply. 'Only we know Kai's AWOL.'

'I agree,' Liam says. 'The odds they've realised Kai has done a runner are about five to one.'

I exhale slowly as I write 'yes' and wait for the response. After a couple of seconds, a single word appears. *Liars!*

Liam's mouth falls open. 'How do they know we're lying? Are they watching us?' He jumps to his feet and strides over to the window.

'They're unlikely to be in a boat at sea!' I remark 'They must be bluffing.'

'They're messaging!' Layla exclaims.

Liam returns and sinks into his chair. My chest constricts, pushing the air out of my lungs, as it flashes up.

We have eyes on Kai in Bristol. He dies tonight if you lie again. How much £££ do you have?

'They're one step ahead of us!' Liam exclaims. '*We* didn't know Kai's there!'

'They must have followed him out of Sandstown,' Layla says, her voice trembling.

I glance away to hide my relief. Kai is within their crosshairs, which means I'm not top of the hit list.

'We need to warn him. He might not check this WhatsApp group.' Layla grabs her phone and messages furiously.

Her mobile pings a few seconds later.

'Kai says he's on the move.'

Liam breathes out heavily. 'Which means he's safe.'

'Not necessarily,' Layla replies. 'They could still be following him.'

Her face has paled; she looks like she's going to be sick. I *almost* feel sympathetic after I've ruled them out as my blackmailers. My quick torch test last night revealed that neither Layla, Liam nor Kai touched the cash. Their hands were clean of residue. That means someone else was hiding in plain sight. I probably saw them in the car park when the Jeep was on fire and hadn't realised I was staring at my blackmailer. They messaged again this morning, demanding an extra £10,000 for the 'inconvenience' of DC Walker and the fire brigade turning up.

'Maybe we should come clean and say exactly how much money we have,' Layla says croakily.

'That will definitely get Kai killed,' Liam points out. 'It's too risky.'

'I agree – we lie to protect him,' I say emphatically.

It's important they believe we're united if my plan is to succeed.

'I guess.' Layla rubs her face. 'But he can't die. I just can't . . .' Her voice disappears into a sob.

'He won't,' Liam says, squeezing her shoulder. 'The probability of him surviving increases proportionally with every extra pound we promise.'

The corners of her mouth twitch. 'Thanks, Liam. Your maths is a comfort!'

He smiles. 'You're welcome.'

I lean forward in my chair. 'Shall I tell them the magic figure: seven hundred and sixty-two thousand pounds?'

'Affirmative. It's enough to protect Kai and keep us alive . . . for now.'

Layla nods.

I tap out the message and press 'send'.

We watch as the person types.

Will send location and time once Kai returns to Sandstown.

'I'll tell him to come back. He won't let us down.' Layla fires off a message, and stares at her phone, willing him to reply.

'Anything?' Liam asks.

She shakes her head. 'He hasn't read it yet. I'll call him in a bit.'

'We have twenty-four hours to persuade him,' I say slowly. 'We can't let on to the gang that he's not playing ball.'

Layla bites her lip. 'They need to believe we're all in this together.'

I write, *Kai says he's coming back*, and show the screen to the others.

They nod. I grip the side of the chair as the message disappears into the ether.

My phone vibrates.

He has 24 hours. We'll be watching him.

'What if you can't talk him round, Layla?' Liam asks hoarsely.

Our answer arrives a few seconds later.

We know you're at the Sea Haven. If Kai doesn't return with his share of the £££, you three die first.

35

KAI

Layla's voice wobbles with fear as she explains the plan.

'What do you think?' she asks hopefully. 'It could work if we all stick together, right? We'll be safe.'

I sit down on the bed and stand up again after spotting suspicious stains on the duvet cover. I've been dead careful since leaving Mum's. I walked around for hours, sticking to crowded places. I've shelled out fifties for a room at this B&B, which doesn't have CCTV or, apparently, hot water. I made the taxi driver take a detour here and paid in cash after Layla's warning. No one was tailing me from the city centre. I'm positive. But I don't feel safe. In truth, I don't feel anything at all. I'm dead inside. It's like I've left my body and I'm staring down on someone who looks and talks like me.

'You can't trust Fliss or Liam,' I say finally. 'I'd be willing to bet my share they're both planning to give the gang decoy

303

rucksacks. Why would they hand over real money when they can fake it? I had a quick search of Fliss's suite on Tuesday – I couldn't find the gun but I'm sure she has it. And I think Liam staged his car break-in the night we went back for the holdall.'

Layla catches her breath. 'W-w-what? Why?'

'So we'd think he was backing out, instead of laundering the cash. It came to me that night at the carwash – why would a thief break into the driver's side, when they're trying to get to the glovebox? They'd smash the passenger window.'

'That's even more of a reason for you to return! You're the only one who has my back. Well, at least I thought you did . . .'

'Of course I do!'

'I can't do this on my own. We need you.' She chokes back a sob. '*I* need you, Kai!'

I'd decided to empty my bank account and head to London tomorrow. I have enough money for about four months' rent and could get a job waiting tables before flying to Hawaii or Australia. I'd figured the rest of my cash would be safe in Mrs Gibson's grounds long-term. I could unearth the money when everything has quietened down. But my resolve weakens as Layla weeps.

'Please don't cry!'

'Then help me. I have no one!'

Shit! How can I leave her alone with the others? Would it hurt to return for one day? I could dig up another couple of thousand and stay long enough to protect her, and for the gang to think I'm going along with their plan, before I leave again.

'If I come back tomorrow, it won't be for Liam and Fliss.' I clutch my mobile tighter. 'It will only be for you.'

'Thank you! That means a lot. I wish I'd . . . I mean that we . . .'

'I know. Me too.' I sigh. 'You should go back to the others. Tell them you've talked me round.'

'Wait! Message me your address. If something happens, I can . . .' Her voice trails off into another muffled cry.

She means she can tell the police my last-known whereabouts if I disappear.

'Will do.' I gulp. 'Let's speak early tomorrow, make arrangements. Be careful, Layla.'

'And you.'

I wipe my eyes with the back of my sleeve as I tap out my address and press 'send'. I notice a new message from Lou. They've sent a broken-heart emoji, which makes me feel worse. I've hurt Lou, lost Mum and Crystal, and placed Layla and the others in danger. My stomach lurches, not only due to the smell in here – an unpleasant mixture of wet dog and fried eggs. I run to the en-suite and throw up in the toilet. Wiping my mouth, I slump to the floor.

9.51 p.m.

My stomach growls with hunger.

I scrape myself up and turn off the bathroom light. I chuck my rucksack in the bottom of the rickety old wardrobe. The landing floorboards creak as I pause after locking my door. Burt, the manager, said only two other rooms are occupied. That's probably because he has the social skills of a serial killer, and no one wants to stay here. Techno music booms from behind the far door while a couple are having a loud row in another 'suite'. I checked in unnoticed – no one will hear me slip out.

Downstairs, the grubby reception is empty. Burt must be in the back room; his TV blares in the background. I'm hit by a sheet of rain as I open the front door. I shove my baseball cap low over my face and pull up the collar of my anorak before breaking into a run. As I turn the corner, a man wearing a long coat ducks into a shop entrance. I hesitate. That's normal, right? He's escaping the rain. To be on the safe side, I cross the road, dodging cars with wipers swiping furiously.

I nip inside the chippy I'd spotted on the way here in the taxi. The window's steamed up with condensation and I can't see out as I wait for my haddock and chips. I'm hoping I can keep dinner down.

'Have you got anything smaller?' The guy holds my fifty-pound note up to the light.

'Sorry.'

He shoves a fistful of notes and loose coins at me. I don't bother to check the change – I've spotted a CCTV camera above the door.

It's raining harder by the time I've picked up my order. My trainers and socks are instantly soaked as I misjudge a puddle, crossing the road.

There he is again!

A man in a dark-coloured raincoat shelters in a shop doorway, talking on his phone. He turns away as he spots me. I run faster, not caring about the water splashing up my jeans. I'm not safe. I could sleep rough in a bus shelter or an underpass – it's not appealing in a storm but taking myself off grid could save my life.

I burst through the door to the B&B, startling Burt, who has returned to the reception desk. He adjusts his glasses and attempts a lopsided smile. The few teeth he has are yellowed from tobacco.

'It's raining cats and dogs out there.' His gaze rests on my plastic bag, which is wafting an unmistakably chippy smell. *Dammit!* I'm busted. Takeaways are strictly forbidden, according to the laminated rules in the room. I'll have to eat it in the doorway. I turn round, but Burt calls after me.

'Don't worry. It's okay as a one-off.' He pushes the glasses up his nose. 'Are you staying in for the rest of the night?

I frown. Maybe he's plotting to kill me later for my takeaway sin.

'Yeah. I guess.'

'I'll say goodnight then.' He scuttles off into the rear room. Within seconds the TV booms out at high volume.

I take the stairs three at a time, holding my breath as the smell of damp grows. I'm out of here as soon as I've grabbed my stuff. The two other rooms are eerily quiet. The guests must be having an early night. I jiggle the key to let myself in and check the wardrobe. My rucksack's where I left it. As I sling it over my shoulder, I hear the thud of heavy footsteps coming up the stairs.

Shiit!

I race to the window, trying to force the latch. It's stuck!

The floorboards creak outside my door. It must be that man in the dark-coloured coat. Frantically I look around, but there's no way to escape. I pad quietly back to the door; I'll have to charge out and knock him off guard. I just need a few seconds' head start down the stairs.

Suddenly a voice booms out, 'Armed police! Come out with your hands raised!'

What the hell? Hands trembling, I throw open the door. Police officers dressed in black uniforms and helmets train their guns on me, flanked by colleagues holding shields.

'Drop the rucksack!' one shouts.

It slides from my shoulders as I step out on to the landing. Everything happens in double time after that – I'm face down on the sour-smelling carpet, my hands handcuffed behind my back and a police officer is repeatedly barking, 'Where's the firearm, Kai?'

I'm too shocked to reply. Black boots thunder past into my room.

'We've had a report of you pointing a gun out of the window,' the officer says.

I clear my throat. 'I don't have a gun! I've never had one.'

'We have intelligence you're in possession of stolen money. Where is it?'

Before I can think of a reply, a voice says, 'The room is clear. No sign of a firearm, but his rucksack contains fifties.'

Hands help me into a sitting-up position and another police officer talks, confirming my name and why they're here.

'We're arresting you on suspicion of theft and money laundering.'

My mind whirrs as he cautions me. This *cannot* be happening. How did they find me? Why do they think I have a gun?

The realisation dawns on me, as painful as a punch.

One person knows *exactly* where I am.

Only they could have tipped off the police with my address.

Layla.

36

LAYLA: *Can't sleep. Didn't tell u something important earlier . . . Not safe to put in writing. R u awake?*
02:47

LAYLA: *landed. Mrs C met guests at helipad. Holidaymakers, right? Not drug-gang members. Am stressing out!!!*
02:49

LAYLA: *Want 2 be 100 pc honest with u. Please call me when u wake up? Will explain everything Xx*
02:51

LAYLA: Will try u in morning. Need 2 talk b4

others find out what I've done. 😱 Night-night xxx
02:54

KAI: *Last seen yesterday at 21:45*

37

LIAM

An object strikes my head. Then another.

'Stop it!' a voice rings out. 'Leave him alone!

I wake with a start, trip and land spread-eagled on the floor. My heart is racing. Paper aeroplanes are scattered around. I'm lying next to the legs of a chair. I'm not under attack from the drug gang. I'm in my form room. I'd fallen asleep at my desk.

'W-w-what's going on?'

A hand reaches down and pulls me up as another missile lands at my feet. I stare into Lou's kind brown eyes, and feel my heart skip a beat.

'It's someone's idea of a joke – sorry.'

Lou reaches over my shoulder. I feel their warm breath on my neck as they pull off the piece of paper that's taped to my back.

My cheeks warm furiously, and not just from the note. 'Who did that?'

'Probably one of the usual suspects?'

I follow their gaze to Spencer and Lisa, who are laughing loudly in the corner.

'Can we speak outside? I need to ask you something, Liam. In private.'

'Sure.'

Lou scoops up my rucksack; I'm grateful for the quick exit. I don't want anyone to notice my watery eyes. I rub my face in the corridor, self-conscious about how bad I must look. I barely got any sleep after seeing that helicopter land at the hotel in the middle of the night. I'd paced up and down my room for hours, terrified that gang members had arrived, not wealthy off-season guests.

I jump as my phone vibrates and scan the message frantically.

'Is everything okay?' Lou holds up the piece of paper. 'Apart from being used as target practice obviously.'

'It's my mum, not . . . anything else.'

A lump grows in my throat. She's apologising for yesterday's row even though it wasn't her fault. She needs the car before her afternoon shift. I left it by the causeway overnight. I'll need to nip out at lunchtime. I search my rucksack and find the keys at the bottom, but my EarPods aren't in the side compartment. I must have left them in my hotel room.

'I don't think you are okay,' Lou says quietly. 'You look mega stressed and I'm worried about Kai. Then there's Fliss . . .'

My heart beats quicker. 'What about her?'

'I know you were driven to school with her this morning.'

Wow! The gossip mill works fast. Her driver had dropped us off ridiculously early – none of us had wanted to bump into the night-time arrivals or Mrs C.

Lou's bottom lip quivers. 'Everyone's saying the Sea Haven Survivors have become inseparable – the photo in the paper, the meet-ups, the limo rides.'

'Are people calling us that?'

Lou nods.

'It was one ride,' I say, sighing. 'Fliss offered to pick up Layla and me. It helps to talk to fellow survivors.' I'd rehearsed my lie in case anyone asked.

'Kai didn't get a lift?' Lou asks, frowning harder.

'He's not around.' I cough awkwardly. 'He won't be in school today.'

Lou studies my face. 'But he's with Fliss? They're a couple?'

'Hardly! They hate each other. We've been thrown together because of the crash. That doesn't mean any of us have become friends, let alone intimate.'

Their eyes narrow. 'Kai claimed Fliss was his girlfriend. He acted scared yesterday.'

I sway and steady myself against the wall. Kai has tried to protect Lou by driving them away, the way I did with Mum.

'He's in trouble, isn't he? It's something to do with the burglary.' They scrutinise my face. 'Or the bus crash? He's been acting oddly ever since.'

I glance away. 'I don't know, sorry.'

'You're lying. I think you're *all* lying – it *must* be to do with the accident. That's why you're spending so much time together. You're hiding something that happened that day.'

I can't meet Lou's gaze. It's like they can see straight through me.

'Fine. Don't tell me. But this is important.' They lower their voice as a pupil walks past into the classroom. 'Can I trust you not to repeat what I'm about to say? This *cannot* spread around the sixth form. You've seen how quickly gossip travels.'

316

'Of course!' I say automatically, despite the fact I barely trust myself.

'I had a worrying message about Kai this morning. I thought about speaking to Fliss, but if she's not really his girlfriend—'

'Hey! What's going on?'

I spin round as Tristram approaches. A frown is fixed on his face.

'We were just discussing who stuck this note on Liam's back,' Lou says quickly, brandishing the piece of paper.

Tristram bursts out laughing. 'Mystery over! It was banter – something to lighten the mood.'

'Wait . . . It was you?' My eyes widen.

'Yes, before I nipped to the toilet.' He smirks. 'Oh, lighten up! Why can't you ever take a joke?'

I bite my lip.

'Why don't *you* lighten up?' Lou says. 'Or, better still, get more depth. I've met puddles deeper than you. What kind of person does that to their boyfriend?'

Tristram's fists tighten into balls. His eyes glitter dangerously as he stares at Lou and then me. I take a step backwards but Lou doesn't move.

'What are you all doing here?' Mr Wilson calls out, walking briskly down the corridor. 'Get inside for registration.'

Lou shares a sympathetic smile, but Tristram storms into the classroom without a backwards glance. I'm about to follow but Mr Wilson touches my arm.

'I'm glad to see you're still in one piece, Liam. I'll mark you as here, but you're needed in the head's office.'

My body tenses.

'I'm sure it's a personal welcome back, not a week of detentions!'

As I'm walking away, Lou pokes their head round the door. 'Find me later!'

'Affirmative. And thank you.'

My eyes sting with tears as I wind through the empty corridors. Was Tristram punishing me for refusing him beer at the Lobster Bar or not texting yesterday? But he never messaged me either! Maybe he's right and I lack a sense of humour. But there was nothing funny about the way he looked at Lou. Tristram was like a completely different person. His eyes were as cold as crystallised nitrogen.

My mood takes a further drop in temperature as I reach Mr Gordon's office. Fliss and Layla are waiting in the seats of doom: the red chairs that kids sit in before being given detentions or worse.

'Do you know what this is about?' Layla asks as I draw closer.

I shrug, trying not to appear nervous. 'My form teacher thinks Mr Gordon wants to check we're doing all right.'

Fliss tosses her hair. 'He might offer counselling or half-days.'

Thomas, the PA, keeps his gaze fixed on the computer screen as he picks up the telephone and informs Mr Gordon we've arrived.

'You can go in,' he says solemnly.

Fliss knocks and enters first. I almost walk into her as she stops abruptly. Stepping round her, I see Mr Gordon. His arms are folded. Standing next to him are two police officers. I recognise the policewoman – she helped us at the clifftop.

'Thank you for coming so promptly,' she says.

Fliss bristles. 'Did we have a choice? I don't appreciate an ambush.' She glances between the officers. 'We've answered your questions about the accident. We don't have anything to add, especially without legal representation.'

The policewoman nods. 'You can request a solicitor at the police station. We're arresting you all on suspicion of theft and money laundering.'

Layla gasps. 'What?'

She gapes at Mr Gordon. His face is pinched with worry.

'This can't be right!' Fliss shouts. 'What the hell's going on?'

'DC Walker wants to reinterview the four of you about the bus crash,' she explains.

'All four of us?' Layla repeats numbly.

'Kai was arrested in Bristol last night. He's currently in custody and being interviewed at Kingsborough police station.'

A strangled cry escapes from Fliss's lips as the policewoman cautions us. She bends over, gripping her side.

In the distance, I hear the officer say Fliss is hyperventilating. Mr Gordon thinks she needs an ambulance.

My ears buzz.

Fear gnaws at the pit of my stomach.

I close my eyes as the room tilts.

Time shifts.

I feel like I'm being sucked into a black hole. There's no escape.

38

RESTRICTED

RECORD OF INTERVIEW

Person interviewed: Kai Marsden

Place of interview: Kingsborough Police Station

Date of interview: Monday, 30 September

Time commenced: 11 a.m.

Time concluded: 11.30 a.m.

Duration of interview: 30 minutes

Interviewers: DC Walker, DC Eastern

Other persons present: Howard Childs, Solicitor. Eleanor Longfield, Appropriate Adult

DC Walker: This is a continuation of the interview of Kai Marsden. Can you confirm that you have accepted new legal representation since this morning's first interview?

Kai: Yeah. I mean, I'm not going to turn down a free hotshot lawyer, am I?

DC Walker: And can you confirm we haven't spoken to you about the matter for which you're being questioned since that first interview?

Kai: I told you a few things this morning about the fifties I found after the crash, but not since . . .

Mr Childs: I would advise you not to say anything else.

DC Eastern: For the benefit of the tape, Kai has shrugged his shoulders and muttered 'okay'.

DC Walker: I would like to pick up where we left off. This morning we showed CCTV footage of you paying for items in several Sandstown shops with fifty-pound notes. You admitted you found £16,000 where the bus went over the cliff – which accounts for your cash expenditure and the contents of your rucksack.

Kai: Mmmm.

DC Walker: We have run financial records and discovered multiple bank accounts in your name, containing a total of £6,800. You used these accounts to pay for a house rental. Can you explain where this money originated from?

Mr Childs: I would advise my client to make no further comment.

Kai: Exactly that.

DC Walker: The next subject matter is regarding the three other survivors – Layla Abdullatif, Fliss Cavendish and Liam

King. Can you confirm how much money they came across at the crash scene?

Mr Childs: My client will make no comment.

Kai: Did Layla betray me? Did she give you my address in Bristol and pretend I was waving a gun around? Seriously, I've never had a weapon.

DC Walker: I'm not at liberty to say who tipped us off about your whereabouts – after I told you not to leave Sandstown.

Kai: Sorry about that. I forgot. I also forgot to say 'no comment'.

DC Eastern: Moving on. Do you know how Liam managed to pay £20,000 in cash for a Jeep? Or how Layla's brother's JustGiving page received £210,000 days after the crash?

Kai: On taking legal advice, I'm saying nothing.

DC Walker: You're a bright boy, Kai.

Kai: Are you taking the piss?

DC Walker: No, I'm being straight with you. You're clever enough to realise that you're in a jam. I'm offering you a way out if you help us and tell the truth about what happened that day. We think a large amount of money was being transported in the school bus by Silas Greenhill and that the four of you discovered it shortly before or after the crash and decided to split it for various reasons.

Kai: I've no idea what you're talking about.

DC Walker: We've traced the source of your bank deposits to a carwash, the same premises that paid deposits into Liam's bank accounts and a large sum – £210,000 – into Layla's JustGiving fundraising account. We are making attempts to speak to the owners of the carwash.

Mr Childs: That's a statement, not a question, and my client has nothing to add.

Kai: I have a question. . . are you saying, you don't know where they are?

DC Walker: The business has closed and the owners have vanished. Do you have any information about why that might be the case?

Kai: Why would I? I don't own a car. I never visit carwashes.

Mr Childs: Kai!

Kai: What?

DC Walker: Thank you for confirming that fact. We will check the CCTV system left on the premises to verify whether you ever visited.

Kai: Oh. I didn't mean . . . I meant . . .

Mr Childs: Stop talking.

DC Eastern: We believe all four of you have committed theft, but Fliss covered her tracks more successfully than the rest of you. She didn't go mad and flash the cash around. But we're asking her about that directly.

Kai: You're questioning Fliss?

DC Walker: Yes – and Layla and Liam. All three have been arrested. They're being interviewed separately with their legal representation.

Kai: Oh.

Mr Childs: I'm only interested in what's happening to my client. Where is the evidence he laundered or stole money? You haven't traced the carwash owners. You're fishing for information and my client has no further comment.

DC Walker: Well, let's see about that. I want to help you, Kai.

Kai: Yeah. Sure you do.

DC Walker: Think about it. Four of you are here today. One of you will inevitably talk. It's going to look much, much better for the person who tells us the truth first, because we will get to the truth, Kai, eventually.

Kai: Are you offering me some sort of deal?

DC Eastern: We're not allowed to offer you a deal. What we're telling you is that things tend to turn out better for people who are honest from the outset.

Mr Childs: Say nothing.

DC Walker: I think, deep down, you want to do the right thing. Tell us what the four of you did that day.

Kai: I . . . I'm not sure . . .

Mr Childs: My client needs another comfort break.

DC Walker: Sure – and during your break have a good think about what we've said. But don't leave it long. One of the others might decide to tell the truth first.

Kai: Thanks. I used to think you were nice.

DC Walker: No, you didn't. You used to think I was stupid. The others too.

Kai: Yeah. I get that a lot.

DC Eastern: I think we'll stop the tape there. The time by my watch is 11.30 a.m. and we're turning off the machine.

39

FLISS

Who took the deal?

It wasn't offered in those terms exactly, but I could read between the lines in the interview. During a break, my solicitor explained that a court will look more favourably on the person who comes clean first out of the four of us.

It was tempting to throw the others under the bus, so to speak, but that would have meant losing my money. *And theirs*. I have other plans. Hopefully they toed the line as instructed. I'd faked a panic attack when we were arrested. As Mr Gordon radioed for an ambulance, I mouthed 'say nothing' to Layla and Liam.

Kai is a different matter. God knows what his crappy duty solicitor allowed him to let slip. Mother paid for the best legal representation for me – a lawyer charging £1,000 an hour – who stonewalled every question with 'no comment'. It was the least she could do since she didn't turn up.

I lean against the side of Aaron's Range Rover. He's listening to music with his eyes shut. Layla walks out first. Her shoulders are curved, as if she's trying to make herself appear smaller. That's not the demeanour of someone in the clear. Kai is next – limping but his chin is thrust upwards defiantly. He could have brazened it out. Liam leaves last with his mum. She puts her arm round him, guiding him down the steps as if he's incapable of walking by himself.

Who betrayed me?

They exchange a few words after spotting me across the street, and Liam's mum walks to her car. Layla, Kai and Liam head over.

As they approach, Layla calls out, 'Did you take the deal?'

Liam sighs. 'I keep telling you, they weren't offering a deal!'

I stand ramrod straight, like Kai, ready for battle, breathing through the sudden stabbing pain in my ribs.

'Do you think I'd be waiting for you here if I'd spilled the beans?'

'Well, *we* didn't cooperate either,' Kai says coolly.

'I find that hard to believe,' I counter.

I stare at them, attempting to judge their reactions. But they're not giving much away. They all look exhausted.

'Maybe you're calling our bluff and stitching *us* up,' Kai continues.

'I swear I didn't. I'm not in the clear yet – I've been released under investigation and have to hand over my phone within twenty-four hours.'

Kai nods, shoving his hands in his pockets. 'Sounds familiar. Plus, I have no idea when they might haul me back.'

Layla tries to make eye contact with him, but he won't meet her gaze.

'Same here,' she says quietly.

'Ditto,' Liam adds. 'They found my bank accounts but didn't charge me, thanks to the solicitor who offered to represent me for free, instead of the duty one. She shut down their lines of questioning and claimed I hadn't brought my phone to school.'

'Mine too. He said the police don't have enough evidence to charge us *yet*.' Layla takes a deep breath, as her eyes well with tears. 'But they've searched my house for evidence and want to examine my mobile. Obviously they haven't found anything incriminating so far, but if they discover the rest of the stash, we'll probably all go to jail. We should dump it, as agreed, while we can.'

'It all makes sense, Layla,' Kai drawls. 'You wanted the police to catch me red-handed with the cash in Bristol so the rest of you could get off scot-free?' He glares at her. 'You're just like everyone else. You betrayed me.'

Her eyes widen. 'You honestly think I'd do that?'

'Only you knew exactly where I was – I coughed up my address like a total moron because . . .' He bites his lip. 'Not long after, I had guns pointed in my face.'

She gulps, shaking her head. 'It wasn't me, I swear! I'd never betray you.'

Kai frowns. 'So how did they know?' He turns to Liam. 'Did you see my address on Layla's phone?'

'No!'

'Why should I believe you after you faked your car break-in?'

'You did what?!' I say. 'You little—'

Layla cuts in, crossing her arms. '*Did* you lie about that?'

He hesitates. 'Yeah, I'm sorry. But I promise I didn't do this!'

'Unbelievable!' Layla exclaims. 'I was worried you'd be targeted after my burglary, and it was all a lie!'

'I'm not proud of what I did. I wanted to tell you everything.' He reaches out to touch her arm, but she backs away.

I bite back a smile. When they turn on each other, they forget about me.

'There is another explanation,' I point out. 'The gang found out where Kai was hiding and tipped off the police.'

'Why would they do that?' Liam interjects. 'Why didn't they torture him until he told them where the money is hidden?'

'Thanks a million! I guess that's what you'd have done in their shoes?'

'I'm saying it doesn't make sense to get you arrested when you could confess.'

Kai glares at him. 'Are you sure *you* haven't secretly blabbed?'

'I gave nothing away. But what did you accidentally let slip that incriminates the rest of us? The money laundering? I've calculated the chances of you—'

'I swear to God if you come out with an equation, I'll flatten you.'

Layla steps between them before World War Three erupts.

'Maybe the gang was unsure Kai definitely would return,' I say. 'Tipping off the police guaranteed he'd be here today. They have all four of us, together with the money and out of custody.'

As if on cue, our mobile phones vibrate.

Liam's voice trembles as he reads out the *Thieves* WhatsApp message:

Hope Kai, Liam and Layla appreciated our lawyers. At 2 a.m. leave all the cash in black rucksacks inside the sea tractor. We'll be watching. Tip off the police and we'll kill your loved ones. Starting with Liam's mum. We know when she's off shift.

40

LIAM

I wish I could use my knowledge of quantum physics to turn back time.

I'd tell DC Walker everything. Or I'd rewind further and never agree to split the money in the first place. I'd hand over the holdall to the police. Actually this £1 million is cursed. I should have hurled it off the cliff and my life would be normal.

But now Mum could die and it's my fault.

I'll never forget the look on her face inside the police station – a mixture of hurt, shock and shame. *Please tell me these detectives are wrong – you didn't steal that money?*

Telling her the truth was out of the question and I stuck to my scratchcard story, saying a Plymouth shopkeeper never challenged my age. I'm hoping a confidentiality clause will prevent DC Walker from checking my alleged claim with the lottery company. Anyway, it'll give me enough time to get rid of my incriminating notes. I've ditched my original plan to switch the real bank notes with duds. Next, I must persuade the others not to call the police after we make the drop. They wouldn't listen earlier, or when I messaged, but I'll do whatever it takes to protect my mum.

I put the torch between my teeth as I carefully lift the panelling and open the storage space beneath the holiday home. This is where I'd dropped off Kai after we'd picked up the holdall – he must have been staying here while it was empty. But tonight two BMWs are sitting in the driveway. The owners may have unexpectedly returned from London, or they're out-of-season holidaymakers. Either way, I could be caught red-handed retrieving thousands of pounds of stolen cash if I'm not careful. Something rustles in the bushes behind me. My heart beats faster as I swing my torch, picking out menacing dark shapes.

A fox streaks across the lawn.

I breathe out deeply and turn back, reaching into the space to feel for my rucksack, which is lodged behind kayaks and bodyboards. A twig snaps and the outside light flickers on, brightly illuminating the garden.

This is bad – the security light has been triggered by movement and it's not mine . . . If anyone peers out of the window, I'll be caught. I stretch in further as another light goes on. This time it's inside the house.

My fingers curl round the strap. I brace myself to protect my back and pull it hard. The bag's heavy with cash.

I manage to drag it out and stumble to my feet. I don't have time to replace the panelling. I hear the click of the back door.

'Who's there?' a man shouts.

I press myself against the wall.

That's when I see movement by the hedge.

A shadowy figure.

I hold my breath until my lungs feel like they're about to burst, as the person straightens up. They back away, deeper into the shadows.

Someone else is in the garden, watching my every move.

41

LAYLA

'Did you bring all the money?' My torch picks out Kai in the inky darkness, making his way across the deserted car park.

I'm torn between wanting to hug or slap him. I swallow the painful lump in my throat. How could he think I'd betray him? I thought something was developing between us, that he had feelings for me, but I must have misread the signs.

He shields his eyes from the beam. 'You're blinding me.'

I don't lower the torch. 'Well, did you?'

'Don't you trust me?' He holds up the bulky black rucksack.

'You don't trust *me*,' I stress.

He lowers the bag to the ground, blinking. I aim the beam at his hands until he fumbles with the straps. Throwing it open, he points at the piles of notes.

'And the rest,' I tell him.

'I didn't bring decoys.' He plunges his hand deeper and pulls out wads of fifties. 'Do you believe me now?'

'Sure, *Kyle*.'

'Funny.' Kai fastens his bag. 'Look, I've apologised. How many more times do you need to hear it before you forgive me?'

I fold my arms.

'I'm truly sorry, I lost my rag.' He takes a step closer. 'I went through some stuff in Bristol and wasn't thinking straight.' His eyes mist over. 'It was wrong of me to take it out on you. Please, Layla. I can't bear the thought of you hating me.'

'Of course I don't!' I sigh. It's impossible to stay angry with him for long. 'You're forgiven.'

I manage a small smile. It's good to see him, plus *I* haven't been completely honest since the crash.

'Thank you. I thought I'd been careful, but you're right, the gang must have followed me back to the B&B. That's the only explanation apart from—' The words catch in his throat.

'What?'

I shine the torch on his face again.

He shakes his head. 'Nothing.'

So much for trusting each other! He's holding something back.

We both swing round at approaching footsteps and the flickering light of a torch. My beam picks out Fliss, dressed from top to toe in black, no doubt designer gear. She glares at me until I lower the beam. She does the same.

'I think I've put my back out.' She swings her rucksack to the ground.

Hmmm. I wonder if Kai was right. Does it contain real fifty-pound notes, or has she loaded it with something heavy?

'Before you ask, it's *all* the cash and not fakes.' She bends down, flicking open the strap. 'Take a look if you want.'

Kai steps forward and digs his hands deep inside the rucksack. 'We never doubted you,' he drawls.

'Ha! The feeling's mutual. Show me *your* money.'

'Layla can vouch for me, but sure.'

Fliss searches his rucksack.

'Happy?' he asks.

'Ecstatic.' She pauses for a fraction of a second. 'We're all in this together.'

Are we?

We've never felt further apart. Liam lied about the car break-in and could have fibbed about his police interview. Kai doesn't trust me, and I've deliberately misled him. Fliss would happily stab us all in the back.

'Where's Liam?' Kai asks. 'It's not like him to be late.'

'No idea,' Fliss replies. 'I haven't seen him.'

'Are you sure your plan will work?' I clench my fists to stop my hands from trembling.

'Absolutely not!' she retorts. 'Liam may have told DC Walker everything or the gang will attempt to kill us. We could end up dead or in prison tonight.'

Kai bursts out laughing, breaking the tension. 'Great pep talk. You should become a motivational speaker when you leave school.'

'That's if I'm still alive by then.' Fliss checks her watch. 'Where *is* Liam?'

I pull out the phone from my pocket, but it slips from my grasp and clatters on the ground. I scoop it up – thankfully, the screen is undamaged.

'We don't have time to hang around,' Kai says. 'Let's get these rucksacks down to the sea tractor. Liam can catch up.'

'Agreed!' Fliss flings the rucksack over her shoulder with another small groan and pulls out her mobile.

'I can carry it if you want?' Kai suggests.

'Not a chance!'

'You reckon I'll try to steal it between here and the beach?'

She doesn't reply.

'I'll take that as a yes. Thanks a lot!'

Fliss snorts. 'I bet you've thought about it.'

'Quiet!' I hiss. 'I heard something.'

A light bounces up and down across the car park. Fliss's torchlight fixes on the figure jogging towards us.

Liam.

'Sorry,' he says, panting. 'Almost got caught collecting my cash.'

'By the police?' Kai demands. 'Or worse?'

'Holidaymakers.' He puts his hands on his waist, attempting to get his breath.

'Are you okay?' I ask.

'I will be if we keep the police out of this.' He exhales deeply. 'We let the gang take the money, and don't tell DC Walker. You heard what they could do to my mum. They'll come after your families next.'

'We've been over this on WhatsApp,' Fliss says through gritted teeth. 'We've got less cash than the gang expects, and they'll take revenge. They've got to be caught in the act. It's the only way any of us will be safe, including your mum.'

'She's right,' I tell him. 'I doubt any of us will survive tonight if we don't try to get them arrested with the rucksacks.'

Liam sighs. He must have calculated the odds of us living until tomorrow. They can't be high.

'Let's put it to a vote,' Kai says. 'We tip off the police

and let the gang take the fall, not us. Raise your hand if you agree.'

I feel for Liam. I can't imagine my blind terror if the gang had named anyone from my family, but this is our best shot at survival.

'I honestly think this is the right move.' I lift my hand.

Fliss does the same.

'Three against one,' Kai says. 'I'm sorry, mate.'

Liam turns away, wiping his eyes with the sleeve of his anorak. I try to put my arm round his shoulders, but he shrugs me off. Nothing I say will make him feel better.

'We need a good spot where our mobiles work.' Kai turns to Fliss. 'Did you pick up a burner?'

'Yeah.' She pats her pocket. 'Mother needed spare staff phones over the summer and Aaron paid for them in cash.' She pauses. 'Before we go, we should check Liam's rucksack.'

He spins round, his eyes moist. 'You think I'd risk my mum's life for money?'

'Of course not!' Kai and I say in unison.

Fliss doesn't reply. Liam stares scathingly at her before shoving the rucksack closer with his foot.

She searches it, pulling out tightly bound packs of fifty-pound notes.

'Fine,' she says. 'We're all being honest.'

Are we? I shove my hands into my pockets and avoid eye contact with the others.

Kai puts on a head torch. 'Turn off your torches and phones. They may have an early lookout. This should be enough light to get us down to the beach.'

Fliss gasps as the beam dies in Liam's torch, followed by mine as we both obey.

'I'm not risking breaking my neck for you lot.' She grips her torch firmly, holding her mobile.

Kai sighs and takes the lead down the narrow sandy path, which is enclosed with bramble and trailing weeds. I'm next, followed by Fliss and Liam. The light from her torch dances over my shoulder, revealing sharp jagged stones.

She takes a big gulp of air. What's up with her? Her breathing is becoming ragged. She stumbles, grabbing my arm, and we both almost topple into nettles.

'Careful!'

She hangs on to my arm tightly and doesn't let go.

'Fliss? What's wrong?'

Before she can reply, a loud bang rings out.

'Gunshot!' Kai yells.

42

FLISS

Someone's fired a gun!

I drop my phone and rucksack as a high-pitched animal-like scream pierces the inky blackness. It's coming from my mouth. Layla spins round, horror etched on her face. She mouths 'run'. Her torch falls to the ground. Fear spikes in my chest, but I'm rooted to the spot. My torch picks her out, staggering backwards. She scrambles over Kai's rucksack and half runs, half stumbles after him down the path to the beach. They both disappear as the light from his head torch is snuffed out.

Liam yanks my arm. 'We have to get out of here!'

I trip over his rucksack. Stones stab my hands. He hauls me to my feet. We're heading back up the path, but my legs aren't working properly. They're solid and immovable like concrete.

'Turn off your torch!' he cries.

I scrabble to find the switch, but my hands are shaking uncontrollably. Liam rips it from my fingers. Before the light goes out, I catch a glimpse of red smears on my fingers. *Blood.*

'Keep going!' Liam urges.

I cling on to his arm helplessly. My breath comes out in painful judders.

Something dark and terrible tugs at the corners of my brain. It pulls me back to the clifftop behind the hotel that summer night. I'm running.

Roaring waves crash on the rocks below, but they fail to drown out the pounding of footsteps. I trip, dropping my mobile. Sharp stones slice my fingertips as I scrabble for it before he catches up.

I hear ragged gasps of breath. I try to get my bearings from the light. Have I picked the right path? Panic spikes in my chest.

Dead end! I'm at the northernmost tip of the island, a metre from the edge.

Slowly I turn round. I lift my phone. The light picks out a familiar figure lurching towards me: Robert Brody.

'Why are you running away?' he asks, frowning. 'I thought you wanted this?'

*

I'm trying to fight off the hand on my arm.

A familiar voice hisses in my ear. 'Get down and stop screaming!'

Liam.

I'm back in the present, which is far more terrifying.

He forces me into a crouching position next to him. My heart judders violently against my ribcage.

'We. Have. To. Keep going. Before. They shoot us.' My words escape in gulps, leaving me breathless.

'I'm not certain it was a gunshot,' Liam whispers. 'When I fired the gun last week, the acoustics and reverberation sounded different.'

'What else could it have been? Someone's back there. They want to kill us!'

'Maybe that's what they want us to think,' he replies. 'This could be a trick to make us abandon the rucksacks – and, look, it's worked! We've left hundreds of thousands of pounds on the path. I have to check it's still there.'

'Don't leave me!' I beg.

'I won't be long, I promise. Stay here and I'll come back and find you.'

'No!'

I make a grab for his arm, but he's gone.

I'm alone in the darkness.

With memories of what I did that night.

I retch, emptying the contents of my stomach. My plan has gone badly wrong. Earlier I'd hidden another identical rucksack, packed with stones and newspaper notes, close to the sea tractor, ready to be swapped for the one I was carrying while the others were distracted.

Now I'm too afraid to follow Liam or stay where I am.

I hear a muffled noise nearby. Did someone catch their breath? That sounded human. Is it a member of the gang or my blackmailer? I'd messaged them with the time and place of the drop-off. Either way, I'm not hanging around to find out. I crawl on my hands and knees up the path, terror prickling in my chest.

If I make it out of here, I'll call the police.

Isn't that the promise I made when I was trapped on the bus?

It's what I told Mother we should do after what happened on the clifftop.

If DC Walker arrives quickly, he'll catch whoever's after the cash. I ignore the painful jabs to my knees and fingertips from sharp stones. Eventually the ground levels out. Earth and rocks morph into concrete. The car park! I'm safe. I search my pockets and pull out the burner. It doesn't have a light, but I retrieve the only mobile number added – DC Walker's.

My finger hovers over the call button as I hear the screech of tyres. Bright headlights blind me as a van screeches through the entrance. I drop the phone. My mind screams: *Run!* But my legs aren't moving. The driver is wearing a balaclava. He slams on the brakes. The rear door flies open and a masked man jumps out. My mouth opens wide, but before I can scream, he's grabbed me. A hood covers my head and I'm in a tight bear hug, fighting for my life. I'm kicking and screaming as he hurls me, ragdoll-like, into the back of the van. As I struggle to sit up, his fist looms above me. It comes crashing down. Pain explodes in my temple.

I slump forward.

My head strikes the floor. My hands are yanked behind my back and tied.

Through the fabric I see bright white.

The flash of a camera.

The doors slam shut.

I slip away into darkness.

43

LIAM

I scrabble around the rucksacks in the dark, trying to find one of the dropped torches. When I manage to switch it on, the beam picks out Kai. He flicks on his head torch as he approaches.

'Was that for real?' he whispers, crouching down beside me.

'I'm not sure. I'm thinking it could have been a firecracker, something to scare us off.'

'It worked!'

'Not necessarily.' I jerk my head at the scattered bags. 'Why didn't they take them if this is a hoax?'

'Maybe we weren't supposed to come back?' he replies. 'Or it could have been a random nut playing a prank. Either way, let's get moving. Layla's on the beach, waiting for us.'

He throws a rucksack over each shoulder. I grab the third.

'Did you hear that?' I spin round at a distant shriek.

'No. What?'

'I thought I heard a cry.' I glance up the path.

'Probably an owl.'

I'm not sure. It sounded human.

'I left Fliss up there. She's too scared to come down.'

A rustling noise in the brambles makes us both stop in our tracks.

My heartbeat spikes.

'Is that a fox?' Kai asks.

I shiver as I think about the animal in the garden earlier. It wasn't alone. Someone was watching as I retrieved my hidden cash.

Kai's eyes narrow. 'What is it?'

I shake my head. 'I should fetch Fliss. Let her know what's happening.'

'We don't have time. Let's get to the drop point. Text her and say there's been a change of plan.'

I fish out the mobile from my pocket and send a message, but within seconds there's a ping. Her phone lights up by the side of the path and returns to darkness. She dropped it!

'If she's lost the burner as well, we're screwed,' Kai says. 'We can't tip off DC Walker without using our phones, which identify us.'

I'm glad it's dark and Kai can't see my panic. Our plan is unravelling fast. Whoever was spying on me, could be here.

'Let's get on with this.' I'm counting prime numbers under my breath and attempting to sound calm.

We walk silently down the path, until the rocks under foot become soft sand. Across the shimmering water, the island is mostly shrouded in darkness, but spotlights pick out the distinctive dark grey slate turrets of the Sea Haven.

'Layla?' Kai hisses.

She emerges from the shadows, running towards the torchlight. Her face is taut with worry.

'What was it?' she asks.

'We're not sure,' Kai replies. 'But the plan has changed – it's dump and run.'

She takes a rucksack from Kai and leads the way towards the prehistoric monster shape in the distance – the sea tractor. When we reach it, I climb the metal steps and hurl my rucksack on to the three-metre-high platform. Kai and Layla pass me their bags.

The sound of driftwood snapping rings out as I jump back on to the sand. We spin round.

Goose bumps rise on my skin. The hair on the back of my neck prickles.

We're being watched.

'Who's there?' Kai shouts. 'We've left the money for you.'
He focuses his head torch on the path.

'Let's take the long way round the beach,' Layla urges.
'Avoid that route completely.'

'But Fliss has the burner!' I point out. 'We need to find
her.'

'Shit!' she exclaims.

There's more rustling from the path. Louder this time.

'We don't have a choice!' Layla hisses. 'We have to move!'

A pinging noise pierces the darkness, followed by
vibrations. Kai and Layla fumble for their phones. Me too.
Layla lets out a cry. Kai shudders.

'What is—' I can't finish my sentence.

A photo has landed in the Thieves WhatsApp group. My
stomach is in tight hard knots as I open it.

A girl lies in the back of a vehicle, hands tied behind her
back. A hood covers her face, but I recognise the long flowing
auburn hair and black clothing.

Fliss.

Our phones light up with another message:

Call the police and she dies.

44

FLISS

I'm alive.

My eyelids flutter open, but I can't see anything. It's completely dark.

My brain is sluggish.

What happened? Where am I?

Don't lose control. Focus.

I'm lying on cold uneven ground. I hear water lapping. Strange echoes. I move my arms, but they're tightly bound.

My head throbs and my ribs are in spasm. I try to open my mouth to cry out, but I'm gagged. I swallow hard to stop vomit from rising in my throat. I could choke to death.

Breathe. Stay calm.

Count backwards, the way Liam taught you. Ten, nine, eight . . .

I haven't been through all this for my life to end here. *Alone.*

351

I taste something coppery and bitter in my mouth. Blood.

It takes me back to that hotel suite with Mother's VIP guest, Robert Brody.

I should leave.

Robert was funny and charming in the bar, refilling my glass with the most expensive champagne and showering me with compliments. Up in his suite, things have changed. We'd started making out and pulled off each other's clothes, kissing passionately. We took a few selfies.

Now I want to slow things down, it's like a switch has been flicked. He's a completely different person.

'Are you a prick-tease?' he asks, as I clamber off the bed.

I grab my top from the floor and turn round, attempting to wrestle it over my head. Suddenly pain explodes down the side of my face and I'm lying on the carpet. There's blood in my mouth. He hit me!

My phone is on the bedside table. I can't reach it.

His mobile rings. As he answers the call, I drag myself along the floor towards the door. I'm almost there!

'Where are you going?'

Robert clasps my ankle and drags me back.

I scream and scream, kicking at him. His hand clamps over my mouth, muffling my cries.

Bang, bang, bang.

'Fliss? Are you in there? Open this door!'

Aaron!

A few seconds later Aaron shouts, 'I have the master key.'

Robert lets go of my leg as the door clicks open.

'Get the hell off her!'

Hands pull me into a seated position. The hood, followed by the gag, is ripped off, and my hands untied.

'Help me!' I whisper feebly.

I blink and blink as my eyes adjust to the dim light.

I'm staring into piercing turquoise eyes and . . . Donald Trump. He's dressed in black, pointing a gun and holding a device in his other gloved hand.

'Let me go.' My voice gathers in strength. 'My mother will give you anything you want but don't hurt me!'

His hand slowly reaches to the realistic-looking prosthetic mask.

'No!' I shout.

I screw my eyes tightly shut. I know what this means. I've seen enough Netflix movies. *If you see their face, they don't plan to let you live.*

'Look at me,' a strange distorted voice says.

I shake my head vigorously. 'I don't want to die! I'll do anything. I'll tell you where all the money is!'

'Look at my face,' the voice repeats. It sounds odd, like a computer is talking.

I feel the coldness of the gun barrel against my skin. The weapon lifts my chin, forcing me to look up as he rips off the mask.

A scream dies in my throat. My whole body freezes.

Despite the coloured contact lenses and the disguise I recognise them.

I can't believe it. I *won't* believe it.

'Y-y-you!'

It's the only word I manage to utter before the gloved hand points the gun squarely at the centre of my forehead.

I watch in disbelief as they pull the trigger.

45

KAI

Click!

I've seen enough movies. There's no mistaking that sound – the safety catch being taken off a gun.

It takes me a few more seconds to process who's holding the weapon.

Layla.

Her hands tremble as she points the weapon towards the path.

'It wasn't Fliss,' I splutter. 'You had it all along!'

Her voice wavers. 'I'm sorry. I was going to confess the night you were arrested. I hid it in Salih's soft toy box in my bedroom and, later, beneath the garden shed. The police never found it.' She takes another breath. 'I knew I'd never actually use it. I didn't trust . . .'

The unspoken accusation hangs heavily in the air.

'Any of us,' Liam finishes. 'Thanks very much.'

'Jeez.'

I look away, my cheeks smarting. I remind myself I have no right to be hurt – I accused her of being a snitch, and I'm betraying her terribly tonight.

'We should call the police,' I say, holding my mobile.

'And get Fliss killed? I know you're not her biggest fan . . .' Liam adjusts his glasses as he stares up the cliff face. 'I don't think we can risk it.'

'If they're watching and see you use a phone, they could shoot her,' Layla points out. 'Let's leave the rucksacks and hope that's enough to save her.'

Hope is in short supply tonight. But what else can we do? We're out of options. My finger hovers over 'emergency call'. They're both right. We have no idea where Fliss is being held. By the time police officers get here, she'll be dead.

'Does it have bullets?' Liam nods at the gun.

'I unloaded it, but whoever's out there doesn't know the barrel is empty.'

'It could be handy,' I say. 'Let's get outta here!'

Layla shines her torch across the sands. A dark expanse of water laps on to the beach. My heart contracts. It's high tide. We're trapped!

'We'll have to swim to get over to the next bay.' Layla's voice quakes.

'It's dangerous in the dark,' Liam says. 'There's a rip tide over by the rocks. I haven't been in the sea since I was a kid. I'll get swept out.'

My knee is throbbing, but I don't want to admit I could have difficulties.

'What about you, Layla?' I ask.

Her voice wobbles. 'I'm a weak swimmer.'

'The only way is up.' I point my head torch at the path weaving to the top of the cliff face.

'We'd be sitting ducks,' Layla says.

'We *definitely* are down here.'

'I'm not sure,' Liam says slowly. 'Something doesn't feel right.'

'No shit!' I exclaim. 'Fliss has been kidnapped and they're hunting us.'

'But it doesn't make any sense when you think about it logically.'

I'm too tense to roll my eyes at him.

'Why didn't they ambush us and take the rucksacks while they had the chance?' he continues. 'Unless . . . Oh. This isn't good.'

'What?' I prompt.

'I think they snatched Fliss as *their* backup plan in case we tricked them. I mean, how did they know we would tip off the police? It could have been a lucky guess, but they always manage to predict what we'll do next.' He swallows. 'For example, how did they get Kai's address in Bristol?'

'Someone betrayed him,' Layla replies. 'But it wasn't *me.*'

Or something. The thought had crossed my mind in the car park, but I'd dismissed it. I groan as I check back through our WhatsApp exchanges.

'They've hacked our phones and read our messages.'

'Omigod!' Layla cries. 'Seriously? Fliss said WhatsApp is encrypted!'

'We discussed *everything.* I messaged you my B&B address. Fliss told us she'd ring DC Walker on her burner.'

Another louder scuffling noise makes us jump. Layla's hands shake as she raises the gun, pointing it in the direction of the path.

'We're armed! We have the money. Seven hundred and sixty-two thousand as agreed. Let Fliss go! Please don't hurt her.'

A figure moves in the darkness. My heart thuds painfully. My skin prickles with fear.

'Show your hands,' Layla yells.

The person walks towards us, shielding their eyes.

'Put the gun down,' a familiar voice says.

As they step closer towards the light, Layla's hand lowers.

'Lou!' Liam exclaims.

'W-w-what are you doing here?' I stutter.

'Following you. Or, rather, Liam.'

'M-m-me?' It's his turn to stammer.

'DC Walker messaged, saying Kai had been arrested. That's what I was trying to tell you this morning before you were arrested in Mr Gordon's office.'

Liam gulps, 'You know about that?'

'It spread like wildfire around the sixth form.' They look from Layla to Liam. 'I waited outside the police station after school and saw you talking to Fliss. I figured none of you would tell me what was going on and that I'd have to find out myself.' They turn round and meet my gaze. 'I staked out Mrs Gibson's house – I thought you might lie low in her grounds. Instead, I saw Liam visiting a holiday home further up the road.'

'That was you in the garden?!' he exclaims.

'I was trying to figure out what you were nicking. I followed you here and hid on the path as you came to the beach.'

'I wasn't stealing anything – I was searching for my rucksack,' Liam stresses.

'Which you'd hidden beneath a stranger's house? That sounds dead legit. Almost as legal as the gun Layla's waving around.' Lou folds their arms. 'Well?'

'You need to leave before you get caught up in this,' I tell them.

Their eyes blaze with indignation. 'In what? Don't lie to me again. Fliss isn't your girlfriend. Who's got her? And how the hell do you have seven hundred and sixty-two thousand pounds?'

Layla lays the gun on the sand. 'You should tell them.'

I sigh heavily. She's right.

'The short version is, we found a stack of money the day of the bus crash and decided to split it. We didn't realise it belonged to drug dealers. They want it back.'

Lou raises their eyebrow. 'You put your lives on the line for money?'

'We had our reasons,' Layla says defensively. 'But it was a huge mistake and now they're threatening to kill us. They abducted Fliss from the path.'

'More likely from the car park,' Lou says. 'I heard her stumble past.'

'Well, they have her,' I admit. 'They're coming for the cash and the three of us. I don't want you to get hurt. I never wanted that to happen. I can't let you get involved in any of this.'

'Is that why . . .?' The words catch in their throat. 'You've been trying to protect me?'

'Yes! Please leave while you have a chance.'

'I'm not going when you need me. I'm here to help.'

I turn to Liam. 'Tell them!'

'Lou, go! We all care about you. You have to—'

My stomach drops as a loud roar fills the air. The beach lights up. A speedboat shoots towards the shore, blinding us with a spotlight. My heart hammers violently as my eyes refocus. Two masked figures are pointing guns at us. Past presidents of the USA.

'Don't move!' George Bush Junior booms through a loudspeaker. 'Do exactly as we say or we'll open fire.' His gun is aimed at Liam.

Bill Clinton clambers out and wades towards us. His weapon doesn't waver, despite the waves crashing into his thighs – it's pointed at me. One slip of his finger and I'll be shot. A horrible gasping noise escapes from my throat.

'Bring the rucksacks to the boat,' Clinton orders. 'Any funny business and you're dead.'

Liam flinches. He recognises the Bristolian accent. It's one of the men from the clifftop last week.

The spotlight follows us along the beach as we return to the sea tractor, guarded by Clinton. We scoop up the rucksacks and turn round, raising our hands in the air.

'Slowly,' Clinton says. 'Keep them where I can see them.' He gestures at the boat with his gun.

'I'm sorry,' I whisper to Lou as we walk to the shoreline. 'This will turn ugly when they find out . . .' My voice disappears into a croak.

'What?' Lou asks.

I shake my head.

'Don't worry,' Lou says. 'I'm getting you out of this mess, I promise. I have a plan.'

I shoot a look at them. That's impossible! There's nothing anyone can do.

I wade through the water towards the boat, hating myself with each step.

Everyone, including Lou, will die because I'm a good liar.

46

LAYLA

'Stop talking!' Bill Clinton yells.

Lou is whispering to Kai in the back of the speedboat. *Please, please come up with a plan.* Liam's eyes are screwed shut. He's no help and I have no idea what to do. I stare over the side into the murky depths. I can't jump. My hands are bound behind my back, the same as the others. No way could I hold my breath long enough underwater to avoid being shot. If the men in the freaky masks don't kill me, the cold and the strong tide will finish me off.

How can we escape?

'We're heading to the old smugglers' entrance of the island,' Lou says loudly. 'Beneath the Sea Haven. We're almost there.'

The guy with the George Bush Junior mask jabs Lou in the belly with the butt of his gun. They bend over double, eyes bulging and gasping for breath. Kai rests his head on their shoulder. Why's Lou drawing attention to themself like this? If this is their plan, it's a crap one.

Kai looks up, giving me a pleading look. But what can I do? I'm helpless. I'm shaking with cold and probably shock. Spray stings my eyes, blinding me. The swell builds, sending water crashing against the hull. We narrowly avoid colliding with teeth-like rocks. Panic courses through my body. If we overturn, we'll all drown. I see fear in Lou's eyes as the boat bounces off the crest of another huge wave. I'm thrown to the floor, making my ribs spasm. I curl into a foetal position, trying to breathe through the pain.

The boat slows and the waters become calmer. Hands pull me roughly into a sitting position. Everything looks different in the dark, but from what I remember this is the west side of the island. A single light flickers eerily from the railing of the private jetty. Another lamp shines deeper inside the cave. I've paddle-boarded past here a few times, but the entrance is always sealed.

Tonight it's in use. Someone is waiting for us.

Bill Clinton grabs Lou's arm and yanks them to their feet, followed by Kai. They clamber out as George Bush Junior gathers the rucksacks, tossing them on to the jetty. He returns, seizing my wrists. He hauls me up. 'Don't be tempted to make a run for it!'

Where would we go? The cliff face is exposed – a sheer drop with few hiding places. The howling wind would knock us over any ledge we managed to find, and these guys could easily pick us off with a few bullets.

Liam curses as he slips. 'Hold on! I've lost my glasses.'

'Nice try.' George Bush Junior drags him out.

He lands heavily on his knee, yelping with pain. I can't help him. Bill Clinton has a tight grip on my arm as he marches me to the cave entrance. I open my mouth to plead for my life, but no words come out. I gag at the rancid smell of rotting seaweed as we're pushed through a claustrophobically narrow tunnel covered in barnacles. I scrape my forehead. A droplet of blood lands on my lip as we move slowly in single file, bent over double. I keep my eyes fixed on the uneven rocky ground, following Kai's scuffed trainers.

Water drips. Footsteps tap. Something scuttles and brushes against my ankle. Was that a crab? Or a rat? I bite my lip to stop myself from screaming. I count my footsteps as the tunnel splits in two – maybe I can work out a way to make it back to the jetty and swim round the island to get help. But a small voice in my head says: *You couldn't swim across the bay to the next beach.*

After a few minutes – *three hundred and one footsteps* – we can stand up straight. We're inside a large echoey cave. Strings of construction lights loop around the walls, which glitter with dripping water and streaks of dark green seaweed. A figure wearing a Donald Trump mask stands in front of us. He lifts a device to his mouth. His other hand holds a gun.

'Have you checked the rucksacks?' The voice is electronic.

'Not yet.'

Bill Clinton collects them.

'It's all there,' Liam calls out. 'Everything we have. We're sorry. We should never have taken your money.'

'We had no idea it belonged to you . . .' My voice trails away, but I force myself to speak. 'Can we see Fliss? Is she okay?'

Donald Trump lifts the voice distorter to his mouth. His mask glistens grotesquely. 'That depends on whether the four of you play nice.' He aims the gun at my chest. 'Let's see, shall we?'

Clinton dumps the rucksacks at Trump's feet. George Bush Junior unzips the first bag and rifles through it. My heart thuds painfully and cold shivers run down my spine. Soon they'll realise we've short-changed them.

'How much?' Donald Trump asks.

The guy searches the other two rucksacks.

Is it enough to save our lives? Or is it too late? Is Fliss dead?

'They've double-crossed you,' George Bush Junior replies.

He turns one of the rucksacks upside down. A few dozen notes waft out, followed by stones and newspaper clippings, all tightly bound like blocks of fifties. He empties the next rucksack and the final one. They're the same. *Fake.*

I blink repeatedly.

'Th-th-this can't be possible,' I stutter. 'How . . .?'

'They were stuffed with fifties,' Liam gasps. 'We all saw the money. It was inside the rucksacks in the car park!'

I watch the colour drain from his face. The penny's dropped – someone switched the rucksacks on the path.

'Is this the way you want to play it?' Donald Trump points the gun from one of us to the other.

'No!' I cry. 'We brought the money. I promise it was all there. Whoever else was on the beach tonight must have snatched the *real* rucksacks.'

'Shall we finish this?' George Bush Junior asks.

We wait for an agonising couple of seconds.

'Yes,' Donald Trump says finally. 'But gag them first. I don't want to hear them begging for their lives, the way that girl did. *They* die in silence.'

The figures loom towards us.

'Stop!' Kai shouts. 'Leave them alone! This is my fault.'

He steps in front of me and Lou. Bill Clinton knocks Kai

to the ground then Lou. A gloved hand pushes me next. I lose my balance and lean against Lou, who's trembling violently.

'What did you do?' Liam cries as he's forced to his knees.

The gun points at Kai. 'Talk,' Donald Trump says.

My heart drops as Kai bows his head.

'I left decoy rucksacks close to the beach earlier,' he blurts out. 'I threw a firecracker on the path and, when the others ran off, I switched them.'

A cold shiver passes down my spine. 'How could you?'

'Why would you do that?' Liam says, sobbing. 'After what we agreed?'

'Because—' he begins.

'Where are the *real* rucksacks?' Donald Trump cuts in.

He steps closer, still aiming the gun at Kai's forehead. Slowly he lifts his head and stares straight into the prosthetic mask.

'If you kill me or any of the others, you'll never find out.'

I hold my breath, barely daring to hope for a last reprieve. But Bill Clinton and George Bush Junior are gagging us with foul-smelling strips of material. I cough, trying hard not to choke on my saliva.

The masked men step back, flanking us on either side. Donald Trump's hand wavers. My heart skips a beat. He's decided to let us live!

His hand switches direction. A low moan escapes from my lips as he points the gun at me.

'Not Layla!' Kai screams. 'Shoot me instead.'

The hand doesn't waver.

I love you, Salih, Mum and Teta.

You too, Leon. You're not Baba, but you're a good stepdad.

I'm sorry I put you all through this.

I love you, Baba.

The gun fires.

47

LIAM

Bang!

The legs crumble beneath the forty-second president of the USA: Bill Clinton. He slumps forward, blood spurting from his mask.

Bang!

Before he hits the ground, the gun fires again and George Bush Junior collapses. A red pool spreads from his head across the rocky ground. Layla staggers backwards into the wall. Muffled screams escape from her gag. Kai sinks to his heels, groaning. Lou crouches beside him, their shoulders heaving up and down. I want to run, but my legs are leaden. Red dots dance in front of my eyes.

'That's what happens when people outlive their usefulness,' Donald Trump says through the voice distorter. He points the gun towards a small entrance to our left. 'Go through there, single file. If you try to make a run for it, I'll shoot.'

Lou nudges Kai with their knee until he stands unsteadily. Layla stumbles, banging into the cave wall. Blood trickles down her forehead. She sways and ducks into the tunnel first. Kai and Lou are next. Donald Trump is behind me. Should I try to wrestle the gun off him? Or will I be shot in the struggle? I hear more strangled sobs and cries ahead. I stop. I don't want to go any further. The hand in my back forces me to take another few steps.

My heart beats furiously as I straighten up. My knees immediately weaken. I want to sink to the ground. Lying on the rocks is a stiff shape. The figure is rigid, unmoving. It looks like a shop mannequin.

The hands are chalk white against the black jeans and jumper. The fingernails are manicured. Long hair is splayed out in a coppery auburn fan.

I blink rapidly. My brain's trying to process the sight.

That's not a dummy. It's another body!

I close my eyes, but all I see is bright red. I open them.

Blood pools around the girl's head, forming a hideous crimson cloak.

Panic rises in my throat, threatening to choke me. I have to get out of here.

I can't . . . I can't breathe . . .

I can't . . . end up dead like Fliss Cavendish.

I won't.

I stagger backwards towards the tunnel, but Donald Trump is watching. His gun is trained on me.

Mum. Lou.

Those are the only two words that flash into my mind.

'Stop!' the masked figure shouts.

The gun fires again.

48

KAI

The gunshot echoes horribly. Sharp rock fragments shower down from the cave roof. I press myself harder against the wall. Liam freezes and backs up. He keeps his eyes on the gun and not on Fliss's lifeless body. I'll vomit if I look at her. I got her killed. If I hadn't been greedy and switched the money, she'd be alive. Lou shudders. They don't deserve this. *None* of them do.

The fake president draws closer. 'Where's the money?' He presses the gun to my forehead and rips off the gag.

I swallow the panic rising in my throat and attempt to concentrate on the small details: the contact lenses, the voice distorter, the gloves. That's a good sign, right? He's disguising his appearance, which could mean he'll let us live because we haven't seen his face. My heart beats quicker as I think about what Lou told me in the speedboat. We need to play for time.

Donald Trump trains the weapon on Lou. 'Tell me where you've hidden it.'

A horrible choking sound rings out and the cold metal barrel swerves away from them. The president moves along our line, pulling off the gags, repeating the question. He obviously doesn't believe I'm the only person involved in this deception.

Will one of them confess to a fake hiding place to save their lives?

Lou brushes my shoulder with theirs. Is that a signal? How much time do we have? I listen hard for footsteps, but the cave only echoes with the monotonous drip of water and a faint roar of the tide in the distance. We're completely alone.

'No one? Okay, have it your way. Let's play a game.' The gun swings towards me again. 'Truth or dare.'

'W-w-what?'

The question throws me off guard.

'Don't make me repeat myself.'

'Fine . . . Dare.'

I dare you to take off your mask!

'No, truth. I've always wanted to – from day one. It was the others . . .'

That's another lie, but my delaying tactic works. The gun wavers. He's trying to work out whether I'm genuine or not.

'Let's start with an easy one. Which school do you go to?'

'Kingsborough High School.'

Donald Trump pauses.

'Wrong answer. Dead kids don't go to school.'

I close my eyes as he pulls the trigger.

Nothing happens.

My eyes fly open. He's examining the gun. It's jammed! This is my only chance. I lunge forward, butting the president in the stomach. As he groans and folds up, I kick him hard in the chest. He loses his balance, falling backwards. The gun drops to the ground with a small echo, followed by the voice distorter. A horrible cracking sound follows as his head strikes a rock.

'Help me!' I scream.

Fingers scrabble at my wrists. Lou has their back turned to me, trying to undo my bindings.

'It's too tight,' they say.

'There's a penknife in the front pocket of my anorak,' Layla calls out.

Liam backs up towards her and leans in. 'Move closer. That's it. I can feel it. Hold on, I think I've got it.' He pulls away.

'Flick the small button in the side and it'll open,' Layla says.

'Hurry!' I cry. 'His chest is moving. He's alive. He'll kill us when he wakes.'

'Not helping!' Liam yelps. 'That makes me more jittery. Hold on, it's open. Layla – you first.'

She stretches out her hands behind her back as Liam hacks at the binding. She gasps as her wrists spring apart. She takes the knife from him and works on Lou. Within seconds we're all free of the restraints.

'Who do you think it is?' Layla asks, staring at the motionless president.

'Who cares?!' Liam says. 'Let's go!'

'I have to see his face otherwise I'll have nightmares about Trump for ever,' Lou insists. 'Well, more than usual anyway.'

They're right. I want to see who tried to kill us.

'Do it!' Layla urges.

Lou crouches down and slowly peels off the prosthetic mask. They fall back on their heels.

'Holy shit!' I exclaim.

'No fricking way!' Layla's voice is high-pitched.

Everyone stares, dumbstruck, at the bloodied but familiar face.

'I don't believe it!' Liam shakes his head.

'We've been played from the beginning,' Layla says. 'We fell for it hook, line and sinker.'

'But if that's the case . . .' I begin.

The words die on my tongue as realisation hits.

Nothing is what it seems.

I turn round slowly.

It's too late.

Another bloodstained figure stands behind us, holding Donald Trump's gun.

49

FLISS

A scream dies in my throat as the Donald Trump impersonator rips off his mask.

My whole body freezes.

I can't believe it. I won't believe it.

'Y-y-you!'

It's the only word I manage to utter before both hands are back on the gun, clasping it tightly.

The barrel is aimed at my head.

Their fingers move towards the trigger.

I hear a small click.

'I took out the bullets,' Mother says sharply, 'but consider that a lesson for stealing my money, *our* money.'

I bend over double, spattering the ground with vomit.

'I wish it hadn't turned out like this.' Her tone is softer as she helps me into a sitting position. 'It's a shock, I know.'

She tries to wipe my mouth with a tissue, but I jerk away.

'You think?' I quickly glance around.

'You're safe. We're in the caves beneath the hotel. This was part of the revamp – unearthing the old smugglers' tunnels.' She gestures at the lighting, before passing me a bottle of water.

My hands are shaking too much to grip it. *Safe?*

She holds the bottle to my lips, but I refuse to take a sip, even though my throat is parched.

'How could you?' I splutter. 'Have me kidnapped . . . attacked. He hit me!'

Mother winces. 'I'm sorry. I told them not to hurt you.'

'Look at my fricking face!' I point to my tender, throbbing cheek.

'I'm truly sorry. I'll make them pay for that.' She takes a gulp of water. 'But I *have* to get that money back.'

Questions swirl around my head, but I can only utter, 'You. You were going to kill us. Kill *me*.'

She shakes her head, rubbing her brow. 'I wanted, I *needed* to frighten you all to play along and cooperate with me.' She reaches out to move a tendril of hair stuck to my forehead, but I jolt away.

'Well, it worked. You had me abducted, FFS. I thought I was about to die!'

'That would never have happened, but I had to get you away from the beach. I knew you were planning to alert DC Walker tonight. I read your WhatsApp messages. I've been reading them ever since the crash.'

I stare at her, aghast.

'I installed spyware on the phones I gifted,' she says matter-of-factly. 'I had my suspicions that Silas's holdall hadn't gone over with the bus. I had to know what you were discussing.'

Who *is* this woman?

'Didn't it ever cross your mind to just ask me?'

'Would you have told me the truth?'

I blink as my eyes moisten. 'I was planning to at one point. I wanted to tell you about the cash and the blackmail.'

'What blackmail?'

I swallow a snort. 'Yeah, sure – you're not a part of that either.'

'I have no idea what you're talking about.'

I don't know whether to believe her. Every single thing that has come out of her mouth is a lie.

'I can guess what you're thinking,' she begins.

'I doubt that!'

She sighs. 'The truth is, I didn't want to ask if you'd found the cash. I thought, I mistakenly believed, it was safer to make you think someone else was after you than admit I was involved in this.' She lifts her hands, looking around the cave.

'In what exactly?'

Mother stands, peeling off her gloves. She leans against the glistening wall. 'I made some ill-advised business dealings earlier this year.'

I roll my eyes. 'You think?'

'The renovation costs far exceeded anything we'd anticipated, and the bank wouldn't loan us more money. Your father was in debt and wanted to let the business fold.'

I flinch. 'Daddy was right. You should have walked away.'

She shakes her head. 'I couldn't do that. This was our dream.'

'*Your* dream,' I correct.

'I wanted the Sea Haven to succeed for all our sakes. But after your father left, I was offered a huge investment I couldn't turn down. I thought the investor genuinely planned to make our hotel the country's number-one luxury destination in the UK.' She pauses. 'When I started to have doubts, it was too late to back out. I discovered I'd made a deal with the devil.'

I shudder. I can't look at her.

'When I examined the accounts, the cost of the refurb was astronomical – millions of pounds were being billed for new electrics and plumbing, as well as redecorating every single room.'

I frown. 'None of that happened!'

'It was money laundering – millions and millions being recycled through the hotel each week for a drugs cartel.'

'It's like *Ozark*,' I mutter.

She looks baffled.

'All those lectures you and Daddy gave me about not trying *any* drugs and now it turns out you're this big-time dealer!'

'I can't stress enough how ashamed I am to be involved in this. But when three guys from the cartel arrived and told me this would be the base for their UK operation, I was in too deep to refuse. There was nothing I could do.'

'How about going to the police?'

'They threatened to kill you.' She inhales deeply. 'I allowed them to use the helipad for drugs arrivals. They stored their merchandise down here ahead of distribution.'

'Merchandise? Distribution? You make it sound like this is a legitimate business when it's drug dealing via the school bus!'

'It was convenient.'

My jaw drops.

'Convenient for them,' she adds quickly. 'Once the drugs

were dropped off at different stops along the bus route, they were ferried to London and across the country. But I tried to keep out of what was happening on a day-to-day basis.'

'Like when the old bus driver was killed to allow Silas to take his place?'

'I don't know for sure that's what happened.'

I raise an eyebrow.

'Okay, yes. I presume they killed Bob. It's the most obvious explanation. Shortly after his hit-and-run, they told me a new opportunity had come up for distribution. I didn't ask any questions.'

'How classy.'

Her shoulders tremble. 'Silas became the main man – distributing drugs to dealers and collecting their cash. But he decided to do a runner with the takings. The cartel had become suspicious he might talk to the police . . .' Her voice trails off.

'They were trying to kill him, but he took out one of the cartel members first,' I say, finishing her sentence. 'The driver of the Audi who crashed into our bus.'

She nods. 'And the hunt for the missing cash began. I'm being held personally responsible.'

'Why? It's not your fault Silas went psycho and drove off a cliff.'

'But it is my fault *you* stole their cash afterwards. I told them I'd handle it, but they were angry about that guest's death this summer.'

I gasp as the air disappears from my lungs. Black dots appear before my eyes, multiplying and dancing.

The truth hits me as hard as a punch.

'That's why you wouldn't report Robert Brody to the police for attacking me in his room. You were protecting the cartel!'

'I couldn't risk you being questioned and letting slip something you didn't realise could land us into trouble.'

I struggle to my feet. 'You're unbelievable! Pure evil.'

'I was trying to protect you. That's what I'm doing now.'

'How? I'm in deep shit because of *you*.'

She catches my arm as I attempt to brush past. 'If I don't get their money back, *all of it*, they'll send someone else to kill us. They'll be worse than who you met tonight.'

'*I'm* getting the hell out of here. The others are only bringing six hundred and seventy thousand. That's all we have left.'

Mother closes her eyes as she sinks down the wall. 'That's not enough.'

'Good luck. You'll need it.' I pick my way round rocks.

'I have a backup plan,' she calls out, as I reach the tunnel exit.

'I don't care!'

'I'll kill the men who kidnapped you *and* your friends.'

I spin round.

'We place the blame on them and leave before the big boss – Mr A – finds out. We'll change our names. It's not as much cash as I'd hoped but it'll be enough for a fresh start. We could go to New Zealand or Australia. I'll do anything to make things right with you, sweetie.'

I pretend to hesitate.

'Firstly, they're not my friends.' I take a deep breath. 'And secondly, what exactly do you want me to do?'

50

LAYLA

'Tell me I'm imagining this.' Kai takes a step backwards.

'You're not,' Lou replies. 'It's like that scene from *Saw*.'

Fliss has risen from the dead. Sticky red liquid trickles down her forehead.

'I doubt Mother's watched that movie,' she says, wiping her face with the back of her hand. 'She's not a horror fan. But she did think my "death" and her bottle of Halloween fake blood would make you cooperate. I guess she overestimated how upset you'd be to see me murdered.'

Kai raises his hands as she aims the gun at his forehead.

'I'd planned to tell her where I'd hidden the rucksacks *eventually*,' he says. 'I was playing for time until the police arrived.'

Her gun wavers. 'The police?'

'I rang DC Walker and told him you were on the beach,'

Lou explains. 'He stayed on the line during the boat ride. He knew where we were heading. He must be on his way.'

That's why Lou risked describing our journey! It all makes sense.

Fliss doesn't lower the gun. 'There's hardly any mobile reception close to the island. I doubt he heard.'

'Well, let's ring him and make sure he knows where we are!' I exclaim. 'What are we waiting for? This is over.'

'Is it?' Fliss's tone is glacial. 'Move away from my mother.' She gestures at Kai with the gun.

'I didn't mean to hurt her, but I couldn't stand there and watch the others take a bullet. You must see that?'

'You double-crossed us all tonight. I heard what Mother said – you switched the rucksacks.' She jabs the gun at him. 'Move out of the way.'

This time Kai doesn't argue. He stands meekly next to Lou and Liam as Fliss kneels and checks her mum's pulse.

'How bad is it?' he asks.

'She's breathing. I think she's concussed. Or has a fractured skull.'

'We should get her to a hospital.' Kai gropes around his pockets. 'Dammit. I lost my phone in the boat.'

I pull out my mobile. 'No network coverage.'

'Same here,' Liam says. 'What about yours?'

Lou stares at their screen. 'Nothing. No messages from DC Walker either.'

'It feels like that day on the clifftop,' I say, shivering. 'We couldn't call for help and we decided to split the cash.'

'If you could turn back time, would you have made a different decision?' Fliss's eyes narrow as she turns the gun on me.

I open my mouth to say 'yes' but stop myself. If I hadn't taken the money, Salih could still be waiting for hospital treatment. Even though the bodies are stacking up, how can I regret that?

'I'd take the money,' I admit.

'At least someone is telling the truth,' Fliss says. 'How refreshing.'

'I've had enough of truth or dare for one night.' Liam heads to the opening. 'Let's get out of here and ring DC Walker.'

'You're not going anywhere!' Fliss shouts. 'I'm not done with any of you.'

Liam turns round slowly. 'You'll really shoot me?'

'Do you want to find out?'

'Let's finish this.' Kai walks closer to her, his hands raised. 'We'll come clean to the police. Tell them what we did. Give them back all the money.'

'Sure, we could do that, but first tell me where you hid the *real* rucksacks.'

This time she aims the gun squarely at Lou's forehead.

Kai flinches. 'Lower that! They're still at the beach.'

'Where? *Exactly?*'

'Stop pointing that gun at Lou and I'll tell you!'

Her aim switches to Kai's chest.

'I didn't have much time,' he says, quivering. 'They're in the sand dunes, hidden under some driftwood, not far from the sea tractor.'

'Thank you. For finally telling the truth.' Her hand shakes.

'Seriously?' Liam steps in front of Kai. 'You'll shoot him? All of us? For a few hundred thousand pounds?'

'Just under six hundred and seventy thousand if I'm not mistaken,' Fliss says. 'People have killed for far less.'

'Do it,' a voice says weakly. 'As we discussed.'

I jump, staring down at the ground. Mrs C has regained consciousness. She's propped up on her elbows.

'Kill them all,' she says, louder. 'They're expendable.'

I feel sick to the bottom of my stomach. She *can't* mean that.

Fliss's hand is trembling violently.

'For God's sake!' I shout. 'You're not like your mum. You're not a murderer.'

'Aren't I?' She stares at me with a strange expression on her face.

'Sure, we've had our differences, but I don't believe you're a bad person.'

'You can be *extremely* stupid, Layla,' she says with a hollow laugh.

The sound of barking dogs echoes through the tunnel.

'Police!' a distant voice calls.

'They're here!' Kai exclaims.

'There's still time,' Mrs C calls out. 'Shoot them.'

'Don't listen to her!' I plead. 'For the first time we'll all do the right thing. We'll confess and face the consequences.'

'No,' Mrs C says, panting. 'We can claim my men killed these four before we managed to shoot them. They all betrayed you. Teach them a lesson.'

The voices are tantalisingly close. I hear the crackle of radios, the echo of boots on the ground. More dogs barking. A muffled voice shouts, 'Armed police!'

Safety is minutes away. Our chance of survival.

'You're right,' Fliss says calmly.

'I'm sorry!' Kai bellows. 'Please don't do this!'

'No!' I cry.

Lou throws their arms round Liam. I hug Kai tightly.

Fliss turns and faces her mum.

'Consider this *your* lesson for screwing me over. You always taught me to have a fall guy lined up.'

She pulls the trigger.

51

FLISS

'The air ambulance has touched down at the hospital and your mum's been taken into surgery,' DC Walker explains. 'The doctors say she should regain full movement of her arm.'

'That's good news.' I pretend to stifle a sob into my cuff. 'I thought she was reaching for another weapon. That's why I opened fire.'

I say it loud enough for the others to hear and back up my version of events. We're sitting on the red-velvet chairs in the hotel foyer, waiting for the helicopter to return and take us to hospital. Mother had revealed the location of a secret passageway that leads from the kitchens to the caves. I doubt she'll admit I deliberately shot her in the shoulder. Anyway, it's her word against *ours* – she's hardly a reliable witness.

Layla flinches at my lie but nods her head.

'She'd have killed us all if Fliss hadn't stopped her,' Liam mumbles.

'Yeah, she didn't have a choice.' Kai holds my gaze. 'It was her or us.'

They're still willing to play the game.

We're all in this together.

'We'll go into this in more detail when you're well enough to be formally interviewed.' DC Walker moves away as his radio sputters.

'That's the story you're going with?' Lou whispers. 'What a crock of—'

'Shut up or I'll make sure you're dragged down with them,' I hiss, jerking my head at Layla, Liam and Kai.

DC Walker steps back. 'ETA on the helicopter is four minutes.' He perches on the side of the mini sofa. 'You'll probably say "no comment", but I'm dying to know. How much money *did* you find that morning?'

I'm ready to lie, but Kai cuts in first.

'The holdall split as it fell out of the bus – we found just over three hundred and fifty thousand. We gave Layla the majority – two hundred and fifty thousand and divided the rest of the money between us. Fliss took ten thousand; Liam, sixty thousand to impress his boyfriend and I wanted to launder thirty thousand to rent the house for my mum and sister.'

I try not to register any emotion, but Layla's breathing heavily. Liam places a hand on her arm, his face whitening.

'The drug gang thought we had the full million,' Kai continues. 'That's why they came after us. We couldn't tell you the truth – they were threatening to kill our families. We thought we could get away with leaving fake rucksacks stuffed with rocks and the few hundred pounds we had left. We were planning to tip you off about the pick-up, but obviously it went wrong.'

'Is that true?' DC Walker asks, glancing at the rest of us. 'It sounds pretty convenient that you've spent *all* the money and have nothing left.'

'Yes,' I pipe up. 'We found far less than the gang thought – or hoped. We came to an agreement to take different amounts, based on what we needed.'

'But the gang didn't believe us. They wanted one million pounds and threatened to kill us one by one if we didn't return it.' *Liam.*

That leaves Layla.

We're all in this together.

She sighs deeply. 'The others let me keep most of the cash to help my brother.'

'How generous,' DC Walker mutters. 'But still illegal.'

'I'm sorry.' This time she isn't lying.

A police officer strides into the foyer. 'Can I have a quick word, sir? I need to show you what we've found.'

My heart beats rapidly. This could be my only chance to make certain we're on the same page.

'Hold on a minute,' DC Walker replies. 'I can't leave the witnesses alone.'

He gestures to a colleague, who comes over and stands between us as he heads to the back office.

Dammit!

Luckily the police officer's radio crackles with a voice. As soon as he steps away, distracted, Layla explodes.

'I can't believe you lied again after everything we've been through tonight!'

'Why tell him the truth?' Kai asks.

'Erm? Because we're in enough trouble?'

'If the police discover we found a million it'll make things worse,' he argues. 'No one has to know the truth if we all stick together and tell the same story.'

Layla holds her head in her hands as she slumps back in the chair. Lou kneads their temples, gaze fixed on the floor.

'We'll probably be charged with theft and money

laundering,' Kai says. 'It could look better for us in court if the police believe we took less. That means the lion's share would have gone to Salih's treatment.'

'I agree with Kai,' I say. 'Why admit to more than we have to?'

'Claims the girl who wanted to shoot us dead,' Layla retorts. 'Is it more convenient for you if we don't mention that either?'

'I wouldn't have pulled the trigger,' I insist. 'I wanted to scare you, that's all. Promise.'

And find the location of the money.

Mother was wrong – no way could we get away with killing all four. Forensics would have proven the guns hadn't been fired by her two henchmen. This is a far better option – Mother takes the fall and I'll live with Daddy in the States when this is over. He'll hire the best lawyer in the country to represent me. I doubt I'll get a long sentence for theft – far less than the others who were money laundering. The judge will be sympathetic when I explain about my blackmailer.

'How do we get the rucksacks?' Liam asks.

Lou sighs, shaking their head.

'Whoever gets released first collects them,' Kai says. 'They're hidden by the driftwood and shouldn't be noticed by anyone out walking in the dunes.' He pauses. 'I trust all four of you not to do a runner with the money.'

Jeez. He *is* stupid.

'Okay. Let's do it,' Liam says.

'We're all in this together.' I stretch my hand out.

Lou steps back but Kai places his hand on top, followed by Liam. Reluctantly Layla does the same. We break apart as DC Walker reappears.

'The helicopter's ready. Let's go.'

We follow him out of the hotel, wrapped in blankets. The cold air hits my face like a slap. The darkness is punctuated with the flash of torchlights. Dozens of police officers have arrived by boat, ready to search the hotel for evidence of Mother's drugs empire.

I hug the blanket closer and hang back as a figure approaches. The others continue walking.

'Omigod! I came as soon as I heard.' Aaron puts his arm round my shoulders. 'I swear I had no idea what was going on. Mrs C kept me out of this, I promise. I can't believe it.'

I swallow the lump in my throat. 'Me neither.'

'We're leaving,' DC Walker calls out. 'He can come with you to the hospital if you want?'

'Shall I?' Aaron asks.

'No,' I say, dropping my voice. 'You have to do something for me.'

'Name it.'

I pause, as a forensics team, dressed in white suits, congregates. Most of them head into the hotel.

'I need you to go to the sand dunes close to the sea tractor and look for three black rucksacks hidden under driftwood,' I whisper.

Aaron's eyes widen. 'Okaaaay!'

He lifts his hands to rub his brow, as one of the forensics investigators accidentally sweeps his ultraviolet torch over us before focusing the light on the path.

That's when I see it. The fluorescent yellow residue on his fingers. It's all over his hands.

'You!' I splutter.

'What?'

I back away. 'You're my blackmailer.'

He swallows repeatedly. 'I don't know what you're talking about.'

'Sure you do! You knew about Robert's death. You had access to my phone.' I lunge at him and beat his chest with my fists. 'How could you? I trusted you.'

He opens his mouth to argue but closes it.

'I don't get it. Why? You're like family to me!'

He shakes his head. 'Except I'm not, am I? I'm an employee and I needed the money after Mrs C cut our wages this summer.'

'I'd have helped if you'd asked!'

'Would you? I know what you think of people who are less fortunate – the Poverty Express passengers. I thought you'd ask Mrs C for the cash and she'd pay pronto. I had no idea it would come to this. I'm sorry. Honestly I am. I promise I'll destroy those photos and return your money.'

'That's not enough! It will never make up for what you've done.'

'I'll collect the rucksacks and cash,' he says breathlessly. 'I heard the police talking about missing drug money. I'm guessing you were trying to return it tonight. We can split it fifty-fifty.'

I shake my head.

'Seventy-thirty?'

DC Walker strides towards us, grimacing. 'Come on, Fliss!'

'If you tell him, it'll come out what happened that night,' Aaron whispers.

Robert Brody's death.

'Is everything all right?' DC Walker asks.

No! I want to scream at the top of my voice loud enough

to wake the nesting seagulls. Everyone has betrayed me. The other survivors, Mother, now Aaron. I dig my nails into my palm to control my rising fury. I inhale deeply.

'This man hacked my phone and blackmailed me. I paid him ten thousand pounds from the stolen money to stop my pictures being leaked on the web.'

Aaron shakes his head. 'You're making a mistake.'

Really? It's more of a calculated gamble.

I raise my chin defiantly. 'I want to tell the truth about what I've done.'

DC Walker cautions Aaron and explains he's being arrested on suspicion of blackmail.

Aaron stares pleadingly at me as two officers approach. 'I'm sorry,' he calls out, as he's led away in handcuffs.

I don't reply. My heart is lined with steel. I turn to face DC Walker.

'I have to confess.' I wring my hands. 'I was attacked by a hotel guest, Robert Brody, this summer. Aaron rescued me. He's always looked out for me . . . He used to anyway.' My voice cracks. 'Mother refused to call the police after the assault – I found out tonight it was because she wanted to protect her drugs business.'

'And what happened to Robert Brody?' he asks gently.

'A few hours after it happened, I went for a walk behind

the hotel to clear my head. I didn't know he was outside. He followed me.' My voice trembles.

'We don't have to do this here,' DC Walker says. 'We can wait to talk when we've arranged for an appropriate adult to be present.'

'I've waited long enough to tell the truth.' My voice rises in volume. 'I tried to get away, but he chased me along the clifftop. I took the wrong path and had nowhere to go. I was on the edge. He told me he wanted to pick up where we left off. I knew what would happen and this time Aaron wasn't around to help.'

'Go on.'

'He lunged towards me and grabbed my waist. We struggled. I was fighting for my life. He was stronger than me, but his foot slipped. He lost his balance and fell backwards. I swear I tried to grab his hand.' I take a gulp of air. 'There's no network coverage on that part of the island. I ran back to the hotel to raise the alarm, but Mother found me before I could call the police. She told me I could never tell you what I'd done – that I'd be charged with murder.'

'I doubt that,' he replies. 'It sounds like you used reasonable force to protect yourself. I'm confident the Crown Prosecution Service would have regarded it as self-defence.'

Tears stream down my face as he puts his arm round me.

'You've done the right thing by telling the truth. Your account will be investigated, but we'll sort this, I promise.'

'Th-th-thank you.'

'We'd better go.'

His arm remains round my shoulders as he leads me to the helipad. I knew he'd feel sorry for me.

My story was a huge success.

DC Walker believes my biggest-ever lie.

52

LOU

I believe Kai. He didn't mean to get mixed up in all this.

That's why I'm helping him. Plus, he was one of the few people who stuck by me when I announced I was non-binary. He didn't treat me like a total freak the way some kids did at school. My pronouns might be different, but I'm the same Lou Tsang at heart – a teenager, a best friend and classmate. I'm a more authentic version of my true self. I'm also a good person. I mean, obviously, I enjoy a good gossip as much as the next kid. But I have my friends' backs. Even when I'm tumbling down dunes and accidentally eating sand.

I'm doing this for Kai. I'm the only person he trusts.

My legs are killing me and wearing my favourite skinny white jeans was a poor sartorial choice. I heard an ominous ripping sound when I fell back there, but I force myself to keep going. The rucksacks *must* be around here. Kai thinks it's unlikely anyone else has stumbled across them. He told me *everything* as we waited by the helipad. The rucksacks aren't near the sea tractor covered by driftwood. He'd lied in case the others were released by the police first. Kai had spent hours digging a massive hole just off the footpath and lined it with panels he'd found in Mrs Gibson's shed. A piece of bamboo cane from her garden marks the spot approximately 50 metres from the car park – around 150 footsteps.

I've counted out the steps, apart from when I fell.

I flash the torch up the dune. I feel like an extra in a horror movie who is lured into an ambush. *Aargh!* Those storylines never end well. If I see anyone else around, I swear I'll crap my pants. That will finish off my jeans.

I shine the light to my right. *Found it!* A tall stick rises out of the sand. I scramble towards it like I'm Indiana Jones and this is the Holy Grail. I search for Mum's trowel in my bag. I couldn't face bringing a spade because I'd definitely feel like an expendable character in a slasher flick digging my own grave. I shiver. It takes for ever before I hit something solid. I shovel faster until I feel wood. Wrenching it off, I shine my torch into the cavity.

Three black rucksacks!

I put the torch to one side and pull one out. The zip catches on the material as I open it. Inside are bricks and bricks of fifty-pound notes. The other two rucksacks are packed tightly with fifties too.

I shudder. *Gross.*

It's fitting the notes are red because this is blood money. It's ruined lives. I don't want anything to do with the drug dealers' dirty cash.

I stuff the notes into the rucksack and wipe my hands on my no-longer-white jeans. Kai says he'll be in more trouble if the police find this stash. He thinks all four of them will be charged with theft. They could get longer jail sentences if they appear greedy. I don't think they were – Layla was trying to help her little brother and Kai wanted to bring his mum and Crystal home. HMG, or rather lovely Liam, was attempting to keep a boyfriend who doesn't deserve him. When will he learn he's better off without Tristram? I can't judge any of them.

Okay, I totally judge Fliss. I warned Kai before: this isn't a boringly predictable movie where the bad girl is redeemed – she'll be thoroughly evil until the end. I don't believe a word that comes out of her mouth. But I'll help the other three.

I won't lie to the police, though. DC Walker told me to return to the station at 8 a.m. with Mum or Dad to give a detailed statement. I'll tell him what happened earlier, but I won't admit to this post-credits scene. It's my secret. Mine and Kai's.

I throw two rucksacks over each shoulder and clutch the other to my chest. My trainers sink into the sand. I swear to God, I have no idea how I'll make it back to Mum's car. I need to hide the cash until Kai can deal with it. Since Mum and Dad are barely talking to me, my bedroom is a good bet. I'll cover the rucksacks with bedding at the top of my wardrobe. I don't like the thought of the money being nearby, but it won't be for long.

Kai says he'll hide it as soon as the police have finished with him. Later, in a year or two, when things have quietened down, he'll give the money away. I want him to use the cash to support trans and non-binary people. Kai has promised that he and the others won't keep a single note.

All the cash will go to charity.

He says he's telling the truth.

I trust him.

53

LIAM

'Will there be a court case?'

Tristram leans against his bedroom wall, which his parents recently redecorated using Christian Lacroix's latest wallpaper designs. Bile rises in my throat as he checks his phone. I've barely been able to sleep for more than a few hours each night or keep any food down since I was charged with theft and money laundering, along with Layla and Kai. Fliss only faces the theft charge. We're not allowed to talk, and I'm keeping my distance from Lou to protect them. Kai is probably doing the same.

I've googled worst-case-scenario sentences and my mind is taking me to a dark place – being sent to a young offenders institution after the case comes to youth court next year.

I clear my throat. 'This isn't going away just because I confessed.'

I catch a glimpse of hollowed cheeks and haunted eyes in his mirror. I barely recognise myself.

'I could get a custodial sentence,' I explain. 'Kai and Layla as well, but they might receive lighter sentences.'

'Why? That's hardly fair when you were all in this together!'

'They had less selfish reasons for taking the money. I wanted . . . Well, mainly I wanted to make you happy.'

'Is that such a bad thing, babe?' he asks, laughing.

'Don't you see? My life could be ruined!'

I turn round so he can't see the tears welling in my eyes. I hear footsteps. Now he's hugging my waist. I stiffen guiltily beneath his touch. I remember clinging on to Lou when we thought we were about to be executed.

'I'm sorry. I'm dead impressed you'd do all this for me.' His arms tighten. 'Have the police asked you about Bob's death? Is that likely to come up in the court case?'

I frown. He's never shown any interest in our old bus driver. He didn't come to the memorial either – it clashed with a rugby match.

'DC Walker thinks either Silas or one of the cartel guys deliberately mowed him down to take over his route for drug dealing.'

'The police investigation is over?'

'I guess.'

Tristram lets go. He sits down heavily on the bed.

'What is it?'

He shakes his head. 'I've been thinking about things lately.'

My stomach shifts uneasily, the way it does whenever he mentions Lou.

'Like what?'

'School, acting, university applications – how best to launch my sporting career. I'm planning to stop drama club and concentrate on rugby seriously.'

'That's good,' I say flatly. 'I might not get into any university after this, let alone Cambridge.'

'Of course you will! You're a genius.' He runs a hand through his hair. 'But you don't need relationship distractions. My parents agree – it's a good idea to cool things.'

I gape at him. 'Are you breaking up with me? When I'm preparing for a life-changing court case?'

I can't believe it. I've been feeling guilty for thinking about Lou when Tristram has been planning to dump me! I can't breathe. I fumble with my shirt collar, attempting to undo the top button.

'I'm trying to help you.'

'By leaving me to face this on my own?'

'You're stronger than you think. Jesus, you messed with a drug gang.'

I inhale sharply as I notice my envelope with the ski holiday deposit on his bedside table. He never had any intention of paying it into his account! He follows my gaze.

'You should take that.' He picks it up. 'My coach said to keep out of . . . *this*. Rugby scouts are coming to my next few matches. I could get picked by one of the big clubs, but they won't touch me if there's a hint of scandal.'

I steady myself against the wall as he passes me the envelope.

'I'm sorry, babe. Truly I am. I never wanted it to end like this, I promise.'

He opens the door. Invisible bayonets stab my chest as I notice his wrist. He's wearing the Breitling watch his parents gave him, not my Samsung Galaxy.

I don't move. I'm trying to make sense of everything: how we got together and why we're splitting. I'm drawing a spreadsheet of dates, times and *motives* in my head.

Cold shivers run up and down my spine as the mask slips from his face.

'This has nothing to do with rugby or your reputation.'

Tristram's hand tightens on the door handle. 'I've no idea what you mean.'

'It finally makes sense – why you'd ask me out. Someone who's not perfect, who doesn't have money or fit in with your friends.'

'You know why – I fancied you. Still do.'

I shake my head. 'You're a good actor. You knew I worshipped you from afar. That's why you came on to me, even though you hate my scar.'

He opens his mouth to speak, but I continue.

'You avoid touching it. You make me feel like I should keep it covered. But you were prepared to look past it because you were using me.'

Tristram shakes his head. 'You're imagining things as usual, babe.'

'I'm done with the gaslighting and being called that dumb name.'

'Whatever. My friends warned me you'd take this badly.' He examines his phone.

'The dates are important,' I say slowly. 'You asked me to lie about where and when your car was stolen because it was the same night as Bob's hit-and-run.'

'I told you: Dad would have gone ballistic if he'd found out I'd left it outside a pub with the keys inside.' He takes a breath. 'Why do you have to make a drama out of everything? This isn't a big deal.'

'It's huge.'

'Why?'

I stare at him. 'You tell me.'

He strides towards me, fists clenched. 'You think I killed Bob?'

I remember how Lou didn't step away when they were threatened. I'm not backing down either. Or looking the other way when Tristram says or does terrible things. I'm not ignoring red flags any more.

'Yes.' I thrust my chin in the air. 'That's why you're interested in the police investigation. You knocked over Bob in your dad's car and asked me out because you knew I'd give you an alibi unquestioningly.'

Tristram's fist hovers inches from my face. I brace myself for it to come crashing down, but he lets out an anguished howl and slumps to the floor, sobbing.

'I never meant for it to happen. Please believe me.'

I crouch down beside him, reaching for a tissue from my pocket. My fingers brush against my mobile.

'Tell me! I want to understand. I can help.'

He takes a deep breath. 'I'd had a few beers, but I swear I wasn't drunk. I didn't see Bob by the side of the road. I heard a bang and thought I'd hit a deer. I went to check.' He shudders violently. 'Then I panicked and got back in the car.'

'You could have tried to save him! You should have rung for an ambulance.'

He shakes his head. 'The injuries were . . . He couldn't survive, and I was worried I'd fail a breathalyser. I decided to get rid of the car. I drove out to Connersbury, set fire to it and walked five miles home.'

'And asked me out to help cover your tracks!'

'Sure, at the beginning. But I've grown to like you, to *love you*.'

My mouth falls open. It's the first time he's ever said that. I stare into his bluish-green eyes. Usually my insides melt. But not today. Never again. He left Bob to die at the side of the road, like an animal.

'Give yourself in to the police. Tell the truth. You'll feel better for it.'

'Are you insane? That doesn't bring Bob back. The investigation is over. I'm in the clear.'

'That's not the point. It's the right thing to do.'

'I'm not ruining my life because I made one bad decision, the way you did.'

'This isn't the same!'

'Isn't it? You lied to everyone, including me, to save your own skin.'

'I never killed anyone.'

'Touché.' He bites his lip. 'Deep down we have more in common than my mates think. We have the same instinct for survival.'

I shake my head. 'That's a line I'd never cross.'

He stands and hauls me to my feet. 'It doesn't matter. We stick to our stories, as agreed.'

I yank my arm away. 'I'm not covering for you! I hate that you think you can get away with killing someone. I hate your cruel jokes and the way you treat people. I hate the way you make me feel about my scar. Why should I be ashamed of it? It's part of me. It's who I am. But people are disposable to you – Bob, me, *everyone*.'

'You can't betray me, Liam. You helped cover up a crime. Your sentence will be longer!'

I walk out of the door.

'Don't do this!' he calls after me. 'We can work this out. Let's get back together. I didn't mean those things I said. You're more important than rugby. I swear I don't care about your scar. *I love you*.'

I keep walking.

I'm done with the lying and the deceit. I'm done with Tristram.

I check my phone as I run down the stairs. The voice

recorder I'd flicked on is still whirring. I'm handing over Tristram's confession to DC Walker.

I try to focus on putting one foot in front of the other. *Not falling.*

My chest tightens. The pain is excruciating. But for the first time in months Mum and Lou will be proud of me.

I've made the right decision.

SEA HAVEN BOSS GETS LIFE SENTENCE!

Sophia Cavendish, the former owner of the Sea Haven hotel, was jailed for life yesterday after being convicted of a double murder at Kingsborough Crown Court. Cavendish was also found guilty of five counts of kidnapping, conspiracy to supply class A drugs, money laundering and possession of a firearm with intent to commit an indictable offence. Cavendish had helped distribute heroin and cocaine across the south-west via a local school bus network. She had allowed her luxury hotel to be used as a base for a drug gang and arranged the kidnapping of teenagers she suspected of stealing money from her boss, 'Mr A'.

Judge Sam Taylor handed down a mandatory life sentence, with a minimum term of 20 years before Cavendish can be considered for release.

Separately four teenagers have appeared at Kingsborough Youth Court where they admitted the theft of £350,000 of stolen drug money after a horrific school bus crash. The court was told that the young people, who cannot be identified for legal reasons, discovered the cash in a holdall belonging to their deceased bus driver. The district judge took pity on the four due to their ordeals, ages, lack of previous convictions and the fact that the theft was opportunistic. They mainly spent the cash on family and friends.

Due to their previous good characters, three received nine-month referral orders for theft and money laundering, and a fourth gained a seven-month referral order for theft.

DC Andy Walker said, 'Our inquiries into the head of the drug gang, "Mr A", are continuing.'

- Tristram Campbell-Levitt, 18, has been jailed for two years at Kingsborough Crown Court after admitting causing the death by careless driving of former school bus driver Bob Swanson.

54

KAI

The swell is huge – over two metres – and too dangerous for the tourists who have hired surfboards despite the lifeguards' warning flags billowing in the wind. Experienced locals were wiped out this afternoon. I surfed a few hours ago – I'd wanted to chase the elusive wave I'd always remember. But it's a myth. Nothing in life is perfect. Instead, I just tried to avoid getting battered to death.

The storm ripped through here last night, tearing tiles off the roofs of beachside rental homes, overturning boats and washing up huge blankets of seaweed, plastic bottles and debris. Litter pickers are on the beach today, scooping up the rubbish. A couple armed with metal detectors are nearby, hoping to discover a long-buried gold coin or ring. Good luck with that! Not all treasure is worth the hassle. Sometimes you should leave loot exactly where you find it.

I lean further over the wall as I catch sight of Layla. Her mouth is parted in a wide smile, her hair streaming behind her back. Her brother shrieks with laughter as she chases him. The clinical trial was successful – I heard Salih is in remission. His hair has grown back and he's buzzing with energy. Layla glances at the promenade, shielding her eyes from the sun. I wave but she doesn't see me. Some things never change.

'Do you need binoculars?'

I spin round. Lou passes me a double espresso – I can't kick my caffeine habit even though exams are over and we've broken up for summer. I didn't do badly, considering everything that's happened.

'Thank you!' I hug Lou tightly. I don't want to let go.

'Whooooaaa! It's a coffee, not a million pounds.'

'Funny.'

'Please don't pour it down my back.'

I let go and dig out a friendship bracelet from my pocket.

'This is for you. I have the same one.' I hold up my wrist and show them the turquoise threads.

'Thanks!' Their eyes narrow, as they pull it on. 'What's the occasion?'

I shake my head. 'Just a thank-you for being there for me.'

'Where else would I be?' Lou smiles. 'I'll always be here for you.'

My heart pounds painfully. I stare hard at the beach as my eyes moisten.

'You should ask Layla out now you've put your criminal days behind you,' Lou says, following my gaze.

I manage a small smile. My solicitor advised against contact with the others before the court case and now . . . well, none of us has messaged since.

'I think the time has passed,' I admit. 'We've been through so much. Going to youth court together wasn't exactly the best first date.'

The back of my neck is slick with sweat at the thought of that afternoon, waiting to hear the district judge's sentence. My mum had half-heartedly offered to come along, but I was afraid she'd let me down. I'd asked Mrs Gibson to support me in court as I'd needed an adult present while Lou waited outside. Tears prick my eyes. I miss Mrs Gibson more than I'd ever imagined. She died of a heart attack just over a week after my sentencing.

'Well, look on the bright side – at least you're free to date *someone*, instead of being banged up. Harder to see *any* girlfriend on the inside.'

'I'm not sure I'm ready for dating,' I tell them firmly.

Liam appears, removing his EarPods and clutching a suspiciously healthy green shake. His hair is longer and he's wearing a pink and mauve tie-dye hoodie and jeans. 'You're dating someone?'

I sigh deeply. 'No.'

'That's the problem.' Lou rolls their eyes. 'Help me persuade him to ask out Layla.' They pause. 'You've both got your lives ahead of you. What's stopping you? Why waste time?'

'My thoughts exactly,' Liam says.

He pulls Lou closer and kisses them on the lips. They're having a full-on snog. They became an item after the court case. I've never seen Lou happier. We're living together now. Lou's mum was fed up with all the rows between Lou and their dad at home and loaned us the cash for the rental on a small two-bedroom flat – I'd had to cancel the lease on Torside Lodge as it was funded by stolen money.

'Okay, enough!' I say, groaning. 'Jeez. I'd say get a room, but you might go back to our place. I've seen enough of the pair of you this week.'

They spring apart, laughing. It's not only the clothes that have changed. Liam looks like a weight has been lifted from his shoulders after breaking free from Tristram. He shocked everyone by turning in his ex-boyfriend to the police. Another surprise was Fliss leaving the country after she got her short referral order. I thought she'd stay to look for the rucksacks, but maybe she doesn't care about the money.

'You'll have a reprieve from me this evening,' Liam says. 'I've promised Mum a classic horror-movie night.'

'Not *Saw*!' Lou says. 'No more "bodies" rising from the dead, thank you very much.'

Liam shudders. 'God, no!'

They're about to kiss again when Layla calls out. She's making her way up the steps with Salih. My heart beats faster. Why does it have to do that? It's too late for anything to happen.

'Hey, you!' I say loudly.

Layla blushes. 'Hi!'

An awkward silence grows between us.

'So, Salih, how about we buy an ice cream?' Lou suggests.

'Sure.' Salih smiles mischievously at us. 'Don't plot to rob a bank! I'm not visiting any of you in prison.'

'Hilarious,' Layla mutters.

'Talk to each other. About non-criminal, interesting topics.' Lou shoots a meaningful look at me before they follow Salih.

Layla nudges an abandoned cigarette butt with the edge of her sandal. Liam sighs and crosses his arms while I rack my brains for something to say. We've been through so much, but we've never seemed further apart.

Layla breaks the silence. 'It's good to see you both after
. . .' She pushes her hair behind her ears. 'What happens
now?'

Liam glances at Lou and Salih. They're joining the queue
at the ice-cream kiosk.

'Not getting rearrested and dragged back to court is high
on my wish list,' he stresses.

She nods. 'Ditto.'

The district judge had warned us that we'll get far less
lenient sentences if we offend again.

'We have to keep our noses clean until the end of sixth
form at least,' he adds.

'That shouldn't be hard,' Layla replies. 'Mum barely lets
me out of the house by myself, apart from to dance and music
classes. She doesn't trust me. Not that I blame her. And
Teta—'

'Who?' I ask.

'My grandma in Egypt. She's on the phone to Mum
virtually every day, checking I'm staying out of trouble.'

'My mum has stopped short of giving me a lie detector
test every morning,' Liam admits. 'What about yours?'

I flinch.

'Sorry. That was insensitive. I didn't mean . . .'

'It's fine.'

Obviously it's not. We lapse into another awkward silence until Liam speaks again.

'Are you sure the money's safe? I'm worried . . .'

'Nobody will ever find it, I promise,' I say quickly.

I picture the metal boxes buried beneath the shed in Mrs Gibson's garden. No one knows where the money is, not even Lou. Mrs Gibson made it clear in her will that the property can't be sold to developers and her son, Charles, is unlikely to dig up the grounds. He's down from London. He admitted his family's not moving here permanently so the house will be empty for most of the year. I can keep an eye on the shed without making DC Walker suspicious. He told the court he believed we'd discovered more money than had been accounted for, but he can't prove anything.

My eyes well as I remember Mrs Gibson's kind words as we left court. *You can make something of your life, Kai. This doesn't have to define you.*

I never got around to thanking her properly for her support. Ten days later, a police officer found her dead from a heart attack on the sofa in her sitting room. She'd made a 999 call, probably about her chest pain, but hadn't been able to speak. The pathologist ruled her death was from natural causes. I'd slipped in the back of the church for her service because the Sea Haven Survivors still attract unwelcome attention around here, but I have visited her grave and left flowers.

'Will you ever tell us where the cash is hidden?' Liam asks. 'No, wait, I don't think I want to know.'

'Me neither,' Layla says.

'That's probably for the best in case you're ever tortured,' I say drily.

Layla slaps my arm playfully. 'Not funny!'

Liam rolls his eyes. 'Yes, very bad taste.'

'You have to trust me,' I say forcefully. 'You can both do that, surely?'

'Of course!' Layla exclaims.

Liam nods. 'Sure. But we should decide what to do with the money. Will we give it all away? Or are we going to split it between the three of us?'

I bite my lip as he studies my face. I'd promised Lou I'd donate all the cash to charity in return for them retrieving the rucksacks last year.

'Do we have to decide today?' I ask warily. 'We could agree to come back in, say, five years' time and thrash it out.'

Layla exhales heavily. 'That suits me. I can't be dealing with all the stress and worrying that DC Walker is still watching us.'

'It should be long enough to throw him off our scent.'

Liam wrinkles his nose. 'Fliss too. She'd never guess we could sit on it after last time.'

'I wonder what happened to Tom and Gerry?' Layla muses.

'Who knows?' Liam says.

The police were never able to trace the money launderers. The court was told they'd deserted the carwash and moved on, probably abroad.

'Let's shake on it.' Layla stretches out her hand.

'We're all in this together,' Liam says, unmoving.

It feels like a lifetime since we first spoke those words. I lay my hand on Layla's, shivering at the touch of her skin.

'Wherever we end up, whatever we're doing, we'll meet back here on the nineteenth of July in five years' time,' she says brightly.

'Another thieves' reunion.' Liam puts his hand on mine.

'*Together,*' I say.

I want to weep as Layla flashes an unsuspecting smile.

'I wonder what we'll all be doing in five years,' she says. 'You first, Kai!'

I pull my hand away. 'Hopefully trying to launch a surfing business.' I cough, attempting to disguise my emotions. 'I want to give it a shot.'

'Are you still applying to Newquay Uni?'

'Yep! Surf science and technology.'

I'm dying inside, but I *can't* tell her the truth.

'What about you?' I ask, as Lou and Salih wander back with ice creams.

'I suppose I'll have graduated from music college. I'll be trying to make it as a musician or singer-songwriter.'

'Cool!' Lou says, joining the conversation. 'Where do you want to study?'

She mentions a few colleges in London while Liam silently examines his EarPods. He's tuned out, probably trying to solve a mathematical problem in his head. Thankfully we've stopped talking about the money. The truth is, I'm planning to unearth the boxes tonight and take it all – just under £650,000. I'd managed to get Gerry's new mobile number before he and Tom fled. They're running a new carwash business in Liverpool and have agreed to launder the cash and give me a forged passport for an exorbitant fee. After that, I'm flying to Hawaii, where I'll open that surf shop.

I should be beating myself up for double-crossing Layla and Liam, but the honest-to-God truth is I feel almost nothing. There's a vast dark heavy hole in my chest where my heart used to be. Being deserted by Mum taught me one thing: I'm better off on my own. Trusting no one. That way I can never get hurt again. Mrs Gibson is dead. Lou no longer needs me. I feel like a spare wheel with Liam around. Hopefully Lou will forgive me eventually for keeping the money instead of giving it to charity. As for Layla, I don't believe I ever had a chance with her. She'll find someone far better than me who can make her happy.

If Mum doesn't want me, why would anyone else?

I'm unlovable. Someone who is discarded like rubbish.

I catch Liam scrutinising my face, as if he's looking for an answer to a question. He has no idea what's going on in my head as usual. I smile back.

I'm an equation he'll never solve.

By the time he's worked it out, I'll be long gone.

55

LIAM

Kai is talking about studying surf science and technology at Newquay Uni. The old Liam would have laughed and questioned how surfing qualifies as a degree course, but the new, better version of me no longer looks down on him. *On anyone.* Who am I to judge after what I've done? I still have pangs of guilt over Tristram's jail sentence, but Bob deserved justice. And asking Lou out was the best decision of my life. I don't have to pretend to be someone else. I'm meeting my old friends and have donated my short-sleeved shirts to a charity shop. I'm no longer ashamed of showing my scar. Lou says it shows my journey: where I've come from and what I've been through. It's my personal map and I'm proud of it.

'What about you, Layla?' Kai shifts from foot to foot.

Why won't he ask her out? It would be great to see him

as happy as me – and *occupied*. He hasn't hidden the rucksacks in their flat – I searched all the rooms when he and Lou slipped out to the launderette a few weeks ago. Layla doesn't appear to know where the money is hidden. It's been obvious since the day of the crash that Kai fancies her. Surely he wouldn't stitch her up by stealing the money? When I asked what we should do with the cash, he wouldn't commit to giving it to charity. Maybe he plans to confide in Layla at some point and split it with her.

I don't trust them. How can I? We're all good liars. We got off lightly in youth court by playing the 'innocent kids made bad decisions' act with the district judge – a family man with teenage children. The experience has taught me that I can only truly trust two people: my mum and Lou. The stolen cash will never make either of them happy, but if I find the missing rucksacks, Kai and Layla can't be tempted to spend the money in the future – just under £650,000 by my calculations. Lou can decide which charities will receive anonymous windfalls.

The question is where would Kai hide the stash? He'd need to keep it close by. I've been secretly following him and have created a spreadsheet to keep track of his movements. The only places he regularly visits are the beach (virtually every day) and the surf shop (two to three times a week).

It's not in the space beneath the shop or the old holiday home he was staying in – I've checked both thoroughly – and he wouldn't have left the haul at Torside Lodge.

That leaves Mrs Gibson's house or gardens. It's the ideal hiding place now she's passed away. Kai's got the run of the property most of the time. He works on the grounds for two hours every Saturday morning – usually between 10.30 a.m. and 12.30 p.m. – apart from during the last fortnight. Mrs Gibson's son and family have arrived for the summer while building work takes place. Mrs Gibson probably let the place get run down.

I've pretended Mum wants to binge-watch old *Scream* movies, but I'll scout about tonight. I can't let Kai cheat charities out of the money. Lou smiles at me affectionately. They mustn't find out what I'm planning. They want a relationship based on mutual respect and trust. But this is necessary – I'm protecting the cash, and them. I put my EarPods in the case and place them in the side compartment of my rucksack, where they won't accidentally fall out – the old ones never turned up and Lou bought me a replacement.

'I'm hungry and bored,' Salih says abruptly. 'Can we get a veggie burger?'

Layla bursts out laughing. 'Tactful, as usual. Sorry, I forgot my purse.'

'I can lend you a twenty,' Kai says.

I raise an eyebrow. 'Can you afford the interest payments on Kai's loan?'

'I guess I'll pay it off,' she replies. 'Maybe, in five years' time?'

She and Kai dissolve into giggles, which heightens my suspicions. I calculate the chances they double-cross me as two to one.

'What's so funny?' Salih demands.

'Beats me,' Lou says. 'Let's go.'

We trail after Salih and Lou, past the shops to the vegan food stall. We pass a newsstand with the words: *Villagers Up in Arms Over New Property Development.*

Kai doubles back and buys a paper, his hands trembling. He scans the front page again and again, as if he's trying to absorb the words properly.

'Oh God.' His face pales to a deathly white.

Layla reads over his shoulder. 'Isn't that Mrs Gibson's house?'

Kai nods numbly. In that split second I know my hunch is correct. This is where he's buried the cash.

'What's going on?' I ask.

He raises his gaze from the newspaper. 'We're about to lose everything!'

VILLAGERS UP IN ARMS OVER NEW PROPERTY DEVELOPMENT

The sudden death of Sandstown parish council member Flora Gibson has sparked a furious row among locals.

Mrs Gibson, who lived in Sandstown all her life, suffered a fatal heart attack last month. She was found to have died of natural causes aged 89.

Mrs Gibson had campaigned for years against second homeowners buying properties in the area and pricing out locals. She had resisted attempts by developers to purchase her property, which boasts two acres and has stunning views of the Sea Haven hotel across the causeway. However, her land had historic planning permission for the building of luxury flats – the legal documents were obtained by the previous owners in 1969.

Mrs Gibson's close friends have accused her son, Charles, an investment banker from Clapham, south London, of going against the wishes of her will by secretly selling the house and land to a property-development company. He is currently helping oversee building work.

Local resident Miriam Walker said, 'Flora would be turning in her grave if she knew what was happening. Charles promised to fulfil her last wishes by not selling to developers, but he turned out to be a good liar. He's double-crossed us all!'

The land has been bought by Cavendish Developments, the US company owned by Warren Cavendish, ex-husband of Sophia Cavendish, who previously ran the Sea Haven. She is currently serving a life sentence for double murder and other offences.

Mr Cavendish was unavailable for comment last night. But a spokesman for Cavendish Developments said, 'We look forward to creating a luxury complex that will make everyone in Sandstown extremely proud. We are excavating the grounds and will move on to the main building shortly. We believe villagers will be pleasantly surprised when we reveal our vision for the plot.'

56

FLISS

'Surprise, surprise! Here you are. Didn't you hear me calling?'

Daddy joins me on the balcony as I gaze out at the sparkling Pacific Ocean. He's tanned and impeccably dressed in a crisp white shirt, tan chinos and brown Gucci brogues. He instinctively touches his little finger, but his gold signet ring is missing.

'Sorry!' I plant a kiss on his cheek because that's what dutiful, grateful daughters are supposed to do. 'I can't get enough of your amazing view.'

'It's *our* view. This is your home.'

I'd chosen my words purposefully to allow him to correct me. Men – particularly rich, powerful ones – love doing that and Daddy's no exception.

I squeeze his arm. 'Thank you.'

'I'd do anything for you, Flicky.' His voice cracks. 'After what you've been through, you simply have to ask.'

I reward him with a dazzling smile. Honestly I'd never anticipated everything would turn out this well. The reappearance of Mother's estranged sister after she had been jailed for life had thrown a spanner into the works. Aunt Lindsay had offered to take me back to Newcastle – *a fate worse than death*. I'd played on Daddy's guilty conscience for abandoning me and cried bitterly down the phone.

I barely know Aunt Lindsay. I was a toddler when I last saw her. I want to be with you, Daddy!

Eventually he'd caved.

You must live with us in Malibu.

I hadn't expected him to break up with Amanda – that was a welcome bonus. I'd thought it might take a few months to quietly undermine her, but she moved out before I arrived.

Daddy leans over the balcony, staring out to sea. 'I know it's hard for you being here. You must miss your mother terribly – and your friends in Sandstown.'

I manage to swallow a snort. Mother deserves her life sentence after putting me through that fake kidnapping and not protecting me from Robert Brody. She put drugs before me. She *had* to be punished. So did Aaron, who's currently serving a seven-year sentence for blackmail.

'It's hard.' I manage to squeeze a tear into the corner of my eye. 'I'm coping as best as I can and taking it one day at a time.'

Everything about Malibu is better than north Devon – the permanent vivid blue of the sky and sea, the shopping malls, the people, even the air smells better, *richer.* All the houses on this stretch are worth at least $5 million and I don't bump into riffraff during my early-morning jogs.

'We can check on the development when we go back to see your youth offending service worker.' Daddy fishes out the phone from his pocket. He taps at the screen, pulling up a newspaper story from the *Kingsborough Gazette.* 'The locals will come round when they see my plans.'

I read the article, trying not to laugh. I'd give anything to see the looks on the others' faces. Did they think they could trick me? I knew they'd collected and hidden the cash. I hired a private investigator to keep tabs on them before and after the court case. Through a process of elimination, I'd worked out the money must be concealed inside Mrs Gibson's house or buried in her grounds – the Lobster Bar and surf shop were far too public.

Kai has his own key to the garden and can regularly keep an eye on the hiding place without arousing suspicion. After working it out, all I had to do was make Daddy think it was *his* idea to invest in the area. He'd contacted Mrs Gibson's son years ago about the land, and I suggested trying again after her death. Daddy made another offer he couldn't refuse, even if it did mean betraying his dead mother.

'I can't wait to see the development!' I say brightly. 'When will the sheds and outhouses be knocked down? I wonder what's underneath them?'

'I doubt there's hidden treasure,' Daddy says, laughing.

The corners of my mouth twitch. I'm not so sure. Kai visits the shed on the east side of the property the most, according to the private investigator who took photos with a long-lens camera from outside Mrs Gibson's house. I've discreetly paid the site manager to secretly tip me off if anything is unearthed and persuaded Daddy to fork out for extra security. Kai can't get anywhere near the property. This isn't about the money. Daddy's monthly allowance is far more generous than Mother's. This is revenge. Liam, Kai and Layla should never have left me on the bus that day and double-crossed me over the money – twice! Now they'll lose it all.

Daddy puts his phone away. 'I need to pop into the office. I'll buy breakfast first. Croissants or fruit salad?'

'Croissants!'

'Coming right up.' He walks away, patting his pocket. 'Wait, I just remembered. I found this under the sofa. It

438

doesn't look like something you'd wear, but I thought I'd check before I message Amanda. One of her friends may have dropped it a few months back.'

He pulls out an opal ring. I'd completely forgotten about this monstrosity – it must have slipped through the lining of my handbag. I pluck it from his palm.

'Mother gave it to me. But you're right, it's old-fashioned. Can we get the opal taken out and put in a new platinum setting?'

'Sure. I'll find a jeweller.'

He blows me a kiss as he slips through the sliding doors. I hold the ring up to the sun, watching the light streak from the gemstone. It's hideous, but I'd enjoyed the rush of stealing it from that elderly guest's bedside table at the Sea Haven while she was at breakfast. I take it to my bedroom and slide out the shoebox from the bottom of my wardrobe. No convenient loose wooden panels here – I'll need to find a better hiding place. I examine my trophies: Mother's rose-gold bracelet, her former PA Maura's favourite china cockapoo, trinkets from holidaymakers' rooms, Robert Brody's Rolex, Liam's EarPods and Daddy's ring. He thinks it slipped off his finger during his morning beach run, but he'd left it in the shower. I unroll the silver leopard, which is wrapped in a hotel bath towel. *Sooo tacky!*

It's not like I wanted any of these items – I took them because I *could*.

I place the opal ring inside the box. I'd told Mother I'd seen Layla going into the suite the day it went missing. It wasn't personal – Mother was freaking out about the thefts. I couldn't own up. She'd have hired another psychiatrist, which would have wasted everyone's time; I don't need a diagnosis. *I know exactly what I am.* Stealing guests' jewellery – or £1 million – isn't the worst thing I've done by far. I return the shoebox to my closet and head to the balcony, peeling off my shorts and T-shirt. I rub suntan lotion over my body, careful to avoid getting cream on my new Chanel bikini. I lie on the sun lounger, adjusting the Jimmy Choo sunglasses Daddy bought me.

I feel guilty, of course. I'm not a *total* psychopath. I never meant for Mrs Gibson to die. She wasn't supposed to be home that night. Every Thursday evening, without fail, she went to her weekly bridge club, according to the parish magazine. I'd slipped inside her house at 7.30 p.m. – the back door wasn't locked, but that's not unusual in Shitstown. I was testing the floorboards in the sitting room, searching for Kai's hiding place, when she walked in. Seriously, she almost gave *me* a heart attack.

'*What are you doing in my house?*'

I watch, stunned, as she pulls out a mobile from her pocket.

'Looking for Kai's hidden money,' I reply truthfully.

*'I don't know what you're talking about. Please leave.'
She frowns, pointing at the door.*

'Not yet.'

*I lunge for her phone but trip on the rug. Mrs Gibson lets
out a cry and staggers backwards, bumping into the side of
the sofa. She slumps on to the cushions, groaning and
clutching the mobile to her chest. She manages to tap
'emergency call' before I come to my senses and pluck the
phone out of her fingers.*

'Let me do that for you.'

'Can't breathe,' she says, gasping.

'I'll help. Do you know where the money is?'

She shakes her head. 'Please. Ring. Ambulance.'

*Obviously that can't happen. I could be hauled back to
court for illegally entering her house. I pretend to dial the
number and speak to an imaginary operator, reeling off her
address.*

*'Can I tell you a story while we wait for the paramedics?'
I ask, holding her hand, and she nods.*

*'I killed a man. It didn't happen the way I told DC Walker
– it was cold-blooded murder.'*

Her face pales as I briefly describe Robert Brody's attack in the hotel suite and how Mother had refused to call the police.

I squeeze Mrs Gibson's hand. 'He'd got away with hitting me! I had to get my revenge. Later that night, I pushed a note under his door, telling him to meet me behind the hotel. I said I wanted to talk. I ran away when he approached and led him to the cliff. I knew it was a dead end. But he had no idea what was coming. One hard push and he went over!'

A strange noise escapes from Mrs Gibson's lips.

'He deserved it. The world's a better place without him. I had a lucky escape, but the next girl he met in a bar could have ended up in hospital, beaten and raped.' I take another breath. 'I went back to his room and retrieved the note. I thought it was safer to ring the police and offer a self-defence story – that we'd struggled by the edge – in case anyone had seen us together. But Mother made me keep quiet.'

Mrs Gibson groans.

'Hold on! The paramedics are outside. They're coming.'

Her eyelids flutter, then close.

I wipe the phone down and place it between her fingers.

I kiss her on the forehead.

I leave empty-handed.

I brush tears from my eyes – they're real this time, not

fake. Confessing to Mrs Gibson made me feel lighter and she helpfully took my secret to her grave. I'll buy a big expensive bouquet of flowers and throw it into the ocean as a thank-you. Kai said she loved the sea. It's a fitting memorial – old people love soppy shit like that.

I pick up one of the glossies from the table and flick through as the doorbell rings. That must be Daddy. He's forgotten his office keys. I pull on my clothes and pad barefoot downstairs.

'That was quick! Did you manage to get . . .?' My voice trails away at the sight of two police officers.

'Fliss Cavendish?' The younger, hotter one, removes his sunglasses.

I flutter my eyelashes at him. 'Yes? How can I help you?'

'We're here to arrest you,' he says sharply.

I attempt to close the door, but he reaches out and stops it from shutting.

'Please cooperate with us. Turn round.'

I feel the coldness of metal against my wrists and there's a loud click as the handcuffs are fastened.

'What's going on?' a familiar voice rings out. 'Let go of my daughter!'

Daddy! Thank God.

'Please step away, sir. Your daughter is under arrest.'

He drops the bag. Croissants spill on to the floor. 'What on earth for?'

'On suspicion of burglary, manslaughter and –' he pauses, fixing me with a hard stare as I face him – 'murder.'

'What?' I scream. 'I've done nothing wrong. Get these freaks off me!'

Daddy frowns as he jabs at his phone. 'I'm ringing my lawyer and we'll sue the police department for wrongful arrest.'

'Your daughter has confirmed her identity. We're arresting her under an extradition warrant on behalf of the UK's Devon and Cornwall police following the deaths of Mrs Flora Gibson and Mr Robert Brody in Sandstown, north Devon.'

My jaw drops. 'Why? The Crown Prosecution Service agreed with DC Walker – I acted in self-defence. The coroner reopened Robert Brody's inquest and found a verdict of lawful killing.'

'That's right,' Daddy insists. 'She faced no charges in relation to his death.'

'*And* I had nothing to do with Mrs Gibson's heart attack!' I stress. 'She died of natural causes. You can't pin that on me.' I break down into tears. 'Daddy, do something!'

He glares at the officers. 'This is clearly a mix-up. You're not taking my little girl anywhere until you tell me *exactly* what's going on.'

'We'll run through the full details of the alleged offences at the precinct,' he says. 'But a DC Walker has provided new evidence regarding the deaths of Mr Brody and Mrs Gibson.'

'W-w-what evidence?' I stammer.

'We can show you footage from the hidden camera later.'

Daddy looks from me to the police officer.

'I have no idea what he's talking about!' I cry.

'Clearly,' the officer says drily. 'We've been told Mrs Gibson's son recently cleared out her house and came across a camera with audio, which she'd installed in her sitting room. DC Walker says she'd seen a man with a camera hanging around outside and was worried about being burgled. The footage captured your daughter entering Mrs Gibson's house, quizzing her about missing cash, falsely claiming to ring for an ambulance when she was dying – and confessing to murder.'

My knees weaken. I sink to the floor.

Daddy's eyes widen as he stares at me. 'Is this true, Flicky?'

I shake my head vigorously. 'No! You have to believe me, Daddy. I'm innocent. I would never do anything like this!'

I'm a good liar.

Far better than the other three.

I'm the absolute best.

57

LAYLA

I'm not the best runner.

Kai is streaking miles ahead, with Liam and Lou a short distance behind. Salih has more energy and is back to playing football after the success of the medical trial. He's only keeping up with me out of sympathy, or possibly because he's worried I'm about to collapse and he'll have to perform CPR.

'What's important about this house anyway?' Salih grumbles. 'And why do we have to see it now instead of grabbing a snack first?'

'Can't . . . run . . . and . . . speak.'

'You're tragic.'

'Thanks, *habibi*.'

I stop since I'm only slow jogging/walking moderately fast. Seagulls hopping around, searching for scraps, could probably overtake me. Or squirrels.

'Do you like Kai?' Salih asks abruptly.

'W-w-what?'

I should have kept 'running'.

'Why . . . do you ask?' I rub the stitch in my side.

'I see the way he looks at you when he doesn't think you're watching. He's well into you.' He pauses. 'You don't have to look out for me any more, you know. You can have a life.'

'I do have a life, thanks.'

'Have you been kissed by a boy, like, ever?'

'You can't ask questions like that!'

'Why not? I'm your brother.'

'That's exactly why, *habibi*!'

Salih snorts. He's about to hit me with another smart-arse remark when we hear the high-pitched whine of an emergency vehicle in the distance. A man tears past. More people are heading in the same direction as us – up the hill towards Mrs Gibson's house. The muscles in my legs are screaming, but I force myself to follow as the siren grows louder and louder. At the top a group of workmen are standing outside a large cream house with phones stuck to their ears. A woman in a hard hat runs into the back garden. Salih is hot on her heels.

'Hold on!' I shout.

Before I can tell him we're not allowed on private property, he's disappeared through the gate. I half jog after him, resting briefly against the fence. I take another deep breath and limp into the gardens. This is huge – far bigger than anything I've seen in Sandstown. Dozens of people are lined up, watching something on the east side. Dust spirals in the air above them. *What's going on?*

Salih speeds towards Kai, Liam and Lou. I chase after him.

'Watch it!' A man grabs his arm and wrenches him back as he reaches them.

'Hey!' he cries.

I'm about to yell at the guy when I reel backwards.

'Whooaa!'

We're standing at the edge of a huge drop. Below, waves are crashing into the side of the cliff. Pieces of wood float on the surface of the water.

'What happened?' I say, coughing as dust enters my lungs.

'The cliff face collapsed – taking a huge chunk of this land with it,' a woman in a hard hat explains. 'You kids need to get back. It's not safe.'

'What . . .? How?'

'It's probably been eroding for years, but the storm loosened the earth,' a second construction worker cuts in.

'Cool!' Salih exclaims. 'Weren't there any defences on the cliff?'

I try to pull him away, but he's back at school full-time and his favourite subject is geography. He's learning about coastal erosion.

As Salih fires off another question, I catch sight of Kai. His face is ghostly pale as he talks to Lou and Liam further away from the drop.

'Are you okay?' I ask, as I join them.

Kai nods numbly.

Salih is back by my side, tugging my sleeve. 'I want to take a closer look.'

'I'll go with you, but don't get too close to the edge!' Lou leads him away.

'Is the money safe?' Liam says softly. 'Because I know you've hidden it here. It's the only possible place!'

Kai shakes his head. 'I can't . . . believe it. I'd buried it all beneath the shed.'

'Please tell me you don't mean the one floating away there?' Liam points at the sea.

Kai breathes out slowly.

'Seriously?' I exclaim.

Kai and Liam's faces are ashen

light as a feather. I want to s

distinctive laughter ringin

No more worryin

or being scared stiff that DC Walker will drag us back to court. No more debating the right thing to do. Everything has come full circle – the cash is in the ocean, where it belongs. The corners of my mouth twitch. I'm giggling. Now I'm howling with laughter.

'It's not funny!' Liam retorts. 'The money was supposed to go to charity.'

My belly hurts, but I can't stop. My eyes are blurry with tears. I honestly think I'll wet myself. Kai is laughing, but Liam looks at us as if we're both completely mad.

'I feel sick,' Liam says, shaking his head. 'Or numb. Maybe both.'

'Me too.' his is what *I*

own

with shock, but I feel as

ng and dance. I hear Baba's

g inside my head.

g about lying to my family and friends

ur haul?'
e lying.'
s going

449

ou're

'I couldn't see a future now Mum and Crystal are gone. I'd lost hope that anyone would want me. That they . . .' His voice breaks. 'That *you* could ever love—'

Before he finishes his sentence, my lips are on his and I'm kissing him. He startles before relaxing into my touch. He's kissing me back and my stomach is somersaulting. My head is spinning. This feels wrong . . . yet in a strange way it feels right at the same time. How can I judge him? I know what it's like to have your back against the wall and believe you've run out of options.

'I hate to interrupt your "boy gets together with girl in touching end of movie" moment, but Salih's gawping,' Liam points out.

I'm shivering, but in a good way, as we spring apart. Salih waves at us across the grounds.

'I *am* sorry,' Kai says. 'I mean it.'

Liam sighs deeply. 'If we're all being honest, I'd guessed the cash was hidden here. *I* was planning to steal it tonight.'

'W-w-what?' Kai stutters.

'Important plot twist – I wanted to give it all away to Lou's favourite charities. I'd worked out people are more important than cash.' He turns to me. 'Were you planning to betray your boyfriend and come here with a shovel?'

Is that what he is?

I shake my head. 'If I'd known the cash was here, I wouldn't have touched it.'

'You suggested splitting it in the first place,' Liam remarks.

'Yeah! Look where that got us.' I wince. 'What I did was wrong, but it helped save Salih, which I'll always be grateful for, but I regret everything else.'

Kai nods. 'Me too.'

'At least Fliss didn't win,' Liam says slowly. 'She must have guessed the cash was here and persuaded her dad to buy the land. I'd love to see her face when she finds out it's at the bottom of the sea.'

'That would be priceless,' I agree.

'Maybe the universe will be happy now everything's come full circle,' Kai says. 'It will cut us some slack hopefully for the rest of our lives.'

Liam runs a hand through his hair. 'Have you been binge-watching old *Final Destination* movies?'

We laugh as Salih and Lou approach.

'What's so funny?' Lou asks.

'More importantly is Kai a good kisser?' Salih says. 'How would you rate him out of ten?'

I slap his arm. 'Mind your own business.'

'What about if I pay?' He holds up a fifty-pound note.

'Today is my lucky day! I found it at the edge of the cliff. Do you think I'm allowed to keep it?'

I inhale sharply. This cannot be happening!

The others groan.

'No!' we say in unison.

'It doesn't belong to you,' I tell him. 'Return it to Mr Gibson. This is his land.'

Salih groans. 'What about finders keepers, losers weepers?' He places the emphasis on 'losers' as he fixes me with a hard stare.

I shake my head. 'Doing the right thing is more important.'

'You should listen to your sister,' Liam says. 'She's one hundred per cent correct.'

'Yeah,' Kai agrees. 'Money doesn't bring you happiness.'

'Sure it does,' Salih says cheerfully. 'It means more Lego!'

'I'll help you find Mr Gibson.' I stretch out my hand, but he recoils, like he's been stung.

'Stop treating me like a baby, *habibti*.'

That's the first time he's *ever* called me that. My cheeks glow.

'Sorry. I forgot you're all grown up.'

Salih hums one of Baba's songs I've been playing to him as we walk towards the house, passing more firefighters and workmen carrying metal barriers and hazard warning tape.

As I glance back, Kai, Liam and Lou are having a group hug.

The upper sixth will be a fresh start for everyone. It's going to be wild!

I can't stop smiling. All my senses feel alive. The sky is a deep cobalt blue. I smell freshly cut grass amid the rising dust cloud and taste salt on my lips. The seagulls caw cheerfully overhead, switching pitch. The ocean accompanies them with a gentle undulating tempo. It sounds comforting and hopeful. I started hearing music again a few weeks after the court case, and notes swirl around my head, vying for attention. I reclaimed Baba's oud and kawala from the pawnbroker last year. I'll compose a new song on them when we get home.

I'll call it 'The Day We Started Over' or, better still, 'We Didn't All Die at the End'.

I think everyone's going to love it – particularly Mum and Leon, who are scouting empty shops to turn into a bookstore. I'll play it to Teta when we visit at Christmas – she's invited us all to stay and Mum and Leon are saving for flights.

Salih sticks his hands in his pockets as we reach the top. I flinch at the crackling noise.

'Did you find any more notes?' I say sharply, glancing down.

'Nah!' He holds his hands behind his back.

'Pinkie promise?'

'Of course, *habibti*!' A guilty smile hovers on his lips.

As he slips through the gate, he uncrosses his fingers.

ACKNOWLEDGEMENTS

My idea for *Four Good Liars* came from holidaying in Devon and imagining a dramatic clifftop school bus crash, with students forced to put aside their personal differences to escape. I used a fictional location – the village, hotel and restaurant don't exist – but the dilemmas facing the characters felt very real, and I couldn't wait to start exploring them. The novel wouldn't have been possible without the support, hard work and talent of my agents, Izzy Gahan and Alice Lutyens at Curtis Brown. Thank you for making dreams come true.

Writing is a solitary process, but publishing requires a massive team effort. I'm very lucky and grateful to be working with the best possible team at HarperCollins Children's Books. Thank you to my brilliant editor, Natalie Doherty, and to Michelle Misra who was my first champion – both of you have shown such passion for my writing.

Thank you to Jennie Roman for your incredible eye for detail during copy edits and editor, Jane Baldock, and publisher, Nick Lake, for all your support. A special shout out must go to Matt Kelly for designing my wonderful cover – I love it!

Thank you to the wider team that has worked so hard to bring *Four Good Liars* to the bookshelves: Jasmeet Fyfe, Charis White, Aisling Beddy, Rosie Hawkins, Ruth Burrow in UK sales; Victoria Boodle and Caroline Fisher in international sales, and Kirsty Bradbury in publishing strategy. A huge thanks also to Geraldine Stroud, Elisa Offord, Alex Cowan, Sarah Lough and Isobel Coonjah in marketing and communications.

I'd like to thank my friend, Hala Khalil, for her invaluable help with Layla's Egyptian heritage and use of Arabic. Once again, I turned to crime fiction advisor, Graham Bartlett, for assistance with the police procedural scenes – the former chief superintendent has helped me with my previous adult books, and I'd highly recommend his services to authors.

I also received help from Natalie Cooper, communications officer at Scoliosis Association UK, for scenes involving Liam's scoliosis. Thank you for answering all my queries.

Kai is a product of my imagination but, sadly, there are many teenagers like him who are homeless through no fault of their own. Latest government data shows there are more than 125,000 homeless children living in temporary accommodation with their families in England today – a 67 per cent rise in ten years. They can be stuck in emergency hostels, B&Bs, one-room bedsits and cramped flats for months or years on end due to a shortage of affordable homes. The country should do much better for these young people and their families. For more information about the problem, visit www.shelter.org.uk

Thank you to my friends who read early drafts – Victoria Crook, Jo Megaw and Rosie Megaw, along with my author friends, Lindsay Galvin, Sarah Govett and Faye Bird. I found all your feedback incredibly helpful during redrafting.

A huge thank you to my family – my mum and husband, Darren, are always my first readers and your opinions are invaluable. With much love also to my dad, sister Rachel, mother-in-law, Maureen and sons, James and Luke. Finally, none of this is possible without you, the reader. Thank you for choosing to read my book!